CRYSTAL DARKE

Everfae and Titans

Book 1

I dedicate this book to everyone who has pushed and nudged me along this path. To keep on moving towards the goal of being a full-time writer. It's truly a pleasure to write books and to see them out and about in people's hands. So thank you to you all.

CONTENTS

CHAPTER 1

There I sat, by myself on a very uncomfortable bench. My fingers gripped around the handle of my bag. All my clothes were inside as well as some books. The information that was delivered all through my village came last week. Telling us that everyone between the ages of sixteen and eighteen would need to attend the next two months at Fawkes Institute of Training. A fancy way of saying they will train us to fight.

It was our sectors turn to receive this school. A large building that was travelling around the continent, Mythoria. Moving from sector to sector. Training almost adults to fight and use magic. To explore whether they have what it takes to join the most elite unit in the army. I had no interest in fighting or even learning how to fight. Annoyed that I would miss learning about our history. Science and maths. Useful things that will help me create a future.

I had no interest in taking another person's life. To kill or even hurt. And now I would need to spend the next two months of my life in a place like that. Perhaps I would do so bad they will send me home. Back to my safe little bedroom and my father.

A foot coming along and hitting my bag. Snapping me out of my thoughts. Eyes lifting to the girl scowling at me. "Why is your bag in my way?"

"Sorry." Lowering my eyes and tugging my

belongings a little closer. Looking at her and apologising for a second time before she walked off. She was two years younger than me, seeing off her older brother. Biting my lip and cursing under my breath. I could never stand up for myself.

A loud whistle made me jump as a train pulled into the station. My eyes rising up to the electric board above the platform. This wasn't my train which meant I was on the wrong side. It was a small station with just two tracks and I had still managed to get the wrong one.

Standing up I straightened my black skirt out with a wiggle. There was no information what we needed to wear. So I had put on my school uniform.

The black blazer had the symbol for our school on it. A yellow bird crossing the white sun. Fingers pulling at the collar of my white shirt. Tucking a few strands of my hair behind my ear. Making sure I was neat and tidy before slinging my big bag over my shoulder. Wiggling my hips as I walked slowly. Trying to wake up my butt cheeks as I moved.

Watching other boys and girls running around. Most of them seemed excited at what we were being demanded to do. The word mandatory was written in big letters on the information sheet.

As I came around the old steam train I spotted my brother and his groups of mates. They were having a laugh, happy that he was able to have his friends with him. Me on the other hand had only turned sixteen three days ago. The two kids I could call my some-what friends were too young to attend this school and by next year it would have moved on to a different sector.

As I came to the group I was yanked into the circle. Being hugged by one of his oldest friends. Luckily they all saw me as their younger sister and treated me as such. Having multiple big brothers had it's bonuses and at least I wouldn't be truly alone at this new school.

"I didn't realise you would be coming as well."

Looking up at the boy. His green eyes wide as he smiled, looking very cute. Flicking a stand of his long blonde hair from his eyes. "Lawrence, is that your way of saying sorry for missing my birthday?"

He laughed, "Have I actually remembered one yet?"

"Not yet but I'm still holding out hope."

The tannoy binging on with a loud annoying noise. A voice coming through but the static made it impossible to understand a single word. My brother speaking loudly. "We should get to the platform."

The group scrambling to grab their bags. Feeling the weight on my shoulder lifting. Giggling as Lawrence held it so easily. "You need to get some muscles if you're going to lug around so many books."

Both of us smiling but it was quickly interrupted when my brother snatched the bag from him. Lawrence just laughed it off and headed for the train.

"You know how I feel about you and the guys."

"It's not my fault he keeps flirting with me." Lance shone a huge grin and pulled me in for a tight hug. "Always the big brother."

"I promised father I would always look out for you and honestly, you're not as annoying as the other little sisters the guys have."

"That's because I'm not an air-head who cares about looking the prettiest."

"It couldn't hurt a little." I balled up my fist and slammed it into his belly. Yelping in pain, holding my hand to my chest. "You have to stop doing that. One day you'll break your hand."

"Maybe I'll just kick you in the balls."

"Alright, for that you can carry your own bag." He slumped it onto my shoulder, almost toppling me over onto my butt. "The trains coming, come on." An arm curling around my shoulder as we walked.

He took after our father with his height and the short brown hair. I was the spitting image of my mother. Short with the long blonde curls. Or at least, that's what the photos showed. Our mother died shortly after I was born. All I had were those photos. Having them were the closest I would get to my mum and I had brought them with me.

Moving my way around to the other platform as the train came into the station. Coming to a halt next to the usual mode of transport that visited our village. It was like night and day. Old times meeting new.

The train that had been here first was an old steam train. A massive funnel at the front bellowing that smoke as it started moving off. The wheels spinning on the rails, screeching trying to find purchase.

The second looked like it was made from plastic the metal was so smooth. Running my hand over it as I moved towards the closest door. The windows were all black but the most amazing thing was the levitation from the metal rails.

Seeing the pulse of the purple rings that sat underneath the train. The whole thing having a slow bob up and down. Coming to the closest door and climbing on board, surprised the whole thing didn't waver with the sudden movement of all the other students.

Inside the seating was extremely comfortable. Grabbing a set of four to myself which was then quickly filled with other kids. None of them even bothering to say hello in any way. So I put my bag by my feet and pulled out one of my books. Taking out the photograph I had inside. All my books had one inside, keeping them flat and pristine.

Looking at how happy my parents looked. Standing on the edge of a cliff. A massive shot of the horizon reaching out below them. The sun just about to disappear, painting the sky in bright orange. My father towering over her like my brother did me.

Wiping a quick tear away before anyone noticed. Slipping the photo into the back cover, curling my legs underneath me I started reading. Getting lost into the world of romance. Not noticing how much time had gone by until the driver came over the speakers in each car.

"We will be arriving at the school very shortly. If you look out the left, you will have the pleasure of seeing the amazing building standing tall."

All the passengers rushed over to the left side of the train, my fingers gripping onto my book as I was nudged by the one sitting beside me. Looking out the window like everyone else. The view of this building made the floating train look like a toy.

The futuristic school looked amazing. The curvy, metal walls of the building catching the sun, shining bright. The massive tower in the middle had glass running down the back and the front. The bottom floor was three times as big as the rest. Six rounded roofs surrounded the middle structure. Looking like an upside down flower.

The view suddenly taken away by a tunnel. The sun getting blocked and the kids all returned to their seats. Placing my book back in my bag. Our transport coming out the other side of the rock. Slowing down next to a makeshift platform.

The building even taller than before. Looking up and hoping I wouldn't have to ascend too high. My legs feeling like jelly at the thought. Not moving until most people had disembarked.

Slinging my bag over my shoulder and moving off. Following the crowd of kids, hearing a voice coming from the front. "Welcome to Fawkes Institute of Training. You are the last to arrive so we will move straight into the hall for the welcome assembly. You can place your bags on the trolleys just inside the entrance and they will be moved up into your rooms once they have been selected. If you haven't written your name on them yet, please do so now. You will find pens by the trolleys."

I shuffled my bag around and found my name written along the handle. Smiling as we all entered the massive school. Placing my bag on a trolley. Trying to catch sight of my brother or his friends but my lack of height made it a problem. The crowds moving through the massive lobby.

Either side of us were two grated openings. A small room that held a shop of sorts. Snacks and food on one side. Empty shelves taking up the rest. Opposite was a massive canteen. Tables and chairs just like in school back home.

As we all filled the area I saw the steps that led up to the middle shaft. An elevator sat at the bottom which could have housed at least half of us. My eyes moving higher, the sunlight coming through the glass sides. Seeing the many many levels high above. My legs almost giving way so I quickly looked down.

The herd of students changing direction as someone saw a set of doors with, Hall, written above it. Pushing through the double doors and inside one of those round shaped buildings. So many boys and girls already seated around the middle stage. We shuffled around until we filled up the last section.

Picking out the other villages and towns who had been invited. My village was right on the edge of the sector eight. We didn't get many visitors out there so it was a shock to see so many different species here. Some looked similar to us humans but others looked like they belonged to another planet.

The seats were benches covered in a cushiony layer which was better than the one I had been occupying at the train station. In the middle was a stage like we were about to watch a live band. Five white booths sitting there at the back. Stairs leading up the front and then behind those five boxes. A single man climbed up to stand in front of the microphone. Out came some note cards from his fancy, black jacket.

His trousers looked just as nice, a red bow tie around his shirt collar. A hand was run through his wavy brown hair. A clearing of the throat echoed around the massive hall before he spoke. "First I would like to welcome you all to Fawkes. As I'm sure you know we are travelling around the continent to find fighters and soldiers for our toughest army unit. To prevent another war breaking out on our land."

He was on about the fifty year war against the

original inhabitants of Mythoria. We came in and tried to take over. It wasn't at all surprising that we were met with anger and war. Sadly they were wiped off the face of this land and we deemed it a win. For some peculiar reason, I didn't agree with that sentiment.

"I am the president of this school, Ethan West. Since you will be training in combat and some of you will have the pleasure of learning magic as well. We don't tolerate fighting outside of the class room. You will be ejected from the school and sent back home. I hope I've made that very clear."

There was a silence that rolled around the massive hall. The president flipped to another card before continuing. "You will be called down by your schools. Inside each of these booths is a crystal. They will not only determine your particular affinity. They will also unlock your potential. Making it much much easier to learn these things. Something that has helped speed up our process which brought great recognition from the government. Not to mention a generous grant."

He waved a hand to the booths and started calling out the schools. Ours being the last one since we were the last to arrive. The rows of benches being emptied, joining the queue that led down the stairs towards the stage.

Finally it being my turn I entered the booth. Opening and closing the white curtain. Looking down at a pedestal. Sitting atop was an electronic pad and a crystal. The clear top of the booth shone light down upon it. Bouncing it across the material around me. So captivating.

Words popped up on the screen, giving me

instructions on how to proceed. Cradling the crystal carefully in my palms. Watching as the middle started to shift. A cloud spreading inside that gem. Watching as my palms started tingling where the crystal touched. Those clouds began to change colour. Glowing from within with a red light. Seeing it storming around in circles.

The redness getting brighter, filling the whole thing. Wondering if that was it when there was something else at the centre. A darkness, just like the red. Growing until it was a little ball in the middle. Half red and half black.

Then the crystal started calming, going back to that clear colour so I placed it back on top of the pedestal. I tapped the pad and it came to life. It first asked me my name which I entered. Then I had to fill in how many different colours appeared in the crystal. Entering two and hitting next.

A keyboard popped up and I filled in the two spaces with my colours. Hitting next a final time and I was giving instructions to head for the canteen. The screen went blank and I left my booth. Walking back across the stage. Looking at the reactions of others coming out of the booths. Some looking confused, just how I felt.

Heading out the hall the way we had entered. Most of the students were hanging around the elevator. Some inside waiting for it rise up the column. I moved towards the cafeteria finding the gate unlocked. The lights on, shining down on the tables. My eyes rose to the menu above the counter.

There were no prices and the pictures looked amazing. My stomach grumbling despite having breakfast before getting on the train. Some of the other students here were chatting to each other. Sitting down near the corner away from them all. Wishing I had my book with me, since I didn't I decided to watch the others. Recognising one of them from my village. The other three I had no clue about.

One of the guys seeing me looking came walking over with a big grin. His chubby features filled out his shirt and trousers. Surprised that top button hadn't popped off already. Giving him a shy smile then looking away. Seeing the outside world through the massive window that ran the whole wall. Loving the green that stretched on for miles.

"I saw you looking at me."

"Sorry, won't happen again." Turning further away from him. Hoping he would just walk away.

"It's okay. I like you to. We should definitely be boyfriend and girlfriend."

I couldn't stop the laugh that shot out of my mouth. Seeing his hurt reaction. "That wasn't very nice of me."

"It's okay. I forgive you. To make it up to me you should definitely dress nicer when we go out for a date."

"I'm not going to go out with you."

"Not yet maybe. You'll soon change your mind. I won't give up so easily. I know when a girl wants to go out with me."

Looking up at him, hoping to see he was joking. "Does this usually work?"

"All the time."

"Then why don't you have a girlfriend right now?"

There was a moment of confusion on his face.

Then an idea clearly popped in there. "I had to leave her behind. She was only fifteen."

"So was I a few days ago."

"But you're sixteen now. So it's alright."

I gave as soft of a smile I could muster. "I don't think you and I are going to work out. Let's not even give it a try."

"Why not. Look." Suddenly he reached down and grabbed my wrist. Pulling me up to his body making me yelp out in pain.

A voice coming from behind him. "Let her go, Troy!"

The chubby boy turned with anger. But seeing his expression quickly changing when he saw who was speaking to him. "Kilroy."

"Let her go." My wrist being released, rolling it around and wriggling my fingers. "Now run along."

"You know, you don't have your father to save you here. It's just us boys."

"I never needed my father to kick your arse. Or your friends. Who I've noticed, most couldn't make it because they haven't gone through puberty yet."

The red headed boy walked and nudged his elbow into Kilroy. Now he was out of the way I got a good look at my saviour. Blonde hair just like me, curly as well. Just a lot shorter than mine. Swept back so the short curls stood up a little. Giving him a boyish cuteness that I couldn't stop staring at.

Out came a hand towards me. Taking it and taken by surprise when he leant down and kissed the back of it. "Kilroy, William. And you are?"

"Her name is Crystal." Another interaction got interrupted but this time I was annoyed. Looking past

William to see my brother standing there. He was one of the tallest in our village and it looked like that could be the case here as well.

Looking down at William with his big arms across his chest. Only my new friend here didn't bother looking around or even acknowledging my brother's presence. "Crystal is a very pretty name."

"Thanks. This is my brother, Lance."

"That's a less pretty name. Not my type." William's bright blue eyes locked on mine. "You are very cute. I love your curls."

As a hand came up to touch a strand of my hair my brother pulled him around to face him. Wanting to interject but I saw the look in his eyes. The need to protect me had always been in him. Sometimes it did go a little too far. "Lance, calm down."

"Yeah, Lance." William reached forward, brushing his fingers over my brother's shirt. Giving his tie a little wiggle to straighten it up. "Calm down. We don't want to get kicked out on our first day. Do we?"

"It would be worth it to wipe that smug look off of your face."

I scooted around in between them. Not seeming like it did anything because of my short stature. "That's enough." Placing a hand against my brother's chest. Softly pushing him away which he did. Only out of respect to me. "It was nice to meet you, William."

"You to, see you around. You to, cupcake." A wink to my brother almost sent my sibling in for a punch. But I pressed my hand against him harder.

Just then one of the teachers came walking in. A young looking woman, wearing a bright blue tracksuit. Long brown hair pulled back into a ponytail. The scrunchy bright blue like her outfit. "I hope I don't see any fighting already. That happens in the classroom and during the tournament. Only then. Got it!"

Her sudden increase in volume had most of us jumping. Not surprising it was my brother and William who didn't. Both of them seeming like they just wanted to get on with the fighting. The teacher calling the kids forward one at a time. My brother getting brought to the front first.

Trying to hear what she was saying to him, not even knowing how many colours he saw in his own crystal. The others being dismissed away, me being left until last. The teacher coming up to me, her ponytail swinging from side to side with each step. A softer face coming through than before. "What's your name?"

"Crystal Darke."

"Right, Miss Darke. There was something off about your results."

"What do you mean?"

"You put in red and black."

"That's right."

"You mean blank? Like a clear colour?"

"No I mean black. Right in the centre."

"Oh." Seeing her confused look. "Black isn't a colour that can appear. If you would take a seat and excuse me for a moment."

"Um...sure."

"I'll be right back." Off she scurried. Doing something between a fast walk and a jog. Wondering what I had done wrong. Feeling even more like an outcast since everyone else had already gone off to their rooms.

Instead of taking a seat I walked over to the

large window. Looking out and spotting what seemed like a ranch in the distance. Animals running around a paddock made out of metal. Not the usual ones you would spot containing horses.

I had no idea how far the train had brought us but I was feeling extremely far from home right now. Wishing I had one of my photos to look at, to bring me a smile when honestly I could have sat down and cried.

Taking a few deep breaths when I heard footsteps coming back, slower than they had gone. The tracksuit wearing teacher popping back through the entrance. "Everything is all sorted. You will be on level twelve, room five. But first the president would like a word with you."

"But, was there something wrong with my results?"

"No, no. Of course there isn't, sweetie." Her demeanour so soft. "He would just like a chat with you. Nothing to worry yourself over. Take the elevator all the way up to the top floor."

"That's really high." Feeling sweat building at the base of my neck just at thought of it.

"Yes, he's a busy man so I would hurry if I was you." Then she turned and left. Leaving me to make my own way up there.

Taking slow steps out of the cafeteria and up to that massive elevator. Moving inside, the vast space seeming even more intimidating being by myself. I hit the top button, the glass doors shutting. The massive round box getting taken up that tower of metal and glass.

Pressing my hands against the side, breathing in and out steadily. Keeping my eyes shut until I felt the stop of motion. The doors opening with a hiss. My fingers reaching for the edge of the doorway and moving out. Sliding my feet over the surface until I felt the metal flooring.

When I opened my eyes I let out a sigh of relief, staring down a short hallway. Giving the elevator a quick glance but quickly moving my feet forwards. Lifting my hand up to knock but the door just slid sideways as I neared it.

Seeing the massive office beyond. My eyes hitting the enormous window at the far end. The whole wall made up of panes of glass. The world beyond looked so small. My legs going like jelly. Using the wall to my left to steady my steps.

My hand knocked into a picture. A piece of tapestry trapped behind glass. The edges burnt like someone tried to destroy it. Too busy trying not to pass out to even try and work out those weird shapes and colours.

Moving along I saw a few old fashioned weapons in cases. Axes from centuries ago. Looking like a tribe had made them. Ignoring the little signs below them and moving along. Turning my back to the window as the room opened up before me.

Looking up to another level when a voice came softly. "Welcome to my office." Seeing the man from the stage, wearing his nice suit still. A book in his hand which explained the new glasses sitting on his nose. "I'll be right down, we can go sit over by my desk."

Looking over my shoulder to where he nodded. The massive desk sitting in front of that window. Turning back quickly, rubbing my hand over the back of neck. Feeling the sweat gathered there. "Is it okay if we talk up there?" Looking up, happy that the small second level he was standing in had walls blocking the outside view.

"Sure. Come on up." Following the wall and up the stairs. Moving until that glass was out of sight. Pressing my back to the wall and acting like I was in a small room on the bottom floor. "Are you afraid of heights?"

Nodding, "Yeah."

"Oh. Our future meetings will have to be somewhere else then."

"Future meetings? I did something wrong, didn't I?"

"Oh no. You should never think that." He placed that book onto a shelf full of them. All of them looking old and dusty. "What do you know about our past. About the fifty year war?"

"I know that we wiped out an entire civilization just because we wanted the land."

"Blunt but also very true." He walked over to a massive painting that stretched all the way up to the high ceiling. Depicting a massive battle with a castle at the top. "This was the final battle where the head of their leader was lopped off. You can probably see a brave knight at the top there holding it up."

"All I see is a barbarian."

"Again, true." A soft smile was sent my way before he carried on. "There aren't many particulars shared about this species that we wiped out. They were more technologically advanced than us. The only way we won is because we betrayed their trust. Attacked during a negotiation. You see, they were going to share the land. Until we found resources. Many of the cities on this continent are built from materials we killed for."

"That makes our past even worse than I thought."

"Much worse. Only, not all is bad news. This species had a defence mechanism that helped them survive. Even until this very day. Do you know what that is?"

"Not a clue. You're saying there are still some of them around?" Looking up at the painting again. The pictures depicting them to be black skinned humanoids. There bright yellow eyes shining. No doubt embellished for the painting but I had seen other pictures showing similar images. Drawings and photos of dead bodies.

"Oh yes, not many but there are some. And of course they have children with humans."

"That doesn't make sense. Why would a human sleep with someone from that species. With the history told the way it has been."

"Because of the defence mechanism." The president of the school rushed off to the bookshelf again. Seeming to be excited discussing history. He pulled out a leather bound journal. The cover kept shut with a string of that same material around a pin. The thing was flipped open and I saw what it contained.

Personal drawings and notes. With how excited Mister West was acting, it could have easily been his writing. "Look, here."

A finger pointed as I drew closer. Seeing drawings of three bodies. One was clearly one of those species with the black skin and the glowing eyes. Seeing that it was changing into a more human looking body. "Are you saying they change into humans?"

"Not just humans. In my research I have figured that they can shape shift. Just the once I imagine. But what better way to hide amongst your enemies than to become them. It's brilliant."

"And you have proof of this?"

Hands were pointed towards me. "You. The crystal turned black for you. That means you have their genes inside you. You're an everfae."

CHAPTER 2

Hearing his words I started backing away. "So, is that what this is all about? The school. To find people like me? I know what the government at the time did to those people. I'm not going to go through something like that."

"No, no. You misunderstand me. It will be better if I show you." I backed away a little bit as he turned. Going to a set of drawers that didn't look deep enough to hold more than a few trinkets. As he turned my body tensed until I saw the crystal he held in his palms. Cupping it and making those cloudy contents swirl around.

The colour becoming darker until the whole thing was filled with that darkness. Shining despite the dark colour of it. "So, you're one as well?"

"Yes I am. On my mum's side, for generations now."

"Why are you telling me this?"

"Because." The crystal was placed back inside that drawer and put away. Next he went back over to the shelving. Pulling out a book. The front cover slipping, only kept intact by a few strands of material. "This contains everything we know about the Titans."

"The Titans?" Trying to take in everything he was saying.

Having trouble keeping up as he carried on

his explanation. "Yes. This was the most powerful technology they had. It was more like sorcery than science but humans have a way with words don't they." He opened the book and placed it on a waist high display case.

As he flicked through the pages I looked at the pictures. Beasts and animals. Both large and small. My eyes going wide when he showed me one that was as big as a city. "This one is the biggest of them, the most dangerous. No one has ever seen it. All that is rumoured is that it turns dark as this thing blocks out the sun. Then the death starts."

"How come people don't see these things around?"

"Some blend in with the monsters we already have roaming around the barelands between settlements. Others are just never seen again. Killed or maybe they die naturally. Perhaps they go into hiding."

"So these can just be rumours."

"Sure, some of them can be. But I've actually seen one." His fingers moved quickly until he opened up the pages. "When I was a boy. This thing was called to me. They can sense when our kind is near."

I studied the picture. Looking like a snake like dragon. A massive head, multiple horns sticking out with two protruding further than the others. The body covered in scales. No legs or feet. A tail topped with a row of spikes. "How young were you?"

"Five. Left me with a nice mark to remember it by." A trousers leg was lifted and I saw the puncture marks it must have made with its teeth. Three scars on either side. "The only reason I survived is because my father rammed our truck into its side."

"And no one noticed this thing?"

"I lived out on a cattle ranch. We were used to having monsters come hunting for our livestock. This was just much bigger and more dangerous."

"And you haven't seen one since?"

The book was closed and he shook his head. "These things call to us just like they are called to us in return. Whenever I felt that calling I would ignore it. Move away until it started disappearing. Now I don't even feel anything."

"So all I have to do is ignore them? They won't attack me then?"

"Actually, I want you to do the opposite to what I did."

"Why?"

"Because there have been reports over the last few decades. Monsters attacking human settlements. People dying and the descriptions are more than your everyday creature. These things are getting restless and wild. They're still here waiting and they're getting bored or something. Taking on their own choices."

"And what does that have to do with me?"

"If you can control them. Stop them and we can show that our kind isn't all bad."

"I don't think I'm the right person for that. I scream when there's a spider in my room. Definitely not someone who can stop these things."

"You can. It's our heritage to do it."

"Then you do it."

"I can't hear them any more."

"Then use me like a radar. I'll tell you if I feel anything and then you can go after it yourself. Keeping me out of danger."

The president seemed to contemplate what I had proposed. Nodding with a big smile. "I guess that could be a good arrangement."

"Alright, is that all you wanted to talk to me about?"

"Yes, thank you."

"Okay. I should get to my room. Most of the other kids didn't wear their uniforms. Think I should probably change."

"We don't have a uniform here. We keep it very casual."

"Alright. Thanks for the chat."

"If you ever need to talk about all this. I'm here for you, I've done plenty of research into the matter."

"Thanks." Giving him a shy smile and making my way back to the elevator. As it moved back down I was lost in my thoughts. Trying to figure it all out, it seemed so outrageous. The elevator bobbed as it stopped on the twelve floor. Hearing chatter coming from behind the doors as I walked. Pressing the button by the fifth door.

Blowing out a sigh as the door shut behind me, eyes closed. My mind racing with the knowledge I now held. The first thought I had was that the president was lying. But that was more wishful thinking.

Pushing off from the door and opening my eyes. Wanting to see what my room was like but all I saw was the thing in here. Dressed like a person but her head was covered in bumps. Looking like horns sticking out of her scaly skin. The image of that thing in the book coming back to me. My heart pounding hard as it just stared at me.

Lips curling to reveal teeth. Then it came at me screeching some kind of noise. Horns growing in length looking so terrifying as I dropped to the floor screaming myself. Hands up in defence, waiting for the attack.

Hearing footsteps bringing that thing closer until they stopped right in front of me. Hearing more screeches, different pitches like it was trying to say something. Cracking my eye and looking through my fingers. Seeing it standing there. A hand reached out towards me.

My heart still racing. Looking into those big eyes it had. Mostly black with a slit of blue down the middle. I slowly reached my hand forwards. Feeling the scaly palm rubbing roughly against mine. Two fingers and a thumb pulling me to my feet.

It suddenly turned, running back to its bed. Rummaging through the two bags sitting there. A small metal object was pulled out. It was placed against the front of its throat. A soft whir of power as it was turned on.

This thing turned and this time the mouth moved it wasn't just the screeching that came out. Words mumbled in with that high-pitched noise until after a few sentences it worked itself out. Words being formed from that little machine. "Oh, that's better." The metallic words sounding weird as I felt a little more at ease. "I do apologise about that. Forgot that I have to be more careful here."

"No kidding. Sorry about my reaction." Feeling embarrassed how I dropped down to the floor.

"Please, if something came running towards me like that, I would react the same." This creature shook it's head softly. Seeing those horns moving back into its head. Looking short again and less frightening. "I feel I can make a better first impression on you now."

"Much." Still feeling my heart pounding. Taking a few deep breaths to calm down. "My name is Crystal. Crys for short."

"Very nice to meet you. My name isn't very easy to pronounce in this language. So perhaps you can just call me D."

"Alright. I can live with that."

"I'm a Dinoser. With the way you reacted, I'm guessing you haven't met one before?"

"No." Letting out a little laugh. "I live in a very tiny village at the edge of the continent, Livenbrook. We don't get other species around there much."

"Well here's to meeting your first." This time when she came forward I didn't cower. Shaking that hand again. "Pleased to meet you, Crys."

"You to, D." Giving her a soft smile.

As she turned to get more stuff out of her bag she spoke over her shoulder. "I'm happy they put me with a girl."

"Do they mix room mates here?" My eyes falling on my own bag sitting on my bed. Joy hitting my heart as I knew what I had inside. Pulling open the top and grabbing my books. Using the shelves built into the wall by my bed to line them up. Pulling out photos from each and leaning them against the wall.

Looking over them making me smile even more. Then turning around to look at my room mate as she spoke again. Her scales showing on her arms as she wore a tight vest top. Looking like it was made out of the material hover bikers would wear. The same went for her trousers. "Well, I wasn't too sure who they would stick me with."

"I hadn't even thought they would put a girl with

a boy. Surely the parents would have a field day."

"I'm not exactly a girl though." My eyes moving over her body. "Dinosers don't have a gender. We're kind of neutral in that respect."

"Um. Oh. That's cool." She gave me a weird look and I gave a smile in return. "Doesn't bother me."

"I'm surprised you're not as judgemental as everyone else. You have no idea the names I get called by the other students at my school."

"Aren't there many more like you there?"

"Nope, I'm the only one there. My parents moved a few years back. Was hard but I made a few friends."

"Any of them here?"

"A couple."

"Lucky you. All my friends were too young."

"I'll introduce you to mine."

"Thanks." Giving her another look. "So...do I...."

D laughed and smiled at me. "I see myself more girl than boy."

"Right, felt so awkward asking that."

"Don't worry yourself."

Turning back around and looking at my photos. My hands pulling out clothing to go into the wardrobe on my side of the room. "So, since you have no gender. Does that mean you like both boys and girls?"

"I don't see it like that. I like who I like but if you're asking about you. I haven't met a human I fancy just yet."

Giving a shy smile over my shoulder. "I don't know whether I should be glad or upset."

A laugh came out of that gadget on her throat. "Just consider yourself human."

Hanging up my clothes my brain latched onto

the last thing she said. According to the president of the school, I wasn't entirely human. But that wasn't something I was planning on sharing. A hug from my brother would work wonders for my emotions right now.

Instead I knew I had to make this work by myself. I couldn't rely on him to keep my spirits up. Hanging the last piece of my clothes up, then I looked through them. Pulling out a pair of green combats, a black vest top and a short zip-up hoody that will shine bright white over my darker clothes.

Stripping without a second thought of the dinoser in my room. Switching outfits just as a screen by our door came to life. Both of us walking over to see it was mentioning a pair of watches. I gave my room mate's bare wrist a quick glance, happy I hadn't missed something.

Two smaller screens came to life just below the monitor. I plucked one off, following the directions we were given. As I pressed it to my wrist a strap zipped around my arm. Clicking into place then pulling snug.

A voice coming out of the wall whilst I marvelled at how cool this thing was. "These watches will help you keep track of your lesson schedule. And right now, it is time for your lesson in weapon training."

The screen went blank and both of our watches lit up. Showing a message that weapon training will start in five minutes on the third level, room one. It vibrated for a little bit before going silent. I gave it a tap but it simply showed the time.

D noticed what I was doing. "They must only come on when we get messages."

"Shame we can't send messages to each other."

"I wouldn't be surprised if they used to. God knows what kind of pictures people were getting with some of the idiot boys about."

I burst out laughing, knowing exactly what she was talking about. "I've already met one of those boys. Idiot called, Troy. Stupid red head."

"Already making friends."

She giggled which made me smile. "Looks like we should get to weapon training."

We moved to the door which slid open automatically after a beep from our watches. Moving out into the hall with the rest of the rabble. "You don't seem too thrilled about weapon training."

"I never even wanted to come to this school. Fighting isn't really my kind of action to take. I'm more for diplomacy and negotiating."

"Did you get green in your crystal then?"

"Green? No it was red and....." My mouth shutting quickly as that second colour almost leaked out. "Why would it have been green?"

"They say that if you're one for diplomacy it glows green."

"No, just the red."

"Then it seems you are more aligned with elemental magic than diplomacy."

I gave her a quick look as we joined the others in the massive elevator. Happy that our whole floor seemed to be all girls. Not seeing that annoying red headed idiot from earlier was a blessing. "I don't like hurting people."

"Magic isn't all about hurting people."

"This school is to train soldiers or whatever. They hurt people."

"They also save people. Don't be so closed minded."

Feeling a little annoyed at her words. Feeling a little judged. "I'll try."

"You might even enjoy yourself."

"I doubt it." The glass doors opened and we piled out into the hallway. Coming up to the bright blue covered teacher again. Her hair still pulled back in that ponytail. "Rooms one to five you're with Holbrook. To your left."

Keeping close to D and moving along the hallway. Moving into the door on this side. Coming into the classroom. A wide open space in front of us. See-through screens hanging down in a large circle. Taking a position with D as the others flooded in.

Looking down the side of the classroom where the space widened. A short stage sat to the left by the wall. Opposite it was racking that curved out of sight. Hearing chatter and conversation from the other side of the room. Another classroom was filling up just like ours.

Then in came Holbrook. Walking with a limp and half an arm missing. His shirt rolled up to show off that mangled stump. His head completely bald with a full on beard covering his face. Two thick scars ran down amongst the hairs making me wonder why he didn't just shave it all off.

Looking like a man at the end of a wedding. Black trousers and a black waistcoat. Long white sleeves folded up to his elbows. He couldn't have stood taller than four foot and he was to teach us about weapons. Watching him walking up to the front. Before talking he hit a button on the wall. The racking I had noticed lit up, showing off the many different weapons. Most of which I couldn't name. Not a single clue how to use any of them.

Holbrook moved among us. "You will all go up to those weapons. Look at each and every one of them. Thanks to the crystal ceremony, deep down. your body will know which one you need. Listen to that instinct."

A girl near the back called out. "How do we know which one we want?"

"You listen!" Holbrook's sudden shout making the whole class jump. "Now get your arses up there and pick a weapon. And I assure you, if you do not listen, you will injure yourself and possibly others. That, I will not tolerate in my class."

Everyone stared at him. Then we all started moving as he pulled an angry face. Sticking close to D as people started to rush. Everyone stood in front of those weapons. Eyes moving over every single one slowly. Seeming even more out of my depth now with no safety net.

Nudging D gently. "You have a clue about any of these?"

"Some."

"Great." Turning and looking. Remembering Holbrook's words. Deciding to take my time, steady my breathing. Wondering if this would actually work. Would I get a ring in my brain or would a weapon talk to me. I had no clue.

My concentration suddenly breaking as I heard an annoying voice. "What the hell are you doing?"

Finding that red headed kid standing there with a smirk. The chubby neck looking a little bit better in a t-shirt. "God, not you again."

"Why are you just staring?"

"That's what our teacher told us to do."

"Ours didn't. She just said grab the first thing that catches your attention."

"I'd prefer to listen to mine." Ignoring him as he made a comment and returned my gaze to the wall. Moving my eyes over each one of those weapons. Then one of them caught my attention. The detailing on the wood looked beautiful. So much of it, it must have taken ages to carve. It was only half a metre long. Not able to tell what kind of weapon it was but somehow I knew it belonged to me.

Reaching out but someone else was too quick. Seeing that weapon being pulled from the rack. My eyes narrowing at that same boy. "Hey, that's mine."

"Looks like it's in my hands. Not yours."

"Give it here."

"Just take another one."

Turning my head and looking at the other two that were sitting there. These were much longer and the detailing wasn't as nice. "That's the one I want."

"Stop being such a baby."

"Something wrong?" Holbrook's sudden closeness made both of us jump. The boy looking frightened by the man. Moving away until he was gone around the corner. "Have you picked a weapon?"

"I did but that boy just took it."

Holbrook rolled his eyes. "Either go get it or pick something else."

"But you said.."

"I said go get it or pick something else!"

Looking into those eyes and feeling them staring back into my soul. "Yes, sir." Turning to the racking.

Seeing a few of the weapons left. Looking to D who was standing there with a pair of nunchuks.

A pair of them were left on the rack so I grabbed those. Even if they weren't calling to me, at least I could study with D about them. Grabbing one end and tugging them from the hook. The other side flipping up and swinging into my finger. Yelping and dropping them to the floor. Holbrook giving me one of those stares again. "Sorry." Grabbing my weapon and hurrying to my friend.

Once everyone was back amongst those screens, Holbrook stood up in front of us and carried on the lesson. "These weapons are different to ones found in the other weapon rooms. Warriors will use something with a little more edge to it. Or a blunt instrument to crush bones. These weapons are ones of finesse. Weapons that go well with mages of elemental magic. You guys."

Holbrook walked up to D and took her weapon. Casually swinging them around with ease, watching the two pieces arcing through the air. Hearing that whipping noise as they moved. It swung around his hand, over his shoulder. A continuous motion until it flipped over into his grip.

He didn't say anything as he gave them back. Moving to another student and taking a stick. Swinging that around just as impressively. Watching in wonder as he seemed to put no effort into it. He did this three more times, showing us how the weapons could be used and moved.

Placing the last one back with its student. "If you have picked the right weapons. It won't take you long to learn them, then only a little longer to master them.

Take a moment to look at your weapons. Get an idea of how they feel in your hands."

Everyone did what they were told. I looked at my weapon. Seeing how end swung back and forth. Not even having the instincts to know what to do with them. A few times I looked up and caught Holbrook staring at me. Giving a shy smile before looking back down.

After a short period Holbrook's voice filled the classroom again. "Just a short lesson today since the welcome ceremony takes a while. When you return for your next lesson, you will get to start training. If you're worried that this seems impossible, don't be. Now, it's lunch time. Return your weapons to the rack and head on out."

Carrying my nunchuks I knew I had made the wrong decision. They felt so clumsy and heavy. Hanging them up and watching how D put hers back. With more confidence like she had been handling them her whole life.

Giving Holbrook a nod as I left but getting nothing but a stare back. Getting into the elevator that took us to the lobby. "Holbrook seems like a real charmer."

"Oh yeah." D laughed as she replied. "He's clearly party central with his friends."

"If he has any friends." We giggled with a few of the other kids joining in. Coming out and moving towards the cafeteria. Some of the other classes had already finished. Tables and chairs filled here and there.

Getting in line as the smell of the food hit my nostrils. Wanting to moan at the sheer bliss of it. Father wasn't the best of cooks. I had learnt a few things here and there with my brother but nothing to this standard.

Doubling that thought as I saw the food sitting there. All different kinds, some clearly from other cultures. Looking over the menu again but I couldn't see any prices for anything. Looking back down as the plates were moving around on a conveyor belt.

Peering down the line that finished by an electronic tablet. Seeing people waving their watches underneath. Jumping as a sweet voice spoke to me. "You look confused."

Seeing a lady dressed in blue. "I was just wondering about prices."

"It doesn't work like that here. You get one plate and a bowl. Plus a drink from the dispensers." She pointed and I saw what she was talking about.

"Thank you."

"No problem, sweetie." She walked off, her red pigtails bouncing. I grabbed a plate with what looked like lasagne on it. Having a bowl of fruit with it. Shuffling along as people picked and moved over to the drinks.

Grabbing a cup and getting some orange juice from the nozzle. Able to smell that fruity scent as it filled my cup. Getting to the tablet I smiled at the woman standing behind it. Wearing the same blue outfit as the redhead.

She punched in what I had and nodded to the scanner at the bottom of the tablet. Waving my watch it beeped back at me. Smiling as she thanked me and I turned. Spotting a table completely empty so I headed over to it. Not touching my food yet, looking over my shoulder to see D heading my way.

Then I heard chairs being moved. Turning back

around to find three girls sitting opposite me. The middle one with long frizzy hair leaning forwards. A huge fake smile plastered across her features. "I absolutely love that hoody."

"Thanks." Pulling my hands under the table, fingers tugging at the end of my sleeves.

"I just wanted to say, it being the first day and all. That you need to choose your friends carefully. It will determine how your time here goes."

"What do you mean?" Eyes moving across them. Seeing how dressed similarly or perhaps the two silent ones copied the brunette in the middle.

"Making friends with the likes of that." Seeing her looking behind me, looking over my shoulder to see D standing there. Seeing the anger in her eyes. "Will put a stain on your reputation."

My new friend went to speak but I quickly turned and beat her to it. "The only people that worry about reputation are the ones who don't matter. The little people who would rather drag others down instead of looking in the mirror and sorting their own life out."

Her jaw dropped open as I spoke to her. "I was the most popular girl in my school."

"You say that like it's a qualification. No doubt you'll be popular here as well. But that doesn't make you important. Just means you're pretty or you're just too friendly when it comes to boys. Either way, it doesn't give you the right to police what other people do. So get the hell off of my table and go sit somewhere else."

The girl pulling one of those fake, hurt looks before getting up and walking off. With her two friends quickly following. D sat down opposite me with a huge grin on her face. "Where the hell did that come from?"

"What?" Picking up my fork and starting to munch my food. My own thoughts mirroring her question. I had never been one for confrontation. That outburst just slipped out.

"That, you know what. You come across as this quiet girl but really you have fire in your veins." Letting out a giggle. "The look on her face was priceless."

"That was truly amazing." Smiling as another girl sat down with us, short black hair covering her head. She looked human like me except for her eyes. They were more like slits with a pretty shade of green showing through. A very tiny black dot like a human's pupil. "I can't believe Larsh missed that. She won't even believe it." She held out her hand, noticing the extremely slender fingers.

Shaking it with a smile. "I'm Crystal. You can call me Crys."

"Just call me Flo." She noticed my eyes dipping to those fingers as they slid across my skin. "I'm half-harkin, half-human. All I got from my groovy side of the family are my fingers, my eyes and my teeth." She pulled her lip down and I saw the lines of sharp points. "Makes eating meat so much easier."

"I bet." Eyes taking in Flo's body. She did seem human apart from the features she mentioned. Her clothes were not the kind I had even seen before. Tight fitting robes, patterns of flowers sewn with golden thread. "Are all your friends.....different? Sorry if that offends."

"We've been called a lot worse but yes."

"Is that going to be a problem?" Flo's reaction clearly coming from experiencing years of bullying.

"No, of course not. It was just a question."

"Sorry." A soft smile shone through the anger. "Over-reacting as usual."

"She does overreact to everything, don't take it personally."

Smiling and putting my eyes down to my food as I ate. Getting through most of my lasagne before I noticed the president of the school standing in the opening of the cafeteria. Staring right at me. He even waved when my eyes landed on him. "I'll be right back, guys."

Heading over to where he was standing, just outside of the entrance. Dropping off my tray at the bin area. Moving towards him with my apple, noticing a book in his fingers. His smile making me smile back. "How did you find your first lesson?"

"Not much doing. Mostly sat and watched videos. I don't see how this school turns out fighters if that's all it does."

"I'm sure your next lesson will be a little more exciting."

"We'll see."

"Here. I found a book on Mythoria. It contains titans that have been rumoured to be in this area."

"Oh. Right." I took it from his hand, gripping the leather cover.

"I also have other books, on the other continents. Read up and it'll help with tracking them down."

"Other continents? Are you expecting me to travel? Helping you find these things? I belong in a little village with my nose in a book. Not travelling around looking for monsters."

"I was just suggesting reading up on some of the titans. Open your eyes to this world you're a part of."

Seeing something in his expression that made me think he wasn't being entirely truthful. "But please, have a look at the book. You might enjoy what you see in there."

"I'll have a look."

"And enjoy your classes." Simply giving him a look as he walked off towards the elevator. My feet moved me as my eyes looked at the cover. Similar to the last one I was shown. Leather bound, a little strap that kept it closed. Heading out of the entrance, the doors opening automatically.

The soft breeze bringing with it the scent of flowers. Even though I couldn't spot any in this area. Moving along the metal wall, looking in through the big window. Seeing the other students chatting and eating. Almost like it was a normal school.

Slumping down to the grass I leant back against the wall. Opened the book and flicked through some of the pages. Seeing the pencil drawn pictures. Ranging from small critters to titans that could knock down a building.

Moving through it until I came to the last page. Seeing the black scribbles that had been scrawled across the page. Making up some kind of shadow monster. No information had been written down like this thing was made up of myth and legend.

Feeling the breeze kicking up harder, flicking the pages against my fingers. That smell of flowers coming harder. I stood as my curly hair was flung up. Pulling my hood up over my head and turning towards the entrance. The wind hitting my back hard, hearing some kind of growl from behind. My whole body freezing with that sound rolling like thunder.

CHAPTER 3

Images in the book flashed in my mind. Picturing some kind of creature ready to rip my throat out. But as I looked over my shoulder I saw nothing. Just an empty horizon of grass. My body getting hit harder by that wind. The growl growing deeper, making my heart beat faster. Stepping backwards as I looked for something in the distance.

But as the growl died so did the wind. Silence so loud as I stood there, confused and surprised. That was until I was hit by a harsh punch of wind. Knocking me back on my butt as a roar rocked my body. Bones shaking from the sheer noise like it was hitting against my body physically.

My feet digging through the grass until I managed to move back through the entrance. Looking over my shoulder like that noise was stalking me. Hitting into someone and sending the book out of my grip.

"Jesus, watch where you're going." Letting out an annoyed sigh when I saw it was the red headed boy. "Oh, what do we have here?"

His fingers grabbing the book from the floor before I could stop him. "Give it back, it's not even mine."

"We stealing other people's stuff?"

"No, I was given it for research."

"Oh?" The book was opened and he laughed at the contents. "This doesn't look like research to me."

"Give it back."

"How about I rip it apart because of your attitude."

Seeing his fingers grabbing a bunch of those pages. "Then you'll have to explain to the president of this school why you damaged his book."

The boy paused, seeing him weighing up his options of trusting what I was saying. Then he quickly chucked the book at me. Catching it as it hit my chest. "There's something about you. Like you're better than everyone else here."

"I don't want to be here. That's all."

"No, from that first time we chatted, I could sense it."

"That wasn't a chat. You hit on me like a creep."

"That's because he is a creep." A strong voice with authority had us both turning. William came walking over to stand next to me. "It's creepy how he hits on every single girl he meets but he would rather spent his alone time with his buddy."

"Shut it, William."

"Don't like the truth do you. You see, Crystal. Our chubby friend here likes boys. Likes to kiss them and feel them up. It's quite disgusting when you think about it."

My eyes going wide as I listened to the way he spoke about him. Shoving my hand into his shoulder which brought a look of surprise. "Don't ever talk like that about anyone in my presence."

"What? You're kidding, right?"

"No I'm not kidding. If I hear you speaking like it

again then I'll tell you just how much it pisses me off."
Hitting his shoulder again before storming off. Heading
away from the cafeteria, coming to a stop in front of the
shop.

Leaning against the shutter that was still
covering the entrance. Looking over to see William
walking back into the cafeteria, shaking his head in
disbelief. Me and the red head exchanged a look before
he walked off in the same direction.

I didn't like the kid but no one deserved to be
spoken to like that. Taking a deep breath as I slowed the
anger running around my thoughts. Jumping a little as
my watch buzzed at me. Looking down and seeing the
message about my next class. Elemental magic on floor
two, room four.

Hearing the sudden noise of the stampede
happening in the lunch hall. Heading for that elevator
before many could do the same. Slipping the little
leather book into my thigh pocket. The elevator
stopping at floor two and heading down the hallway
looking for room four.

Having a couple of girls with me we walked
through the open door. Seeing the vast room beyond.
Holes in the ground like little learning pods. Seeing the
ladders that led down into each of them. A loud voice
making us all jump around to face the teacher standing
in the doorway.

Her tight one-piece outfit looked like something
you would wear swimming. Like a wet-suit made out
of cotton. Short white hair stuck up on end despite her
young looks. She sneered as she spoke. "Who the hell
told you you could enter my class without permission?"

One of the other girls speaking up with

confidence. "No one was here to tell us otherwise."

"I'm sorry I don't keep the same schedule as you. I'm a teacher and I have other things I need to take care of apart from teaching sniffling little kids how to do magic. Now get your arse out of here and line up like the others."

Feeling slightly frightened by this woman. Making my last teacher seem like a cuddly toy. The three of us moving out of the room quickly, looking down as we past by her. Joining the end of the queue, giving D a smile as she came from the elevator.

"Were you talking to the president of the school?"

"Yeah, he's leant me a book. He heard I loved history. Just something fun to read."

"Oh. There was me thinking you knew him from before."

"No. Nothing like that." Thinking about the connection we shared. Our heritage from the original inhabitants of this continent. "Was just a coincidence that I bumped into him."

The teacher calling out to me, "If you've done chatting. You can listen. Enter the room and stand by a pod. These will be for learning magic. I have no intention of getting burnt or drowned. These will keep me safe from your inexperience. Do not enter the pod until I give you the instruction to do so. Now in you go and please, for my sanity, keep the chatter to a minimum. I have no qualm with chucking students out of my class."

The more time I spent here, it seemed less like a school. The teachers almost seeming annoyed that they were here teaching us such things. The line moved forward. As I entered I followed the right wall, me and D picking pods over out the way. Watching as the rest of them were taken.

The teacher stood in the middle. "When you enter, please swipe your watch under the scanner for logging progress. We will be starting with the easiest elements to handle. Wind, fire, water and earth. These can be used defensively or offensively."

She moved to where a desk sat by the far wall. Picking up a clipboard and coming back towards us. A pen appearing in her fingers. "In you go. Make sure you're listening and not falling asleep down there."

Moving to the edge and using the rungs built into the side to descend. The floor made of rubber just like the walls. Finding the scanner and swiping my watch underneath. A beep coming and my name appearing.

Moving to the middle of the pod as the teacher spoke down to us all. "First will be water. Our bodies are made up by a percentage of it. Plus in most cases there is moisture in the air. You can pull on these factors to create a water spell."

As I listened I found it quite peaceful down here. Even the teacher's voice didn't sound so harsh in my pit of learning. Lifting my eyes as I noticed her figure moving above me. My eyes picking up the thick lines that ran down the side of her neck. Seeing them fluctuate a little and gasping.

This time I knew what kind of being I was looking at. Eyes dropping to the hand that held the pen. Seeing the webbing that joined her fingers. Knowing that her toes would be exactly the same. She was an aqualoy. Like a human but with fish features. Able to breath underwater and swim better than any other species.

Her voice coming again, "Our magic comes from our imagination. You need to will this creation into existence. Picture it in your mind and it will happen. You have already proven your affinity with elemental magic with the crystal ceremony. Now you can prove it again."

"You will create a ball of water. Doesn't have to be very big. Once you have it and it's sustained enough I want you to chuck it in the air. Call out so you get my attention. The first to do it will gain the most elite points. They will also gain my restraint. The rest of you won't be so lucky. I'm wasting my time being here, teaching you students how to do magic. So be quick about it."

A quiet fell over the class as we just stood there. The tapping of her feet walking her around in circles stopped. The teacher's voice filling the silence like a hammer smashing through glass. "Come on, get on with it!"

For a moment I just stood there, listening to the others as they tried. Hearing some chanting words like they were in a movie. Looking around at the edges I thought. This wasn't a physical exercise. The way she spoke about it, it was all mental.

So I took a seat in the centre of my floor. Deep breathes being brought in slowly and let out. Cupping my hands together over my lap. Picturing the ball of water forming there. Willing the water from inside my body to form outside.

As I wiggled my fingers I felt the slight splash of water hitting my skin, feeling it cool my hands. Opening my eyes and seeing that small sphere of water.

Letting out a laugh suddenly as I couldn't believe I was actually doing it.

Watching that little thing grow. Water seeping from my skin as I used my magic. The floating shape getting even bigger until it was similar to a football. Willing it to solidify. Lifting my finger, dragging it across the surface of my magic.

Like running your finger through the surface of a lake. The thing still holding that spherical body. Cupping my hands underneath it gently. Like a ball was sitting there. Thinking about chucking it up, to show off my talent but then I was reminded that I didn't want to be here.

I didn't agree with fighting and to use a talent even something like this, to hurt people. Was against my morals. So instead of chucking it up I let go of my concentration and moved my hands out the way.

Before it even dropped it burst apart. Jumping up from my sitting position as it splashed my trainers and trousers. Wiping but it had been more water than I expected. Leaving some damp patches on my thighs.

Only having to wait a few seconds longer before someone called out. Hearing the joy in their voice as the ball was chucked into the air. Then the yelp as it came crashing back down. The scream of shock making me giggle. Wanting to see who it had been and how drenched they were.

The teacher's voice coming from up there. "That's not bad but I'm sure you all can do faster than that. If you're ever in a battle or fight. Your enemy will not take a break whilst you concentrate. The more you practice the quicker it will come."

Whilst she chatted I sat back down. Cupping my

hands come together again, willing that water to come back. Fingertips wiggling and witnessing that ball form from droplets. Coming together much quicker than before. The ball floating above my palms again.

"Now, we'll move onto wind." My fingers flexed, not wanting to splash myself again I willed that ball to slowly shrink. Turning into little droplets by the end which landed on my hands, rubbing them together to get rid of them. "The air around us and our own breath helps us with this magic. Think of it as something you can see, manipulate with your fingers. Remember, it's more about the mind than the body when it comes to magic."

I kept in my sitting position. Steadying my breathing as I thought about the air leaking through my lips. Thinking about it like string. Fingers moving to capture it. Able to feel it running around over my skin like webbing.

Spinning those digits around in a circle. Thinking about a little tornado and was utterly delighted when it started to form. Letting it drift down to the soft floor. Guiding it with my hand to make it orbit around me. Moving to the wall and keeping that distance like it was on a track.

Giggling at how amazing it was to do such a thing. In books I had read about magic but it felt so different doing it myself. Doing the same again. Making that mini-tornado and letting it ring around me.

The wind kicking up in my little pod as they spun. Breathing out and letting them grow a little more. My hood being tugged about every time they past around me. Smiling in wonder until I heard the teacher's footsteps coming in this direction.

Breathing in as I reached my fingers towards the closest tornado. Making it come closer but it wasn't quick enough. Breathing out a sigh of frustration, flicking my fingers at it. The wind suddenly burst out against the walls and my body.

Doing the same for the other, the burst of power flicking the blonde stands of hair hanging down. Looking up as the teacher came to the edge. Staring at her as innocently as possible. "I'm trying, it's just not working for me."

"Uh-huh." She scribbled something on her clipboard and walked off as another student called out. Hearing the delight in their cheer and smiling to myself. Knowing that I had beaten them to it. Wiggling my fingers as I thought about the magic I could wield.

The teacher's voice coming again, "This needs to be much quicker. You have the power. It's right there in your fingers. Believe in yourself."

Hearing D's voice coming from the next pod over. "Crys, how you doing?"

"Struggling, you?"

"Same." She sounded a little disheartened about her struggle. Thinking to myself that I could help her back at the room. Wondering if they had a rule against magic out of the classroom. Then again, it wasn't dangerous. Just some water and wind.

"We can't do earth in the classroom for obvious reasons. The fourth element is fire and this is the most dangerous. It's pure destruction if mishandled. That's why we have a fire suppression system in place."

There was a click and then a whir of power running through the ceiling. Seeing little nozzles up there poking through above each pod. "Fire links to your emotions. It doesn't matter if it's anger or happiness. Sorrow or extreme joy. The stronger it is the more powerful your spell will be. When you think you're ready create friction. Rubbing your hands together seems to be the easiest way."

Waiting to make sure there were no more words before pulling my focus into my own little world. Sifting through my emotions. Being happy most of my life but nothing too extreme. The strongest emotion I had was sadness. The photos I had of my mother did make me smile.

They were also a constant reminder that I never knew her. A gap in my heart that couldn't be filled no matter how amazing my father was. Closing my eyes and picturing her face. Thinking about how I never got to hug her. Feel that warmth of love. Never knowing what her voice sounded like.

A tear came down my cheek and I rubbed my fingers together. Feeling the heat rise before there was a snap of embers flung into the air. Grinning as I watched the flames flickering over my fingertips. Crackling with a few snaps of heat. The warmth felt amazing. No burning or scorching.

Rubbing my fingers against my palm and watching as the fire spread. My whole hand engulfed. Thinking about that emotion again, the longing I felt. Snapping the fingers on my other hand brought another burst of flame. Letting it spread so both hands waved with fire.

Moving them around, watching how the fire shifted with the movement. Wiggling my fingers, making it dance. "You seem to be doing fine with the fire."

As she spoke I jumped out of my concentration. The fire leaping from my hands as I yelped. Seeing it rise up, growing bigger until it hit that nozzle. Looking up, suddenly getting engulfed by white smoke. Feeling it showering down into my pod. Covering my face and coughing.

Seconds later it stopped. Having to wave my hands to see through the fog. Seeing the teacher still standing there. A smile on her lips. Another scribble on her clipboard and she wandered off.

Hearing another kid shouting out about having fire. The teacher calling to us all. "Practice some more, just remember the fire suppression system doesn't smell very nice. And it takes forever to get out of your clothes."

Lifting my arm up and sniffing it, smelling nothing. Getting a cheeky smirk from the teacher as she motioned for me to get out. Following that order she took me over to her desk. Clicking a few buttons and it came on like one massive screen.

Showing multiple shots of me using magic. Creating water and wind. Seeing it from this angle made it even more exciting that it was me doing it. "Why are you hiding your ability?"

"Because I don't want to be put on the elite team. I don't agree with violence."

"Your natural ability with magic seems to disagree with you." Her eyes looked down at me, her nose wiggling left to right as she thought. "I won't give you the highest score but I will be scoring you."

"Scoring?"

"Each class you take you will get a score. In your case, elemental magic and weapon training. You will participate in the tournament, getting a score from that as well. Then the teams for the elite training are picked from the top of the class."

"Oh. Can't I just opt out? Say I don't want to do it?"

"That's not how the rules work. If you're picked, then you're picked. No way out of it."

"I'll just have to do badly in my weapon training and get out during the first round of the tournament."

"If you say so. Talent always finds a way to present itself. Might not be as easy as you think. Back in your pit."

She gave me a smile before walking off. I returned to my hole in the ground. Using my magic to create different kinds of things. Enjoying playing about with it until the teacher told us all to stop and head up a level for weapons training.

Piling into the elevator, giving D a soft nudge as she seemed to be day dreaming. "How did you get on?"

"The fire was the easiest. I have a lot of strong emotions. The other two I couldn't quite get the hang of."

"We can practice in the room tonight."

"Magic isn't allowed outside the class room."

"Where do you read all these rules?" Letting out a little laugh as she smiled.

"I did a lot of research. You can get kicked out if you're caught."

"Alright, no extra learning. But I'm sure you'll get the hang of it."

"Thanks." The large glass box was emptied into the hallway. Holbrook was standing there waiting for us at the door. Moving inside as we got to him. Holbrook took up position in the middle. Motioning towards the curved racking. "Retrieve your weapons."

The group moved like a herd of animals. My eyes landing on that stick with beautiful patterns all over it. My hand reaching for the nunchuks whilst I watched Troy taking my weapon. Wanting to whip my nunchuks at his face but I would probably hurt myself more than him.

Turning my back and shuffling back between the other girls. Holbrook pointing out to different parts of the room. Putting us in groups by weapon. "Face the screens and copy what you see."

There wasn't much more instructions than that. Turning and seeing the screen come to life. Showing someone standing there with a pair of nunchuks. Taking a look over my shoulder showed the rest of the class had the same. Only with their specific weaponry.

The man started speaking, talking about the weapon and how it worked and could be used for defence and attack. It was me, D and another girl who looked just as worried as I did. Standing taller than us two, skinny enough that I was surprised she could lift the weapon at all.

Then as the lesson really started we moved our nunchuks. It felt heavy and awkward. Smacking myself with the swinging end more than once in the first few minutes. Blowing out a frustrated breath. It was what I wanted. This would give me low marks or possibly none at all. The elite team would be a distant worry. I just wished it didn't hurt so much.

Copying the screen and getting cracked in the knee which made me drop down to the floor. Wincing in pain. Looking up I watched as the other two used their nunchuks. Swinging it around, the air whooshing with a whipping noise.

Amazed at how they moved and did it so effortlessly. Moving my eyes around the group I noticed most of the others were doing the same. Using those weapons with ease. There were only a handful of girls having their own problems like I was.

Holbrook came walking over. "Is there a problem?"

"No, sir. Just made a mistake."

"Are you sure that's the weapon you're supposed to have?"

"Definitely. I felt that...feeling."

"Clearly." To the others he went then disappeared around that curved wall into the next class over. Just standing there and watching D spin that weapon around her body and over her shoulders. "You picked this up quickly."

"It's like muscle memory. Just watch and copy."

"Between you and me, I have the wrong weapon. That little bugger took the one I wanted."

D stopped swinging, turning and almost getting whacked by the taller girl. "Oh, so sorry about that."

"Don't worry about it." D gave her a smile showing off her coned teeth. "Why don't you say something?"

"This works out best for me. I don't want to be put on one of those elite teams."

"Really? I can't wait to be put on one."

"I think you'll get top marks for your weapon."

"Just need to get better at magic."

"You will. I have faith in you. And if we go up against each other in the tournament, I won't even put up a fight."

"We won't. It's girls versus boys. Maybe you'll get to go up against the red headed boy you're having so much trouble with."

"Then I'll be torn between wanting to do bad and wanting to wipe that grin off of his face."

"A price to pay."

"Maybe." She grinned and then went back to watching the screen. As I heard Holbrook coming back into our side I straightened up. Moving my weapon just a lot slower so when I made a mistake it didn't hurt as much. Getting very bored of it by the time the class was called to a close. Both sides returning those weapons.

I found myself sticking close to the racking. Seeing that bully placing the weapon back and moving away. I stepped forwards and ran my fingers over the engraved patterns. The weapon feeling smooth. Curling my fingers around it and lifting it up. Expecting a heavy weight but it weighed almost nothing.

Seeing three circles at the centre of the stick. Wondering what they did but a voice made me jump. "What are you doing?"

Jumping around and seeing that boy. His face screwed up like I was trying to steal something from him. "Just looking."

"That's mine. Not yours."

My eyes picking up the red mark on his jaw. "You having trouble with it?"

"No. Of course not. It's easy."

I placed the weapon back in its home."Sure. Whatever you say." Moving past him with a fake smile. "Your jaw looks hurt. Think that might bruise up."

"Shut it." I walked off with a smile and joined

D as we climbed into the elevator. Looking forward to getting some food into my belly. Getting off and following the gorgeous smell. Spotting my brother by the entrance I excused myself and headed over.

Jumping on his back with a tight hug. But his face was full of sadness as he turned around. "What's wrong?"

"They sent Lawrence home."

"What? Why?"

"Defending your honour."

"You're kidding."

"That rich kid, William. He was saying some stuff about you."

"What kind of stuff?" Feeling my brain filling with anger.

"Just about how stuck up you were. How you should keep your mouth shut otherwise no one will go out with you."

"That punk."

"Yeah. Lawrence had a similar reaction. Swung a lance at his head."

"Holy..."

"Exactly. He got kicked out for attacking another student. None of us got to say bye to him."

"William should be the one to be sent home."

"He's lucky I haven't knocked his head off. For you and for Lawrence."

I rubbed my hand over his arm. "It's sad about Lawrence but I can defend myself."

"You're the shy girl that let the girls bully you just because you found it easier."

"It seems I may have changed a little since coming here. This place has opened my eyes to a lot already so maybe it's time I opened myself up as well."

"You're getting on board with violence now are you? Little miss peaceful."

"When it comes to certain boys, maybe." I gave him a little smirk before a tight hug. "We should try and catch up every day."

"Agreed." We entered the cafeteria then went our separate ways. I headed over to the line whereas he joined the rest of the guys at a table. Happy that it was on the opposite side of the massive hall to William.

Annoyed that the rich kid seemed so happy at the moment. Joking around with his friends. The system for tea was very similar to lunch. Only this time the meals were larger. Grabbing a plate covered in roast chicken and all the trimmings. Choosing some melon slices for my desert and a bottle of water.

Heading over to my friends. Seeing the third member of the group sitting next to Flo. My eyes moving over the black skin, hair looking like it was made out of rock. Eyes flicking to me, just white rings in a pool of black.

Smiling wide as I held out my hand. "I'm Crys."

"Larsh."

"Excuse me?"

"Her name is Larsh." Giving Flo an unsure smile. "She's pleased to meet you."

"If you say so." The black skinned lady got up after her comment. Binning the tray she had despite the amount of food still left on it.

I sat down, not sure what had happened. "Did I say something wrong?"

"No, it's me. She's jealous."

"Why?" Laughing as I grabbed my cutlery and

started cutting into the roast.

"Because I said you were cute."

My hand freezing mid-air as I looked up at her. "You told her I was cute. And she's jealous?" Flo nodded with a soft smile. Then it dawned on me. "You two are together."

"Yeah. Did I forget to mention that?"

"You sure did. She knows I'm not into girls, doesn't she?"

"How do you know if you've never tried it?"

Seeing the smile she pulled. Knowing that she was flirting with me and honestly, it had me blushing a little. Feeling the heat in my cheeks as I smiled back. It was completely different to how boys would flirt.

Even the ones who were subtle about it. It still held something, that I was expected to respond mutually. Like their interest in me warranted the same back. But this was just flirting. Flo carried on eating her tea and so did I.

It wasn't a big deal and the three of us chatted about our lessons. Flo's crystal had turned blue which was hand-to-hand combat. She mentioned how they had dummies to attack. Some of them even attacked back which made me laugh at the image.

Nearing the end of my dessert I heard William shouting something across the whole room. Aiming it at my brother's group who were sitting very quietly. Out of character behaviour for their missing friend.

Only the boy's comments were starting to get a rise out of them. Including my brother and I don't think I could witness my brother being sent home. I checked around, not seeing any adults in here apart from the staff serving the food.

So I got out of my chair and walked over to William who was standing at this point. Thinking about the emotion I had used before. The fact I missed my mother brought that heat to my fingertips. Giving them a very slow rub.

As I got to him I wrapped those hot fingers around the back of his neck and shoved him down into his chair. Letting my grip tighten as I pulled more emotion into that magic. Making him wince in pain as he craned his neck to look at me.

My eyes quickly checking the entrance for any teachers. Then lowering my gaze to his, seeing that privileged smirk. "I hear you've been saying some things about me. Behind my back. Are you afraid of saying it to my face?"

"No, I was just getting your friend kicked out."

"Yes, you did. He was a friend and now you've pissed me off. You might get your own way back home where your parents can buy buddies for you to play with. Here, you can't control everything with money. And just so you know, I really don't care about being here. I'd much rather be at home. So when I tell you that I will hurt you. You know I mean it. Right?"

"Sure." There was still that annoying look on his face so I built the magic up. Letting a lick of flame run over his neck which made him yelp in pain. "Ow, alright. Cut it out."

"You know what I want to hear."

"I'll stop talking about you."

"Good boy." Giving him a wink before walking away. As I looked over to my brother he clapped his hands together with a huge grin on his face. Taking a deep breath to cool my thoughts down. This was highly unlike me and it was only the first day. I just hoped I didn't change too much even if it had felt so good.

Grabbing my tray and telling the girls that I was going to grab some fresh air. Exiting out the front like I had done last time. Looking up at the sky which was still bright and blue. Not a single cloud in sight. There was a hint of orange at the horizon as the sun was getting ready to sleep.

Looking at the school watch and seeing that it was almost six in the evening. Turning to head back inside but I was cut off by a group of four boys. The leader having that red hair I was becoming to really hate.

He stepped forwards as the other three stayed back. "Look, you're gay. Maybe you should tell your friends and you can stop acting out because of it."

First there was disbelief on his face. Then he burst out laughing, his buddies joining in. "That's why you think I've been bullying you?" Troy looked over at his friends. "What was the name of my last relationship?"

One of them calling back. "Either Greg or Mark. They kind of overlapped, didn't they?"

"Exactly." The red head grinned at me. "So you see it has nothing to do with me being gay."

"So you're just an arse then."

"Yep. Just an arse. And if I see you trying to take my weapon again. You will see a much meaner side of me."

"Your face is looking even worse."

"At least my face looks worse for a good reason. What's your excuse?" My feet moving me towards him, angry at his comment. Pushing my hands against his chest which just made him laugh again. Then I slapped him and the laughter was cut off.

Seeing his look of rage as he stared at me. Getting pushed, easily dropping to my back on the grass. When he came at me I rolled over and scrambled away. Feeling the tears running down my cheeks as I heard him calling after me with names.

I had no problem standing up for others. Only when it came to myself I had always ran away. Whether it be to hide in a corner or hide in a book. Ignoring the things that were called to me. Only, never did I have someone get physical like that.

Wiping my cheeks as I kept running. Watching as the grass swept underfoot. Breathing heavily as I came to a stop in the middle of the wide open space. Looking over my shoulder at the school that stood so tall.

The boy had gone inside which had me happy. But I didn't want to return there right now. I just wanted to be alone. To just sit and look at the world around me. My eyes turning up as a rumble came from the sky. Seeing a flash as black clouds loomed in the distance.

Giving the school another look but deciding to head towards a cave in the distance. Something seemed welcoming about it and it would do nicely if the storm brought rain upon me. Pulling my hood over my head as my trainers squelched through the mud at the cave mouth.

Setting myself down against the rock and watching those dark clouds. Seeming to black out the sky a little. The sun looking even further down over the horizon. I went to get more comfortable when I heard something coming from the cave.

Looking but only seeing darkness. Letting my

ears listen as I shut my eyes. Hearing that noise coming again but it wasn't steps or a rustle. Nothing moving inside the black but there was something calling to me.

I stood up, rubbing my hands together and bringing that heated magic to my fingertips. Using my hands like torches, lighting up the way as I started walking. Moving deeper through the winding tunnel of rock.

Every now and again were shafts that led right up to the surface of the cliff. Feeling a soft spattering of rain coming down as the storm closed in. My light illuminating the walls as they spread out. Stepping into a massive cavern. Stalagmites scattered around the ground where those shafts led up through the rock.

Moving between them I heard that calling noise even louder. Looking around in here but seeing nothing. Getting towards the middle where there was a plinth of stone. Only sitting atop it wasn't anything ornate or valuable.

Curled up in a ball was a black animal. Only happening to see it as my flame hands shone bright. A long tail hanging down over the edge above my head. As I grew closer the thing started to stir. The light waking it up.

This little animal couldn't have been bigger than a cat. The tail thick and sleek with black fur. A head coming around, showing off those fox like features. Eyes opening and spotting me. Reacting immediately with a growl. The tail flicking up into the air. As it did the whole body started to glow orange.

I put my hands up like I was surrendering but it seemed to react to the flames. Backing away and growling again. As the noise rolled out of its throat the tips of its fur started to glow brighter. The colour spreading to red and yellow as the whole animal starting flicking in flames just like my hands were.

My hands reflected in those eyes. The thing looked amazing and extremely cute. Lowering my voice to a whisper which still echoed around the vast room. "Hey there. You're cute."

Its head tilted to the right, then the left. Lips moving as words came from its mouth. "Cute? What do you think you're talking to?"

My breath getting caught in my throat. Staring at this thing. My mind still comprehending what had just happened. "Did you just speak?"

"Typical human asking stupid questions. The last human that came in here left with burn marks."

"You can talk."

"Thanks for pointing out the obvious. Now leave me in peace."

"I'm sorry. There's a storm. I'm taking shelter."

The animal lifted its head up to those holes. Rain becoming a little heavier. "That's not my problem. This is my home, now leave."

"There's no need to be so rude."

"I said leave!" The body of fire reacting to its anger. Raging harder making the animal grow in size. Brightly shining as the flames flickered harder. "Get out whilst you still can."

Feeling my heart pounding faster. Noticing how its tail divided as it growled deeper. Nine tails flicking out behind it. Getting close to the size of a lion. Looking even bigger and more ferocious from this angle.

"I just came in here looking for shelter."

Without warning it's tails flicked, sending out a

ball of heat that hit a piece of rock beside me, bursting it into pieces. "Hey, that's dangerous." Another came making me dive out the way, hitting the floor hard. Breathing heavily as I turned onto my back. Fear filling my mind as I looked at that fiery animal. Seeing it was ready to attack again.

CHAPTER 4

Taking a deep breath as I felt water trickling down upon me. Looking up and remembering my magic lesson. As another fireball was flung at me, I threw up my hands and thought about the water in the cave. Bringing it in quickly to engulf that attack. Extinguishing it with a singe.

"Think you can defeat me with your magic?" Down it jumped, taking a few steps towards me. "You're just a pathetic human." It opened its mouth and I expected a roar. Instead it was a plume of fire heading towards me.

Pulling on that magic again, a bubble of water forming before me. Holding it there as the stream of flames were doused. Letting it drop as that sudden brightness dimmed. "I don't want to fight but when you're being attacked by something."

Breathing out steadily but it was the cool air coming down those shafts that I held onto. Swinging an arm and hitting this thing with a hard hit of wind. Making the creature sprawl across the floor, skidding until it hit one of those rock formations.

The water coming down through the ceiling dropped on the fire beast. Hearing the singe of embers being put out. The animal twisting and shaking. Where the droplets had hit were lighting up again slowly.

Then it jumped, baring teeth and claws as it

rushed through the air. Taking a deep breath and slamming my palms together. Thinking about all the water coming into the cave. Those little puddles sitting about on the ground.

Bringing every drop I could together and smashing them either side of this creature. Drowning those flames in liquid. Seeing how the light quickly dampened until its fur turned back to black. Not even a glow of warmth at the tips. Letting the magic go and sending the water splashing against the rock walls.

Seeing this thing drop to the floor where it coughed, back to its original size. Water hitting the ground. Preparing my body for another fight but this thing was done. It was wet which seemed to prevent it from growing and attacking again.

I took a step closer, holding out my hand towards it. "Are you okay?" Eyes darted up to mine before it slumped onto the floor. The tip of the tail burst into flames. My body jumping back in defence. Only as the fire engulfed this little animal it disappeared like it was being burnt away.

Those eyes lifting again before the whole thing was gone. Nothing in this cave apart from myself. Looking around feeling very confused. An itching against my wrist made me yelp in surprise. Pulling up my hoody sleeve to see a black mark like a tattoo on the inside of my forearm. A circle an inch across. The pattern made up of black flames, making up the fox-like face of the creature.

Rubbing my thumb over it, feeling completely smooth like it had been there for years. As I circled around it I thought about that creature. What it was able to do, the flames and fire. The mark glowing red before there was a sudden whoosh of power.

Feeling the magic for fire building inside me. Clapping my hands together brought the fire to my touch. Covering my hands completely with such ease. Grinning as I closed my hands into fists and took the magic away.

Laughing which echoed around the cave. When it was joined by a soft voice I jumped with a gasp. Looking down at that fox-like creature standing there before me. Tensing my whole body ready to use that water magic again.

"I said, you're one of them. Aren't you."

"One of what?"

"A wielder. An everfae." The animal walking closer which had me tensing even more. Feeling the dampness of water on my fingertips as I prepared to attack. This thing stopped, dropped its back legs down and looked up at me. "You don't have to be afraid. I won't attack again."

"Why not?"

"Because I belong to you now. You have my power in you." I looked at the mark on my forearm. "Don't you know?"

"I was brought up as human. I only found out what I truly am earlier today."

"Oh. That must have been rough."

"Yeah." Studying this thing as it just looked up at me. "You don't talk like an animal."

"Because we are not animals. We come in all kinds of shapes and sizes."

"Where did you all come from?"

"From the birth of magic. The everfae needed a weapon to retaliate against the humans. We helped turn the tide back. Only it wasn't enough."

A bright white tear trickled from its eye before dropping to the ground and fizzling out. "Did you belong to someone else before?"

"No but my family did. I'm just a young one. I lost my family just like your kind lost their home."

"I'm sorry." I squatted down to the creature. Reaching out and rubbing my hand over it's fur. Worried that the fire would burn me but as I touched all I felt was warmth. As I stroked down its spine the hot fur turned black. Swearing I could feel the vibration of purring despite it being a fox. Or something similar. "What are you exactly?"

"You know I'm a titan right?"

"I know a little but not a lot."

"Alright. I'm a Kitsune. There have been myths written about my kind. I'm a fire type. As you can tell my abilities are pretty clear."

"Yeah, those fire balls you were throwing were no joke."

"You handled yourself pretty well. Everfae have always been good at magic."

"That must be why I pick it up so quickly." Eyes running over the black animal. "So what happens now?"

"That's up to you. I belong to you and you can call upon me at any time."

"How?"

"Just like the water you produced. You use your will and the power will follow."

"Right." Looking over my shoulder, knowing that this thing wouldn't be easy to smuggle into school. "Do I just leave you here then? You come running when you feel me calling?"

"Of course not. I'm within you." It nudged its nose against that black circle of patterns. "Call me in."

"Um. Before I do, what is your name?"

"I've never had one before. I've always been known as a Kitsune."

"Kit. Kit will be perfect for you then."

Those thin lips curling and showing off its sharp teeth, knowing that it was a sign of happiness instead of attack. "I like it."

"Good. Now, I call you in." Taking in a deep breath and thinking about it. Pulling that creature within my heart and watching as it happened. Fire bursting from tail to head and it vanished in a puff of heat that swept over my body.

My black mark winking with red before going back to normal. My lips curling in an uncontrollable smile. I knew nothing of this apart from what the president had told me. All I knew was that I liked it and if given the opportunity to do it again. It would be hard to ignore that urge.

Pulling my sleeve down and heading back to the entrance of the cave. Seeing that the rain had gotten a lot worse so I parked my butt on the floor. Leaning back against the wall and pulling out the little book the president had given me.

Flipping through I found the page on Kit. Seeing that he was one of thirteen kinds of Kitsune. Others included shadow, sound and time. They have multiple tails. The more they have the more powerful they are.

Thinking about how Kit grew in size before it attacked me. Thinking about that kind of power inside my body. Knowing I would be the one to control it. My interest in these Titans peeking slightly.

Turning the pages and looking at the drawings, reading up on the information. Amazed that some of these things could exist out there on this very continent. Coming again to that last page and the massive black being of destruction.

The wind kicking towards the cave entrance harder. Looking up as that growl I heard earlier came again. A noise being carried by the forceful wind from a far off distance. Or maybe I just hoped it was far off. I gained control of Kit through a battle. I couldn't survive against something like this.

Shutting the book and blocking my mind to what I had seen inside. Not letting it call to me and the wind died. Taking a few deep breaths as I stared. The rain making it a little hard to see anything too far away but I was sure nothing stirred out there in the storm. Still, it had my heart racing and my want for safety. Looking over and seeing the school in the distance all lit up.

Floodlights covered the structures around the middle spire. A bright light coming from the president's office like a lighthouse. It was a distance especially in this weather but it would be worth it for that sense of safety.

Tucking the book away in my pocket, tugging down my hood so it blocked my face. Then I started running. The wind hitting me harder once I was clear of my cover. Feet squelching on the drenched grass as I ran. My clothes completely soaked by the time I got back.

Even with my hood up my hair got drenched. Combing it back with my fingers, already seeing the ends going even curlier. Looking around at the place. Inside the cafeteria the chairs had been moved around and a movie was playing from a projector. Like all kids my age, most of them were chatting rather than paying any attention to the film. Some games set up by the wall.

I carried on walking, hoping to get into some dry clothes quickly. Getting up to my room and finding D sitting on the bed. Hearing a sniffle as I walked in. Looking over to her and seeing the tears trickling down her scaly skin. "What's wrong?"

"Forget about me. Where the hell have you been and what happened?"

"It's just some rain. And I was out for a walk."

"Your brother was worried about you. Came over and asked where you were."

"He's a little over-protective."

"He also has a few of the girls crushing on him."

"Typical really." Seeing the look of sadness on her face. Moving over and perching on the edge of her bed. "Did something happen?"

"Just some comments, nothing I haven't heard before."

"Looks like something more than a few comments."

She pulled a soft smile. "I'd rather forget about it."

"Alright but I'm here if you ever do want to chat about it."

"Thanks." She went to hug me but then looked at my wet clothing. "Aren't you cold?"

"Extremely. Please tell me there is a shower in this room that I'm missing."

"Down the hall. There's a communal shower on every floor."

"Great." I pulled my bag from under my bed and

yanked out two towels. One thin for my hair and a nice fluffy one for my body. Picking out a change of clothes as well for the walk back.

"I'll join you. Think I've sat in this room for too long." We both walked down the hall and into the showers. Taking one of the cubicles that sat around the edge of the room.

Pulling the curtain across and stripping out of my drenched outfit. Hanging them up with my towels before turning the water on. Dunking myself under once it was hot enough and letting out a sigh of relaxation.

"God, that feels amazing." Letting it heat up my body. As I stood there I looked at the tattoo on my forearm. Thinking about the Titan that now resided inside my heart. D's voice making me call out, "Huh?"

"Where did your walk take you?"

"I took shelter in a cave. It was Troy and his buddies. Being their usual selves."

"What did they do?"

"He just pushed me over. Was silly to run off just because of that."

"As someone who has had their fair share of bullying. Nothing is ever silly when reacting to it. Don't think like that. He's the one who should be ashamed, not you."

"Thanks. I'm really glad they put us in the same room."

"Me to." I used my toiletries and washed myself. Making it nice and quick and then standing there as the water washed over my body. Letting the heat warm me up perfectly. When D's water shut off I did the same. Drying myself and putting on my pyjamas. A white vest and a pair of shorts. A massive mirror sat on one of the walls with a bunch of sinks.

First brushing my teeth then combing my hair, tugging at a few of the knots I always got after getting caught in the rain. Looking at my friend's reflection. "Having no hair must be so easy."

She laughed in reply. Chucking something onto the counter. "You think it's easy to wash with one of those?"

Picking it up and running my thumb over the thick rigid bristles of metal. "Doesn't that hurt?"

"Not my skin. It just takes a long time. You wouldn't believe the kind of things I get stuck under my scales."

Pulling a face as I gave it back. "Next time tell me that before I touch something." We both laughed. Looking over as she ran her brush under the tap. Thinking about the water magic inside my body. Flicking my fingers and making the water splash up against her face.

She gasped and then burst out laughing. "Watch it, if someone catches you."

"No one is going to come in here. Give it a try."

"We'll get in trouble."

"Do you want to get onto one of the elite teams?"

"Of course."

"Then come on. It's just us here." I turned and leant back against the counter. "Let the water running out the tap link to the water inside your body."

"Alright." She held out her hand and her eyes focused.

"Breath with the magic. Flow with it, the magic and the water. Link yourself to it." Watching as her fingers twitched and the water shifted. Flickering like a wind was catching it. "There you go. Again, bigger."

D looked so happy with herself. The confidence building that magic until she flicked her whole hand and I felt the liquid hitting me. Laughing as I spat some out into the sink. "I did it. I actually did it."

"All you needed to do was focus."

"You have a way of explaining it."

"I've been told I have a knack with magic."

"Thank you."

"Don't worry about it." Smiling at her and feeling the friendship growing.

Sensing an intrusion before a voice called out. "You two practising magic when you're not supposed to?"

Looking over and seeing the frizzy haired girl standing there. She wasn't carrying a towel or anything used to wash. Her presence here was clearly for trouble. D already looked fed up with barely any interaction. "What do you want?"

"We heard some chatter. Thought you two might be in one of the cubicles. Getting to know each other a little better."

"Still can't come up with any new jokes, Alesha."

"They're still funny."

"Not really."

"New girl, what do you think?"

"I'm trying to find the insult in your words. You act like it's such a terrible thing that I could be involved with D. I think you need to get a life."

Seeing her face twisting with disbelief and anger. I simply smiled at her. Knowing that she couldn't say anything that didn't destroy the fact she was just attention seeking. Wanting to belittle someone to make her feel better.

"Look here you little bugger." She stepped forwards and so did the two girls following her. "You are so insignificant, you don't matter."

"Then why are you always pestering me. Twice in one day. Maybe it's you who is attracted to someone. You certainly have girls following you everywhere."

She scoffed so hard some of her spit hit my face. "Don't be so disgusting."

Using my finger to wipe my skin clean. "It's really nothing to be ashamed of."

"Just shut up." Her hand coming out and shoved my shoulder. Then another. "Aren't you going to do anything?"

"What would be the point?"

"Huh?"

"Seriously. What's the point? No matter what happens. If you win or I win, the end will be the same. You'll carry on being an annoying bitch. So why waste my energy?"

"Fine then, I'll just punch you in the face if you're not going to fight back." Watching as she balled up her fist. Not caring, listening to the water running out of the tap behind me. Wiggling my fingers and feeling for that magic. Scooping it around that running liquid and flinging it at the bully.

Seeing it splash all over her face hard. Making her gasp in surprise, sucking down some of that water. Quickly turning to a sink and coughing it up. "Careful. You don't want to choke on something."

A few more coughs and then she turned. Eyes darkened with rage as she ran at me. Arms stretched out towards me. Taking a deep breath I pushed out with that water magic. Grabbing hold of as much as I could.

The showers suddenly turning on with a sharp hiss of power. The taps flowing quickly as I pulled harder. The sudden noise making Alesha stop. Her friends starting to back up towards the door. Bringing my hands together brought all that rushing water towards the middle of the room. Such a huge orb of liquid.

The bully's eyes going wide. "I'm....I'm going to tell."

"I think you need help leaving." Swinging my arms and rushing that ball towards her. Flicking my fingers and letting it lose shape. Becoming a rushing river as it hit her legs and swept her off towards the door. Angling the stream around the corner as her friends fled from the showers.

Giggling as I let the magic go. Not caring if she would stomp right back in here or not. That was the best feeling in the world. Standing up to such an entitled cow had me and D grinning. "That was really stupid of you but I can't stop laughing."

"She deserved it."

"About time she was put in her place. Flo will love this."

"I didn't cause a problem between her and Larsh did I?"

"Why, because Flo thinks you're cute? You can't help that. Don't worry about it. Larsh has been very non-emotional for as long as I can remember."

"I'll try not to worry then."

"Just.....um....when Larsh is there. Don't be too friendly with Flo."

"I'll do my best." Giving her a big smile. Collecting our things and making our way out of the showers. Feeling the rush of water coming back from the door to drain away in the middle of the room. Moving along the hallway and back into our room.

Putting my stuff away I jumped into bed. Laying on my back with the little light that sat underneath my shelving area. Running my thumb over the black tattoo on my forearm, thinking about the little fire fox.

Knowing the other kinds of Titans that were inside the book. Being able to control the elements was cool. I was enjoying it but I couldn't lose myself to that feeling. The elite team members would be picked and I did not want to be on that list.

Laying my head back on my pillow and switching my light off. Letting my mind drift off to sleep. Wishing it hadn't when my dream started. Lost in a storm, feeling the rain on my skin like I had earlier. My vest top and shorts drenched, clinging to my body like a second skin.

Lost in the storm, not knowing which way was safe. Spinning around with each step. Wanting to be somewhere dry and warm. Shivering as I felt that roar of power coming with the wind. Whipping against my body as I stared. A figure out there, moving closer.

Backing away I started moving quickly. Turning as this thing shot forwards. Tripping over nothing and hitting the wet grass hard. That knock to my face making my eyes shoot open. Gasping as I felt the cold on my skin.

When I realised where I was, the warmth came back quickly. But that sense of dread and fear was still there. My eyes picking out the leather book on my shelf.

Shaking my head as I sat up. Swinging my legs over the edge and seeing a bowl of porridge sitting on my side of the desk that sat between our beds.

"Porridge?"

"Yeah, they come with these so it's not that bad." She pushed over a little basket of sachets. Picking out two honeys and mixing them into my breakfast. Scoffing it down, finding it quite nice unlike the porridge I had eaten at home.

Placing the empty bowl on the desk I looked at my watch. Seeing a button had been added to the screen. Pressing the little calendar brought up today's schedule. Seeing we would be outside practising earth magic. Intrigued to see what kind of things we would be able to do.

Opening my wardrobe door then pulling the curtain across for privacy. Getting into some thick jeans and a white vest top. Wearing a black and white chequered shirt which I knotted at the bottom. Doing half the buttons up. Coming back out and seeing my bundle of wet clothes sitting on the floor. "Do they have a place for washing clothes here?"

"I believe it's in the shop but I haven't seen it open yet. They should have the times somewhere."

"If only they loaded that kind of thing on our watches. Would be helpful."

"No kidding." D disappeared behind her own curtain and came out wearing a tight vest top which matched the strange green colour of her leggings. Our watches vibrating, telling us to meet by the entrance.

So we left our room and travelled down the elevator in a big group. My day getting ruined when seeing Troy standing by the entrance with his buddies.

Getting a sneer as we neared him. Ignoring that idiot as best as I could.

Happy when the two teachers arrived and we were taken outside. The storm from last night had disappeared completely and the sun was out. Feeling very nice on my arms as I rolled up my sleeves.

We got taken a few metres from the school into open space before splitting into our genders. I was curious to see if Troy was any good with magic. Hoping that it was something I could beat him at. Mrs Kelp standing in front of us all.

The other teacher looked human from this distance, standing back a bit and letting the whole class listen. "Earth magic is simple. You have a connection with the ground beneath you. It knows you control it. But you must believe this yourself. Just like the other three spells you've done. Now create a simple pillar from right in front of you. Spread out a bit, find your own space and practice."

Moving over to the edge so I wasn't surrounded by people. Fear of getting a pillar of rock knocking me on my arse. Giving a smile to D who looked worried. "Just remember how you controlled the water. It's like that only with rock. You can do this."

Taking a moment just to watch her, not bothering to even try it myself just yet. My eyes peering over to Mrs Kelp who kept glancing my way. I wasn't about to let her mark me up for more points. If anything I could do with losing some points but the only way I could think of doing that was to injure one of the other students.

Whilst I had the perfect candidate for such an action I decided against it. I wasn't that kind of person even though the thoughts were there. Watching as D looked at the floor. Seeing it start to shake a little. Hands pulling up like she had hold of a rope.

Smiling as the ground bumped up a little like a mole was about to poke it's head above ground. My smile growing bigger as rock started to emerge. One long pillar of it coming to stand just above our heads.

Mrs Kelp calling over as she marked her clipboard. "Very good, D." Her eyes flicking to me and I noticed how she wrote two things down. Forgetting it and looking around at the others, seeing that they were all at different stages of completing the task.

Then I saw Troy who was standing there with a huge smirk on his face. Leaning on his pillar like a triumphant warrior. Extending a finger out and touching my magic to his pillar. Making a small circle, imaging a single piece of that pillar coming out. Coaxing it with a wiggle and then it popped free.

Troy leapt back and yelped like a puppy about to be squashed. Laughing as the thing came crashing down. The other teacher yelling at him, "Be careful. You're going to injure someone or knock yourself out. And you can't afford to lose any more brain cells."

Giggling as D nudged me. "Was that you?"

"Maybe."

"Why aren't you trying to do one yourself?"

"Because I don't want to be on the elite team."

"Clearly you are really good at this. I'd want you on my team."

"Sadly you can't. At least you won't have Troy on it either."

"Luckily."

I laughed which brought a glare from Mrs Kelp.

"That's enough of that. Next you will bring up little pieces of rock. Using these you can mould them into anything you want. Can be really useful in tight situations. Especially for defence. You can build a wall of strength."

Watching as she brought her arm up quick. Pieces of rock leaping from the ground and building a thick wall of protection. Letting it crumble back down as she carried on speaking. "You can't pull up a massive piece of rock quick enough to defend yourself. Little pieces. Proceed."

Turning to D who was already trying to conjure pieces of rock. Myself I decided to try but on a much smaller scale. Hoping that the amount of students between me and the teachers kept it a secret.

Turning my back and looking at the floor. Seeing those little pieces on the ground that had been disturbed by D's magic. Extending my fingers down and pulling on them. Using that power to roll them about. Making them run circles around my feet. Then building one on top of the other. All the way up until there was a little totem standing just below my knee.

"Seriously, you should definitely be trying harder. Think of what you could accomplish."

"I know. It is fun, being able to do this kind of thing. Helps me feel less like an outsider I guess. But violence is wrong and even I know what the elite teams do. They fight."

"True." Looking up and seeing her eyes going wide. Something moving in their reflection. "Crys!" Turning and pulling my arms up as I saw a massive rock being hurled towards me.

CHAPTER 5

Watching as the ground was pulled up bit by bit. Blocking just in time as that heavy weight smashed into it. Making me take a step back as the strain hit my magic. Then flinging my arms to the right. Sending that projectile off to the side. Hearing it rip through the ground as it skidded. Taking a step forward, ready to defend myself again.

My whole body losing tension as I saw that it was Mrs Kelp who had thrown that rock. "What the hell!?"

"No more half-arsing my lessons, Crystal. I know what you're capable of. Time you showed it."

Gritting my teeth as she scribbled on her clipboard. "You could have killed me."

"But I didn't." Getting a fake smile before she turned her attention to the rest of the class who had stopped and stared. "Back to it!"

Huffing out a frustrated sigh. Turning around and freezing as I saw the president of the school watching from a few metres away. He wiggled a finger for me to walk over. Rolling my eyes as I did. "Did you just see what that teacher did? She almost killed me."

"Looked like you protected yourself just fine."

"That's not the point. She's insane."

"She's one of the best magic wielders in Mythoria."

"An insane one."

"Needless to say that isn't what I wanted to talk to you about."

Pulling on my sleeve a little to cover up that Kitsune mark. "I haven't felt anything yet."

"No, not that either. I have had a report come onto my desk about magic being used outside of class. More specifically, some kind of water slide in the bathroom on your floor?"

"That frizzy haired....."

"Crystal." Shutting my mouth. "Using magic outside of class is forbidden. Fighting of any kind is in fact forbidden. We've had to send one boy home already."

"I know, he was one of my brother's friends. One of mine as well."

"You're lucky I managed to get a hold on this before it got spread around. I won't be able to protect you every time you step out of line."

"So I'm not kicked out?"

"If I kicked you out, how else will we find Titans?"

"Yeah." My hand pressing to my forearm. Wondering if I should tell him what had happened. I had said I wouldn't take a titan. If I felt something I would tell him and he could take it from there. I didn't want to tell him I liked the feeling. I still didn't want to be here.

"Crystal. Be more careful. This is important work."

"Yeah, okay. I will."

"Good. I got your results from yesterday. Weaponry class could go a lot better but I'm happy to see you're excelling at magic. Comes from your heritage as an everfae."

"I didn't know that." Pulling a fake smile and nodding. Knowing full well that that was the case. "I best get back to class."

"Try and behave. Please."

"I promise." Turning and jogging back as they started learning how to hurl projectiles. Listening to the instructions and proceeding as the teacher wanted me to. Begrudgingly putting in effort and being one of the first to create a projectile and tossing it off into the distance. Getting a well done, the only thing making me happy was that D managed to accomplish it shortly after me.

We got dismissed from class once the teachers were happy with everyone's progress. Heading inside and seeing my brother sitting on one of the benches in the lobby. As soon as he saw me he grabbed my arm and pulled me to the side. "What's up with you?"

"What's going on?"

"I don't know what you're on about."

"I've heard some rumours about you."

"Like what?"

"Attacking girls in the showers."

"I didn't attack them. They were bullying me and my friend. You always said I should stand up for myself. You applauded me when I did it to William."

"That was small. Rumours are flying about this place, about you and the guy at the top."

"The president of the school?"

"Yeah. These aren't good rumours. Not the kind of thing I want hearing about my little sister."

Seeing the look on his face and I knew what he was getting at. "Ew. What the hell. You think me and him are doing stuff?"

"That's the rumour."

"Definitely not. That's disgusting."

"Then explain why he's covering for you."

Feeling eyes on us as we talked. Looking over and seeing a few of the students by the cafeteria entrance. So I grabbed my brother's sleeve and dragged him just outside of the school. "Can you keep a secret?"

"I'm your brother, of course I can."

"Even if it involves mum?" Seeing the sadness hitting his eyes suddenly. "You need to believe what I'm about to tell you."

"Why wouldn't I?" Hearing by his voice that he was already unsure of things.

Lowering my voice to a whisper. "Mum wasn't human. She was an everfae."

"That's not a funny joke."

"I'm being serious. I'm half-everfae and half human. It's why I'm really good at magic. And also why the president has interest in me. I'm helping him because he's half and half as well."

"The president of the school. Half-everfae."

"Yes."

"And you are as well?"

"Isn't that what I just said?"

"Where's the proof?" He crossed his arms and looked down at me like I was about to tell him the most outrageous lie.

"The crystal they had us hold at the start. It had a black centre. Just like the other colours it signals something deep inside me. That's the part of me that can control titans."

"You're talking about titans now. They were

stories made up to make the everfae seem more terrifying."

"They exist."

"No. I know how you feel about the war and what happened to them. Someone is preying on this belief."

"How would the president know about that?"

"Maybe he read some school reports. I don't know. But I don't believe what you're telling me."

"Fine. I'll show you." I thought about the tattoo on my arm, the titan that resided inside my heart. Willing him to appear and feeling that rush of fire as red light erupted from my chest. Seeing it drop and form that fox-like animal.

Eyes darting from me, then to my brother. "Who's this?"

"Kit, this is my brother, Lance."

"Nice to meet you."

My brother looked ready to pass out. "What the hell is that?"

"He's rude. You sure he's your brother? He doesn't smell like an everfae."

"He's all human." Lance's jaw hung open as he kept staring at the titan by his feet. "Just wanted to show him. You okay to go back?"

"Of course." The titan gave my brother's leg a quick sniff and rubbed its face across his trousers. "See you around, Lance."

"Yeah, see you around." His voice squeaky for the first time I could recall.

"Thanks, Kit." I got a wink before he leapt towards me. Shifting back into that red light and he went back to where he lived. Feeling the warmth of the magic he held spread through my body to my tattoo.

"Now do you believe me?"

"What kind of magic was that?"

"Not magic. That was a titan. I found him in a cave not too far away."

"And what, he's now yours? Like a pet?"

"I wouldn't call him a pet. It's a deeper link than that."

"Of course. How silly of me to think otherwise."

"Look, what I said was the truth. It doesn't change anything between me and you. We're still sister and brother. From the same parents."

"Crys." Lance's whole body language changed as he stepped towards me. "Nothing is ever going to change that. You're my sister no matter what. Don't ever think our bond will ever go away."

"I'm glad to hear that."

"Okay, say I believe you. You need to be careful. Not only about keeping this a secret but also what people think. This might be a new kind of school for us but its still a school. The same kind of people and ideas."

"So I've noticed. But don't worry, I've got my friends and it actually feels good to stand up for them. I wish someone had done it for me growing up back home."

"I stood up for you."

"True, you always did." My arms curled around him as I gave him a tight hug. "And I hope you always will."

"Of course. Be careful, alright."

"I will."

A kiss was pressed to my forehead before we entered the school. Heading into the cafeteria, lining up together and then going our separate ways. Finding

Flo and Larsh sitting at the usual table. Parking myself down, "Where's D?"

"She just popped to the toilet."

"Why is she sitting with us?" Looking at Larsh who was staring right back. A slight grimace twisting her mouth. "She shouldn't even be at the school still."

"Come on. We all wish we had the balls to do that to that frizzy haired witch."

"That's not the point. She broke the rules. She should be punished." Carrying on her conversation with her girlfriend despite those eyes still burning into mine. "How about you go sit somewhere else. We don't want you at our table."

"Larsh. That's incredibly mean."

"Flo, it's alright. Wouldn't want Larsh to be seen with me. Would hurt her reputation of being the cuddly one of the group." Giving the nice one a soft smile as I stood. Grabbing the turkey sandwich from the plate and putting my tray away.

Heading into the lobby and parking myself at a bench by the small fountain. Munching away, the peaceful space had it's benefits. But feeling lonely just reminded me of the years growing up at home.

Finishing my sandwich I turned on the bench. Watching the water rippling as the fountain spurted water out of nozzles like it was chasing itself around the circular concrete. Hanging my finger down into the cool liquid. My fingertip getting damp as I used my magic.

Creating a second spurt of water rushing around the surface. Shaping it into a fish, making it jump out and dive back in. Swimming around in circles. Smiling as I lost myself in that motion. A deep voice calling to me softly. "Crystal."

Turning, hoping to see a friendly face but it was in fact my weaponry teacher. Holbrook wore a similar outfit to yesterday. Looking just as grumpy as he always did. "Yes, sir."

"I'm not a sir. May I sit?" The softness coming from his question surprised me. Nodding because my lips refused to move. "Thank you."

"What's wrong?"

"Look, I don't want to over-step. I've heard the rumours."

"Which ones?"

"You and the president?"

"Ugh, there's nothing going on between us." Blowing out a sigh.

"I know. There have been others. From other sectors. Favours and special treatment."

"Oh." I wasn't sure if that was a good thing or if it made me less special. Had he found other's who were half-everfae. It made sense but where the hell were they. "What is your point?"

"The president isn't someone you should fully trust. That's all I will say on the matter. Just be careful and look after yourself."

"If there's something you're not telling me, I'd like to know."

"Just be careful. If you get put into a situation that you're not ready for. You will get yourself hurt or killed. Possibly others as well."

"You're on about the elite teams, aren't you?"

"It wouldn't be the first time it happened." I felt his hand touching over mine. "Don't just follow instructions. Think for yourself."

"Alright. That I can do. But why do you care so

much?"

"What makes you think I care?" His stone expression came back and he stood up. Taking a step before looking over his shoulder. "Oh, after lunch. We're doing fights in class. I hope you've come to master those nunchuks."

"But."

"No buts. Time to show me what you're made of." I didn't want to know what I was capable of. Giving him a scowl as he walked away. Annoyed that everyone seemed to be goading me into doing my best. It's funny how it didn't seem like I had a choice.

My watch vibrated when it was time to head to class. Using the elevator and waiting by the door with some others. Holbrook turned up a few minutes later and showed us in.

We were led to the stage by the weapon racks. Enough space around it for everyone to stand and watch including the students from the boys side. This was like a fight club which put my stomach into twists even more than usual.

Seeing D and quickly moving over to her. "Hey, you okay?"

"Yeah I'm fine."

"This is insane, isn't it?"

"Yep."

Feeling the air between us getting colder with her behaviour. "Is everything okay?"

Her eyes flicking to mine, seeing the annoyance in them. "You lied. About you and the president of the school."

"No I didn't."

"Oh please, I've heard the rumours and I've seen

you two together."

"It's not what it looks like."

"I'm struggling. I want to be on the elite team so bad. You can just do whatever you want. You should have been kicked out for what you did in the showers. But here you are. Special treatment. I've spent my whole life seeing people getting special treatment for how they look or what they do. The complete opposite happening to me."

"D, come on. It's not like that. I'm not like that."

"I don't want to hear it. Don't consider us friends any more. I'm going to ask to be put in another room. Maybe you can bunk with the president in his private room."

"That's ridiculous."

"Whatever. Just stay away from all three of us." Then she walked off. Standing there with my jaw hanging open. Not able to believe what had just happened. I was sad but also extremely angry at her.

After everything that I had done to help her. Shown that I wasn't just another idiot. And this was how she treated me. Not even taking a second to hear what I had to say.

Turning around and looking at the stage. My ears listening but my mind was racing over everything. Thinking about the rumours being spread around. Losing my friend and knowing Flo would follow suit as well. Being put back on my own just because of my mum. Being half-everfae just made being alone even worse.

Hearing my name getting called out. Moving to the front, hearing the whispers, seeing the stares I got. Knowing what they were thinking. Believing that I was being helped along. Given special treatment. I'll just show them how wrong they were.

Getting up on stage and seeing that my opponent was Troy. Smiling as fate seemed to be on my side for a small moment. Of all the students to take my anger out on, he was perfect. Holbrook came up to stand between us.

Handing each one a small vial of purple liquid. "This is a protection spell. You won't receive any damage but it will still hurt. First one to knock the other on the floor wins." Before I would have just let it happen. Only now I had something to prove. "Here are your weapons."

Watching as Holbrook brought over the nunchuks I had been using. Feeling the weight of them as I took them. Letting the one side hang, swinging it back and forth. Knowing that I wanted the other weapon. It belonged to me, not Troy.

Downing the protection spell and handing the vial back to Holbrook. Thinking through my strategy until something popped into my brain. Smiling at Troy, scorching my stare into his eyes. Grabbing both ends of my nunchuks in one hand. Swinging my arm, getting ready to throw them.

Hoping that the small amount of those training videos I had seen with the staff would help me the rest of the way. Hearing the whistle and I ran forwards. Troy did the same but he wasn't ready for what I did next.

Launching the nunchuks right at his face. The look of surprise being erased by pain as they smacked him in the chest. Seeing the protection of that spell keeping them from doing any damage. It wasn't where I had aimed but it was good enough. Troy stumbled back and my hands wrapped around that stick he held.

It was still short unlike the others. Bringing my attention to those buttons. Pressing the one on the right and jumping as one end shot out a metre. Covered in intricate patterns like the middle and my brain clicked as to what the other buttons were for.

Slamming my fist down onto Troy's. Yanking the weapon from his loosened grip and spinning it around. The end just missing his face but that wasn't my intended target. Crouching down and aiming the shortened end at his groin.

My thumb pressed the button and it shot out. Connecting hard enough to drop him to the floor despite the spell. My anger pushed me to attack again. Swinging that staff over my head and bringing it down against his arm. Hearing the weakening of the protection magic.

Hearing Holbrook shouting that the fight was over but I didn't care. My anger was flowing and there was no stopping it. Bringing that weapon down again and again. Hitting that same spot until there was a loud crack of the magic being smashed.

Taking deep breaths and forcing myself not to swing again. Knowing that if I had Troy's arm would get broken. Not even the president could save me from such an act. Leaning over the bully, holding the weapon in my hands and pushing the middle button. Both ends sliding into the middle. "This was mine from the start. Keep your hands off of it."

Stepping away from him and over to Holbrook. Handing over the weapon then walking through the silent crowd. Still breathing heavy to slow my thoughts. Seeing D giving me a look but I ignored it. Not staying in the classroom. Moving into the elevator then down to the lobby. Exiting the school and finding the fresh air outside.

Breathing it in slowly. Filling my lungs and telling myself to calm down. My brain splitting into two. Wanting to be done with this place and return to my quiet life. The other wanting to prove everyone wrong. Show everybody that I deserved what I could do.

Shaking my head, a tear trickling down my cheek. Wanting my father's advice. Even something from my brother would have done. Hearing some kind of vehicle off in the distance. Looking over and seeing a large wagon being pulled by an electric orb. Taking a step back as it veered over towards the school.

Not to the entrance but towards a single door on the back of an out-building. Walking over but freezing when I saw the driver. His ears sticking out sideways with pointed ends. Skin smooth and green. Not a single hair to be seen. Wearing a baggy beige clothes. Yellow eyes flicking to me as I watched.

A high-pitched voice coming out through sharp teeth. "They don't usually send out a pair of hands to help."

"What?"

"To unload."

"Unload what?"

"I guess I was wrong. What are you doing out here? Aren't there classes or something you should be doing?"

Ignoring his words and moving closer. "What are you?"

"Excuse me. Do you often walk around being so rude to strangers. What the hell are you?"

"Not entirely sure right now."

"What?"

"Nothing."

I got a scowl before he disappeared into the back of his wagon. Hearing some rummaging around until he popped back holding a crate. "Make yourself useful if you're going to stare at me like that."

"I wasn't staring."

"Uh-huh." Without warning he dropped the crate. Catching it with a thud to my chest. "Just over by the door."

Carrying and placing it on the ground. Turning around and seeing him ready with another. This went on for a few minutes and I found myself wondering how he fit so many crates in his wagon. There were over twenty of them varying in size and weight.

Down he jumped from the wagon, finding he only came up to my waist. Seeing thin scars running over the back of his head. Those pointy ears with rip marks along the bottom. Staring down at him as he smiled. "Thanks for your help."

"Earlier, I didn't mean to be rude."

"It's alright. I've been told my people skills could do with some work. Probably to do with being a goblin." A bundle of keys were pulled from his pocket. Seeing all the kinds he had like he collected them. Seeing a few of them were just cylinders of glass. Darkened by their deep colours of purple and red.

He opened the door and nodded to the crates. "Bring them in will you. I have to check to make sure nothing was stolen."

"Alright." Not entirely sure why I was agreeing to help. Maybe to take my mind off of what had happened in class. What was going on in my life right now. Bringing the cargo in one by one. Noticing how he simply sat on his tall stool behind the counter. Pointing to the destinations of what I was carrying.

Bringing in the last one which was set down behind the counter. This one he opened immediately with a crowbar. Inside were some kind of fruit I had never seen before. His green fingers plucked one up then chucked it into the air.

Catching it with a smile. "That is a pinto. One of the best fruits on this whole planet. For your troubles."

"Thanks." Giving it a bite and sighing at the immense flavour it held. The juices trickling over my tongue. Swallowing it and smiling wide. "Where did this come from?"

"You wouldn't believe me if I told you."

Taking another bite as I looked around at the shelves. One half of the store was filled with snacks and general things I recognised. As I munched the little shop owner moved around. Popping open crates here and there. "Would it be okay to have a look around?"

"Just keep your fingers to yourself."

"I'm not going to steal anything."

"Some of this stuff isn't your run of the mill trinkets. This isn't just a shop for you students."

"Who else comes here?"

"None of your business."

"Oh." Giving his grumpy face a once over before walking off. Biting into my fruit as I went. Eyes running over the objects sitting in the crates. Not able to tell what any of them were. Making my way around before spotting the laundry section near the back. "You do have machines."

"What's that?"

"Laundry machines."

"Yes, free to the students."

"When are you open?"

"Now that I'm here with my new stock. The shop is open to you guys from morning till sun-down."

"Us guys?"

A grumble came out of his mouth as he chewed his bottom lip. "Yes, you students and teachers. Afterwards, is none of your business."

Studying his look before giving a big smile. "Thanks for the fruit."

"It was payment, no need to thank me."

"I still like to."

"I'll never get you humans with your cheery attitude."

Giving him a smile as I headed for the back door. Making my way around to the entrance. Walking into the lobby and heading towards the elevator. Thinking I should get back into my class but when the elevator arrived the president came walking out.

As he came up to me he grabbed my elbow. Pulling it free much to his confusion. "There are rumours going around that you're favouring me, so don't touch me. My life has already gotten hard enough."

"Crystal, it's your father."

"What? Has something happened?" Already feeling tears gathering at the bottom of my eyes. "Tell me."

"He's not hurt or injured. But someone has reported you for being everfae."

"What? I told my brother but he wouldn't do

something like that."

"Maybe someone over-heard." His hand touched my elbow again and he escorted me towards the entrance. "The government are sending someone over to bring your father in. For questioning. I've cleared it with your teachers for you to be absent. Go to him before they take him."

"What about me?"

"I have some pull with the governors. Told them I would be doing my own investigation into you and your brother. Now go."

"How?"

"Your brother has that covered."

We walked outside and there was Lance, sitting on top of a hoverbike. The long body of it coloured dark blue. The wheels just spheres spinning rapidly. Giving off a shudder of air as they did.

I was handed a helmet and I hopped on the back. Pulling the visor down and feeling the power as the bike suddenly shot off. Curling my arms around my brother to stop from falling off. The wind hitting our bodies like it was trying to send us flying.

The trip was quicker than when we made it by train. The hoverbike moving through the air with ease. Skimming over uneven ground until I saw Livenbrook in the distance. Coming in slower as we neared.

Coming to a complete stop just before the buildings started. The village was so small we didn't even have roads to drive on. Everyone moved on foot. Leaving their vehicles in the communal parking lot at the entrance.

This is where Lance parked the bike and we ran the rest of the way. Coming to the house just as my father was being pulled out by the force. Seeing the cuffs around his wrists. Looking like a criminal for everyone to see. And they were looking.

People stopped and stared, many of them had known both my parents but they didn't say anything or stand up for him. The fear of having an everfae in their community was enough to scare them.

Me and my brother ran up to him but one of the force stood in our way. Holding his arm across my path and placing a hand on my brother's shoulder. He spoke through the black visor that covered his face. "You need to stay back."

"That's our father." Lance pushed the man's hand from his shoulder. "Let us through, now."

"You don't give orders here. We do. Now stand back." My brother kept arguing which took the attention from me. Waiting until that arm was dropped then I ran forwards.

Shoving my body against my father, hugging him tightly. "Where are they taking you?"

"It's just for questioning. Nothing to worry about, pumpkin." He pulled back and looked into my eyes.

Feeling the tears falling down my face but they suddenly stopped when I saw his look. He knew about mum. He knew about my other half. "Dad?"

I was suddenly pulled into another tight hug, his whispering coming through my hair. "In the attic, there's a box. You'll know the right one. She wanted you to have something. I love you."

CHAPTER 6

Feeling his lips pursing to my cheek before he was pushed along. Turning to see him being escorted up the path. Everyone just standing and staring. A walk of humiliation and false accusation. Something he didn't deserve to experience. My brother came to me, arm coming around my shoulders. I buried my face into his t-shirt and cried.

Hearing the vehicle engine whirr to life in the distance. The thing lifting up from the ground and zooming out of sight. My fingers gripped into my brother's jacket.

"What are you all looking at!" Feeling him cuddling me close as he turned. Taking me towards the house. He unlocked the door and took me inside. The walls bright white apart from the sections my father had painted. It was his job so in his spare time he liked to practice.

A huge vineyard scene in the lounge dominated the biggest wall. The kitchen had an ocean theme which I was always loved growing up. His paints sitting on the floor in the hallways. The start of a scene drawn in pencil over the white wall.

I was placed onto a chair in the kitchen. Lance moving around the cupboards, making me a drink out of chocolate sauce and milk. Laughing as he placed it in front of me like he had countless times growing up. He was like a second parent figure to me. "Thanks."

"Everything will be alright. Father isn't an everfae."

"I am though. What if they find out? Now or in the future?"

"They'll have to get through me first." Smiling at him as I sipped my chocolate milk. Feeling like I was ten years old again. "Dad, will be okay, right?"

"Yes, of course. They'll question him. He didn't know mum was everfae and he'll be right back here."

"He knew. In his eyes, I saw that he knew."

"Why didn't he ever tell us?"

"I guess he was scared. With mum gone maybe he didn't want to lose us to."

"Yeah, you saw him grieving. It wasn't a pretty picture."

"True. He actually spent years with her. We've only got pictures."

Lance nodded, wiping a tear away before it could fall. Never having seen him like this before. "He was a great father considering what he was going through."

"I know. Do you ever feel like you're missing something in your life. Like a chunk is missing."

"I know what you mean." My glass was taking up and he stole some of my chocolate milk. "It's part of life. Some people lose their parents or other family members or friends. Nothing we can do to change it."

"Yeah. It's sad." Bringing my hands up to cover my face as I let myself fall into that sadness. Tears falling fast, trying to wipe them away but they just kept coming.

Lance moved to me but there was a knock at the door. His frustration coming out hard. "Some people need to keep their noses out of our business." His stomps echoing as he stormed towards the door. Yanking it open his voice suddenly became lighter. "Lawrence. What are you doing here?"

"I heard you guys were back and what was going on with your father. Thought I'd come round to make sure you two were alright."

I peered from the kitchen. Lance looked over his shoulder at me. "We're okay. Give me a sec." My brother came walking back. "It's Lawrence."

"I don't really want anyone to see me like this right now."

"No, of course not. I'll send him away."

"No, you go out. Have a chat."

"I'm not leaving you by yourself."

Giving him a soft smile. My father's words resonating around my brain. "I'll be alright. Please, I could do with some time by myself."

"Are you sure?"

"Yeah. I'll be fine. I've got my chocolate milk." Taking another sip of it. Lance laughed and wiped the milk from my top lip. "Go. Really, before I chuck you out of here."

"Alright but I won't be long. I'll come right back."

"Take your time. Seriously." He placed a kiss to my forehead, stole some more of my milk then jogged to the door. Taking a walk with Lawrence, probably down to the docks where him and his buddies always hung out.   Jumping off the jetties into the crystal clear water. We very rarely got boats in there so it was pretty safe.

With the door shut I made my way down the hallway. Stopping below the hatch. Giving the string a tug and pulling out the little set of steps attached to the inside.

Even before I started climbing I could feel something up there. I had never noticed it before but with the crystal ceremony it must have awakened that part of me. Taking the steps and moving into the shallow space. Crouching down and shifting from beam to beam towards the boxes in the corner.

That pull getting stronger until I was squatting in front of them. Pulling one forwards and discarding it when that pull brought me to another. Moving through them until I got to the right one. Lifting the flaps and seeing it was filled with screwed up newspapers.

Shifting through them, not having seen one since I was little. The world had switched to electronic news. The paper old and stiff like it had been hiding whatever was inside for decades. My fingers gripping something hard. Pulling it free, my eyes finally seeing what was calling to me.

A beautiful, dark stained wooden jewellery box. My fingers running over the smooth surface. It was perfect. Scooting across the beams holding it. Getting back down from the loft and taking my position at the kitchen table.

Opening the latch after a gulp of chocolate milk. Lifting up the lid and seeing the envelopes inside. Three of them, addressed to dad, Lance and myself. Flipping mine open, seeing the same handwriting that was on the back of all my photos. A tear falling when I read the opening line.

My dearest Crystal. I hate having to write this letter but that's the reality for me right now. I know that when you are born it will be my final day. My final goodbye to your father, to your brother. When my genes are passed down to you, my life will be yours.

And since you're reading this letter it means that you've found out the truth and pray that no one else has. You can't trust people with this. They fear us despite them being the ones who can't be trusted.

You know the abilities you have. Maybe you haven't come across a titan just yet but you will soon. They can sense your power. They call to you and you will call to them. And to help protect you, I've left something behind. Something personal to me.

I love you with all my heart and it crushes me that I will never get to hug you, to watch you grow up. Just know that my heart is with you, all the time. Every single day. I love you.

Each sentence I read the tears came harder. Sobbing by the end of the letter. Wiping them away but they were replaced immediately. I put the letter on the table with the other two, then pulled out another little box, this one much cheaper.

I lifted the top and revealed a piece of jewellery. Her necklace that she is wearing in every single photo I had. A simple thick, silver chain. The pendant was silver as well. A simple locket that opened up, a curved symbol on the front. When I pulled it apart a piece of paper fell out.

Seeing the marking on the inside making the shape of a face. An evil looking face with fur. Sharp teeth marked in the silver and those sharp eyes. I ran my thumb over it, feeling that call like a siren inside my thoughts.

Closing the locket and placing it onto the table. I unfolded the piece of paper, another letter from my mother, this one much shorter. The paper stiffer than the last. Showing it had been written long before.

I don't know if you would know about titans at this point. But they were our most powerful weapons against the invaders. They come in all kinds of forms. Some friendly and some need beating into submission. Once they are ours, they belong to us forever.

I used magic to contain one of mine, Belemoth. One that is very powerful and therefore will take a lot to tame. You must know who you are and believe in yourself otherwise you will fail. Call out his name whilst holding this pendant. I love you and believe in your power. You are my daughter and always will be.

Yet again making me cry, sniffling up my leaking noise. Grabbing a kitchen towel from the side and wiping my face. Taking a few deep breaths. Looking at the locket as it sat on the table. Hearing that call to the titan within.

Jumping as the front door swung open. Lance came walking in alone. Giving him a soft smile as I plucked up that locket and shoved it into my pocket. "Hey, you have a good talk?"

"Yeah. Was nice to chill away from the school. You okay?"

"Yeah, I found this. And these." Handing over his letter. "From mum."

"Really?" Seeing the look of shock on his face as he took a seat. Leaving him alone with his letter and taking a walk down the hallway. Moving into my bedroom and taking a perch on the edge of my bed.

Pulling the locket out and looking at it. That call from the titan within relentlessly pinging to my thoughts. I had to believe in myself and be ready if I was to capture this titan. Mum said it was very powerful and doing that in a place like this was out of the question. I had no idea how big this thing was or what it could do.

I would need to find somewhere quiet and big. Maybe that cave where I found Kit. Then a thought hit me. Breathing in deep and calling to that titan within. Feeling that whoosh of warmth as Kit appeared from that red light.

Dropping to the floor and spinning around to face me. "Hey, Crystal."

"Hey, Kit. I was just wondering, do you know about a titan called Belemoth?"

"Oh yeah, I've heard stories. Very powerful but not very big which I always found funny. He's more like a little imp or goblin."

"Oh. Do you think I could beat him?"

"Definitely not. You're not in full control of yourself. Belemoth isn't an offensive attacker like myself. He uses fear, gets inside your head and messes with you."

"I'm pretty strong minded."

"Maybe but you need to be sure before going up against him."

"Thanks."

"No worries." We shared a smile before I breathed in and brought him back into my heart. Feeling that heat hitting before it faded. Getting up and slowly making my way out to my brother. Lance was sitting at the table staring off into the distance.

"Lance?"

"Yeah." Quickly he wiped his face. "It's alright."

"You okay?"

"Uh-huh. Just mum's words."

"What did she say?"

"She told me to always protect you. Told me about being everfae and that people will try and take you away if they find out."

"You've always protected me anyway. Not because she asked."

"That's because you're my sister." He turned in his chair and looked into my eyes. "And no matter what your heritage you always will be. Mum made dad happy. We're a family and I don't care what other people say."

He stood and I moved into his arms. Hugging in the kitchen. "Should we take dad his letter?"

"No, he'll be back soon enough. Maybe we should get back to the school."

"You think we should?"

"Maybe in a bit." He slipped away and moved to the fridge. Grabbing a tray of dad's home-made lasagne. My belly grumbled at the sight of it. We shared a quick meal before jumping back onto his hover bike and making the trip back. This time much slower which enabled me to enjoy the scenery.

Taking a detour to the edge of the continent. Enjoying the views of the ocean hitting against the beach as we zoomed by. Veering back on route and arriving back at the school. Instead of heading towards the main entrance we arrived at one of those out buildings.

Moving through the shutter door that opened at a push of a button on the bike. We parked up with the rest of the fleet and I climbed off. "The rumour mill is going to be even worse now."

"Don't pay it any attention. If you're that important to the president he'll protect you."

"Maybe. It's not just the rumours though, D thinks I'm up to something."

"Then make her see. Show her Kit."

"That's not a bad idea. Just hope she can keep it to herself."

"That's up to you whether you think she can or not. But don't shy away from a friendship you're willing to get kicked out of school for."

Smiling as he winked at me, we moved out into the lobby, noticing that the shop was finally open. I quickly took the elevator up to my room. Noticing that D's stuff was in her bag which sat on the bed. Feeling a tug of sadness in my heart which got amplified when I spun and saw the photos of my parents. Seeing the locket that sat around her neck. Taking it out of my pocket I placed it behind my books, somewhere safe until I was ready.

Shaking my sadness and grabbing my wet clothes from the day before. Carrying them down and entering the shop. Using the machine to tumble dry them. The little shop owner appearing from the back. "Be back in a hour or I'll be dumping those clothes outside on the floor."

"Has anyone mentioned the importance of customer service to you?"

"Only people that are banned from using my shop."

"Warning taken. I'll make sure I'm back on time." Moving out of the shop and heading over the lobby towards the cafeteria. Just in time to see my brother chucking William onto one of the tables. Everyone shocked as he slammed his fist down into his face.

I quickly rushed over and pulled him off.

Standing between them. "This better not be about me again."

"It's not. He had a few words to say about our father. Saying that he was a dirty everfae and we should be expelled from school."

Turning and seeing the look in William's eyes. "Did you say that?"

"Yeah and it's true." William was too busy giving my brother the evils that he didn't see my fist coming. Smacking him in his jaw and sending him tumbling to the floor. "You're both crazy."

Moving forwards to hit him again but my brother pulled me back. A loud voice coming from the entrance. "What's going on here?"

Everyone turned to look at the teacher standing in the doorway. Mrs Kelp with her wide eyes staring at us. "Nothing is going on."

"Yeah, nothing. I just slipped." William stood up, giving me an angry look before walking off.

"Crystal, over here, please." My eyes down at the ground as I approached her. "I don't know what is going on with you. But you need to be careful. Talent or no talent, I can send you home myself. Understood?"

"Yes. Completely." Breathing in deeply, holding back the anger that I was being spoken to and William wasn't. He was the one running his mouth. Feeling important because his family is rich.

"Grab some tea and come see me in my class. I want to have a chat with you."

"Alright." She walked off with a nod and I headed over to the counter. Grabbing some sausage and mash and forgetting the dessert. Taking my plate and heading over to where D was sitting with the other two.

Putting my plate down but I didn't sit. My eyes scanning each one in turn. Feeling that I could trust D more than the other two however, they might not allow me back into the group even with her approval. And that's if she approved me.

Clearing my throat. "I was wondering if I could show you three something."

"What?" Larsh answered with a tone without looking up from her plate.

"Something private. Could we pop outside or something?"

Flo looked out the window, "It looks a little cold out there." The softness in her voice gave me hope.

"Alright, how about up in the room." Watching as the dinoser didn't move or speak. Pushing forkfuls of pie into her mouth. "D?"

Her eyes finally lifting to mine. "Why should we?"

"It'll explain everything."

Trying to smile but she just stared back. "No. I don't think so."

"Come on, we should at least hear her out. What will be the harm?"

"D said no, Flo." Larsh still hadn't looked up from her plate.

"Well I'm saying yes." She stood up so quick her chair almost toppled over. "Come on, Crys."

Larsh stood, wrapping her black fingers around her girlfriend's wrist. "You're not going with her."

"You have nothing to worry about. This is my decision to listen to what she has to say."

"No."

"Let go of me." Flo yanked her hand back. Not

wanting to start an argument but it was too late. "I'm going." Then she walked off without even waiting for me. Quickly moving out of the hall leaving my plate on the table.

We went up in the elevator with no words being exchanged. Flo looked out of the glass until we arrived. Making our way to my room. Flo sat down on D's bed, looking extremely distracted. So I sat down next to her and wrapped my arms around her.

Hugging her until she hugged me back. Feeling her tears seeping into my shoulder. "I didn't mean to cause an argument between you two."

"It's not our first and it won't be our last. It's not your fault."

"She really hates me. Her and D."

"D doesn't hate you." She pulled back and wiped away her sadness. "I think she's just disappointed."

"Disappointed? Why?"

"She really liked you."

"Now she doesn't because of the rumours of me being an everfae?"

"She doesn't believe that. It was the rumours of you and the president. She didn't like the thought of believing in someone who was going to cheat the system."

"But I wasn't."

"It doesn't matter. As a group we have trust issues. One little crack and we block ourselves from it. We've had friends in the past that have gone off as soon as the popular girls pay them some attention."

"I can understand why you guys act that way. But those rumours aren't true and I wanted to show you all something to explain what was happening. Why me and the president have been chatting."

"Well I'm here. If you still want to show someone." Her lips curling as her eyes looked at me.

"I do." Standing up in front of her. Taking that deep breath and calling to Kit to appear. That warmth and then the whoosh of colour. The kitsune dropping to the floor. Looking up at me then Flo.

Seeing the look of surprise on her face. Then the massive grin. "Holy hell, that's amazing. And he....he?" Nodding in reply. "He's so cute."

"At least your brother didn't call me cute."

"And he talks?"

"He does."

Kit walked around the room sniffing like he was a dog. Jumping up onto D's bed and snuggling up against Flo. She jumped at first but then she realised she wasn't going to get burnt by that fire fur. "So, that means."

"I'm half-everfae. They're the rumours that are true."

"That is insane."

"And that's why I've been getting special treatment from the president. He needs my help and needs me to be around to give it. Hence why I'm still here."

"Right." Watching as she stroked Kit, fingers shifting through that heated fur. "You should definitely show D and Larsh this."

"It's hard to get them to a place where I can. No one else can hear about this. Someone has already reported me once and that's why my father has been taken in."

"Is he okay?"

"My brother says they'll release him when they

realise he isn't everfae and the president has said he will conduct the investigation into and my brother."

"That's good. I'll help any way I can to make them listen."

"Perhaps you could convince D not to move rooms just yet. I can show her at night when no one else will see."

"I'll do my best." She picked Kit up and placed a kiss to his nose. Bringing a smile to his thin lips. "So cute. I best get back. Larsh will think we've run off together."

"Larsh is lucky to have you. She's a little grumpy for me."

"Never knew you were that way inclined."

"I'm not." My cheeks blushing as she looked into my eyes, laughing. "Thanks for understanding all this. And helping."

"Of course. I'll work on D when I get back to the table. They might give me a bit of the cold shoulder but no one can stay mad at me for too long, I'm too sweet."

"Yeah." Her eyes flashing for a moment as I agreed. Giving her a sheepish smile before calling Kit back into my heart. That whoosh of light which Flo watched with delight. Then we made our way back down to the cafeteria.

Seeing that my plate was missing from the table despite the fact my two ex-friends were still sitting there. They did give Flo the quiet treatment but I was happy that she started talking as soon as she sat down.

Heading up to the counter I was glad I only got a main meal. Using my watch to grab an apple and then a bottle of drink. Leaving the cafeteria, giving my brother a quick look. Nice to see his friends took him back into the fold. All of them coming from my village and knew my father quite well.

As I came out of the cantina I looked over to the shop. Popping my head into the entrance, spotting the little owner sitting behind the counter. "How long until the machine is finished?"

"Do I look like your slave?"

"I guess not." Moving through the shop and seeing that the machine had twenty minutes left on its cycle. Heading back out getting a grumpy look from the goblin. About to sit down on one of the benches when a green jeep came skidding to a stop outside the entrance.

The president climbing out and coming through the automatic doors. Waving at me, "Come on, we've got a field trip."

"Oh. You sure it needs to happen now?"

"Yes, I'll explain on the way."

"Okay." Taking my drink and apple and getting into the vehicle. The big thick wheels kicking up the grass and dirt as we shot off. Skimming over the field until we met a road and he veered off to the right. Cutting between the cliff and up a slope.

"So what's going on?"

"I got a report, of an animal attack. Judging by the details it could be a titan and a big one at that."

"Oh, you think I'm ready for this?"

"You won't be ready. We just have to get in and get it done. You'll take me to the right spot and I'll take it from there."

"How?"

"You're not the only one who can do magic, Crystal. I'll be fine."

"Okay. So what have the reports been saying?"

The jeep coming off the road and moving down a dirt track. Knowing now why he picked this particular vehicle. "Something has been coming out at night and eating pets and livestock. We're heading to Vinnerston. A little farming village. Very little luxuries there. All work and no play."

"I've heard of it."

"Of course. They believe something is living under ground. They're finding tunnel entrances around their crop fields. Disturbed dirt, collapsed areas. If it's not a titan, maybe we can still help these people from losing their livelihood."

"Is that what we're doing? Going around helping people?"

"When it's possible, yes. That's the whole idea of the school. To train people, so they can help others who don't have the talent for battle."

"I've never thought of it like that."

"That's because you don't like violence, right? But tell me this." The jeep bouncing around as we started making our way through a thick forest. Hearing the clicks of the manual lock button. "When someone is being hurt by a person or group of people, with violence. How would you defuse the situation?"

"Should I be worried about us driving through this forest?"

"What do you mean?"

"You just locked the doors."

"Just your run of the mill monsters."

"I've never actually seen one. At least, nothing bigger than a bug."

"Have a look around. You might spot one. They tend to steer clear of the road but you never know." The president's upbeat demeanour had it sounding like we were on safari.

"I think I would rather not. The knowledge of something that could eat me being out there is enough to frighten me."

His laughter filling the jeep. "Ignorance isn't a good way to run through life. You miss everything that way."

"I prefer to see it as having some comfort. Not being scared to go for a walk."

"With the training you're getting at the school, you won't be scared either."

"I don't do violence."

"Not from what Holbrook tells me. He said you did amazing in your first fight test."

"I was angry. Wasn't thinking straight."

"Just means you're a natural."

"Like magic? Because I'm half-everfae?"

"No, not at all. It's part of who you are."

"I don't think so." Keeping my eyes looking out the front of the vehicle. The trees breaking and the sight of the farmer's village coming into view. The track we were on sloped down towards it. A circle of buildings in the middle. Behind those were a few packing warehouses. A couple of paddocks for the animal. Then the stretch of crops.

From this height I could see the disturbed dirt and the areas that were threatening to collapse. The pattern showing tunnels running around the whole area. The amount of damage was immense and something big was causing it. Making my heart pound in my chest. "You think we can help them with this?"

"Of course we can. You shouldn't be afraid about

how big your enemy is. There's always a weakness you can exploit. Don't let your fear effect how you act in battle."

"You keep talking about battle like it's a sure thing."

"When hunting for titans, it's inevitable."

"I guess."

"There will be battling involved. And you have a talent for it. That's clear from your elite scores back at the school."

"I also have a talent for drawing. But I'm not going to pursue it as a career."

The president pulled down into the village and parked up over by one of the packing warehouses. We climbed out and I looked around. One of the workers came walking over to my driver. "Are you Ethan West?"

"Yes I am. We're here to have a look at your problem."

"I'm not entirely sure how you expect to help. There's just two of you."

"We're very well prepared for what could happen, don't you worry. We're going to take a little walk through the fields. See if we can find where this thing is living and go from there."

"If you say so." The man headed off back inside. Muttering something about us not taking this seriously.

Turning to the president as he came around to my side of the jeep. "So what do we do?"

"We take a walk around the field. See where this thing is living and take it from there."

"And how do we fight this thing if it attacks?"

"Oh it will attack. And we have magic and you have your little friend."

"My friend?"

My heart skipping a beat as his eyes lowered to my forearm. "Come on, I know you found the kitsune in that cave. I told the governors that I wanted that spot because the monsters don't venture that close to the coast. Really it's because I know about the sightings in that cave. I checked it out last night and when it didn't attack me I knew that you must have gotten there first."

"Yeah, it just happened. Didn't even know what was going on."

His hands gripped my shoulders. "It's in your blood. And now you're better equipped to fight more of them. Plus now you know what it's like to have that kind of power. I bet it's intoxicating."

Giving a shy smile. "If I'm honest, all kinds of magic is pretty alluring."

"Exactly. Give in to it, will make finding them a lot easier if you accept who you truly are."

"I'm still not a violent person."

"I know, I know. That's not what I mean. Come on, let's get walking. The field is quite large and the sun will be heading down soon."

"Yeah, okay." We moved from the compacted dirt and into the fields. The crops of corn sticking up above our heads. Making it hard to see any of the buildings as we ventured deeper. Hearing the soft noises from the packing plant going.

The president leading us until he stopped. The ground dipping down in front of us before levelling out again. "This must be one of its tunnels." He looked one way, then the other.

"So we follow this and find out where it lives?"

"Exactly. But do we go left or right." Quickly he

spun on his feet. "Do you feel a calling to it?"

Taking a moment. Remembering what it was like, being drawn into the cave to find Kit. Shaking my head. "No, nothing yet."

"Alright. Then we split up."

"Split up? Are you serious? What happens if I get attacked?"

"Scream and I'll come running."

"Seriously? That's your advice?"

"I'm kidding. You'll feel the ground shaking before this thing appears. I will to. Follow the trail you take backwards and I'll meet you along the way. Don't be so worried and trust your abilities."

"But."

"Shout if you find something." Then he walked off to the right. Following the shallow trench. Leaving me to take the left. My heart pounding faster as my trail curved through the corn. Taking the president out of sight and leaving me truly on my own.

Wondering what the hell I was doing out here. If this thing is so big and dangerous I'm not going to be able to do anything but die. Feeling lonely I called to Kit and he appeared in front of me. Paws digging into the dirt as he looked up at me. "This is a lovely place."

He lifted a leg and licked at the dirt. The sight of him making me smile. "I could do with some company, if that's alright."

"Of course. I'm your titan."

"Alright." The kitsune stepping in beside me as I walked. Moving through the destroyed area as we followed that tunnel. "Can I ask you something?"

"Yep." His voice upbeat despite the surrounding area.

"How does this whole titan thing work?"

"How do you mean?"

"Well, you attacked me and I beat you in a battle, so to speak. And now you're mine to control."

"Right. What's your question?"

"If I had killed you, what would happen then?"

"I would die."

"Oh."

Kit stopped and cocked his head to the side. "What's with these questions? Didn't this all get explained to you by someone? A parent?"

"No, my mother died giving birth to me. She was the everfae so I never had anyone to teach me about it."

"I'm sorry to hear that, I know what it's like." We started walking again. "Look at it this way. All titans are different. Just like humans, some want to fight and some want peace. Some are intellectual and some are physical. Lots of variations."

"So there's no way of knowing until I come face to face with one."

"Essentially, I'm sure there are others who have done the research but who's to tell what is the truth."

"Agreed. I know the history of everfae has been swept under the rug to make the humans feel better about what happened." Taking a deep breath as I thought about what I had said. Referring to everyone else as humans. Excluding myself from that statement.

Kit stopped suddenly and I felt a twinge in my brain. A calling to something down underground. "Of course there are titans who have lost their way. Without everfae to control us, to look after us. We were hunted and some took offence to that. Gone wild. I'm guessing that's what's going on here."

"You could be right. I can feel it calling out to me."

"Me to."

"You can?"

"Yes, we sense each other. It's why you very rarely find different species of titan living together."

"What do you think we should do?"

Kit looked around at the crops. "This thing is destroying something that is needed. I guess we could ask it to move somewhere else?"

"Would that ever work?"

"Not a clue but I bet no one has tried doing it."

"People tend to run away from large monsters."

"I know the feeling."

We stood there for a moment, staring into the entrance of the underground. Hearing that calling bringing me closer. Taking a step which Kit mirrored. "This is a really stupid idea isn't it?"

"I think you already know the answer to that question." We both did and yet we both kept walking forwards. Moving down into the ground. The fur on my titan's body lighting up the way ahead.

Following that calling tone in my brain, getting lost down here already after a few twists and turns. Coming out into a massive cavern. Looking at the many tunnels leading from this room. That calling was near but I couldn't pick which way to go. "We're near, right?"

Kit started sniffing around the floor in a big circle. "Feels like it. But." A few more sniffs before he started walking back to me. "Something is here."

"It's empty." My eyes moving around the massive area. "Come on, let's head back."

"If you say so." As I turned to leave the ground started shaking. Crumbs of dirt bouncing about. My eyes going wide as dark green fins started coming up out of the floor. Backing away but they were surrounding me.

CHAPTER 7

Getting lifted up as this massive titan came out of the ground. Its back covered in panels of hard skin. Falling to my hands and knees. The titan feeling smooth like a shell. Clinging to one of those fins as Kit came jumping towards me. Cowering by my side I curled an arm around him.

This thing was just as tall as one of those buildings out there. Seeing it's head twisting and looking around. Holding my breath as it turned on the spot. "I think it's looking for us."

My eyes dropping to Kit who looked extremely worried. "Its okay. We'll be fine." Feeling my heart pounding in my ears. The thing seeming to calm down, lowering onto all fours before suddenly sprinting off through one of those tunnels.

My arm wrapping around that fin even tighter. Bouncing as this thing sped through the catacomb. The light at the end coming quick until it bounded up to the surface. Huge feet trampling over the crops until it came to the little village.

Rearing up and screaming out with a screeching noise. Hearing the screams of the workers. Seeing how they ran like little ants. A huge bounce made me lose my grip and I started slipping over that smooth shell.

Hitting fins as I went until I dropped down over its head. Smacking the floor hard, wincing from that pain. Looking up and seeing this things face. The shell came over its head. Black eyes blinking at me. The skin of its face covered in scales.

A long snout came down towards me. A tongue coming out and flickering in the air. Getting sniffed which just made me even more frightened. This thing could step on me and I would be ended. Letting my breathing come out steady as that huge head backed away.

Thinking I was safe until it screeched again. Feeling the stinky air hitting my body. My breath getting stuck in my throat as it moved. Rearing high above ready to bring its two front feet down upon me.

My eyes catching movement then the flicker of fire. Seeing Kit leaping through the air. Twisting and shooting out a fireball with its nine tails. The huge creature stumbling to the side, the ground shaking as it came crashing down.

Climbing to my feet as he landed beside me. His bigger body standing in front of me.

Kit's fur ablaze, flickering like real fire. "Kit, do you think you can beat that thing?"

"Not a chance. Its skin is too hard."

"What if I helped?"

The big titan turning at us, screeching. Then it started running. We turned and fled but I wasn't fast enough. Kit scooping me up with his head and onto his back. Fingers gripping through that hot fur as he sped up. Leaving paw prints of fire behind.

We shot behind one of the huge warehouses. Looking behind me I watched as that creature bashed into the building. Crushing one side of it and anything inside. Hoping everyone got out in time.

121

Kit came to a halt and turned. "What do we do?"

"We need to stop it, hold it back so everyone can escape."

"And the plan to do that, is?"

My memory flashing back to magic class. Using the earth to build defences. "Get me close."

"Not too close I hope."

"Kit, let's go. It's time I started acting like an everfae."

"As you wish." Sharing a quick smile before he shot off. The heat from his body feeling nice against my face as we moved around the building being destroyed.

Jumping off of Kit and standing there. "Get its attention." Kit ran off, leaping through the air and flicking into a forward spin. His tails lighting up before a huge fireball was sent flying through the air. Hitting so hard I heard the crack of fire bursting against the big titan.

It crashed to the ground but was quickly getting back up like the fire didn't hurt it at all. Seeing those black eyes staring at me as it turned. Breathing in deep and reaching down with my earth magic. Pulling on the rock and making it build up. Block by block until a huge wall curved around in front of this thing. Blocking its path to the village.

Then I pushed at one side. Bringing it down upon the titan, then building it back up. Shifting it across the floor as it started to back away towards the crops. Smiling as I couldn't believe it was actually working.

Happy until that ear-piercing screech came again. Feeling the strain on my arms until that thing crashed through my wall. The sudden ping of force knocking me back onto my arse. Feeling the pain running through my body.

Staring as it climbed over the mess the wall had created. Seeing the pieces of metal sitting around from the warehouse. Not wanting to do what had popped into my head, not even sure if it would work.

Scurrying back on the floor but this thing was too large. Too quick for me to escape. Laying back and looking up with my arms extended. "Stop, please. I don't want to do this." Seeing flames hitting into its side but they did nothing.

"Crystal!" Hearing the president's voice but having no clue where he was. The ground shaking with what I thought were the thudding steps of the titan. But I was wrong. Seeing the ground erupting up in pieces. Covering the shell with a dome of stone. I knew it was Mr West.

I climbed up onto my feet, looking over my shoulder. He was standing there. Arms held up but the sweat on his forehead meant he wouldn't be able to hold it much longer. Turning back and walking up to this titan. Looking deep into one of those black eyes. Pleading with it, "Please stop. Go back."

It struggled but then it looked back. That calling I felt, it felt it as well. Like a link between us. I reached out with my hand and pressed it against those scales. Feeling the beast was calm. Hoping I was right. "It's okay. We'll take you somewhere safe. I promise." Rubbing my touch up and down.

My sense of accomplishment was short lived when I heard a massive crack. Thinking it was the rock. Then I saw the break in the shell growing down over its head. Hearing another and it screeched in pain.

Quickly turning to the president. "Wait, you

can't. It's not going to fight."

"I don't have a choice. You saw what it did."

"It won't be a danger any more."

"I can't take that chance." His hands moving together even more. The screech coming again as a crack rung out. Turning and seeing how distressed it was. A tear trickling down my cheek as our eyes connected.

"No, you can't do this." Spinning and pushing at the president's hands but it was too late. Hearing a snap and that beast dropped to the ground with a crash. Looking over my shoulder at the titan. The rock rolling from its back. Seeing the damage, the cracks in its shell. Where it had caved in and killed it.

Rubbing my face with my sleeve, sniffing. "You didn't have to do that."

"I did. This thing was destroying the place."

"It was a living being."

"No, it was a titan and it was out of control."

"You don't know that. You don't feel what I feel."

"You just have to trust me. I know what I'm talking about."

Turning away from him and walking over to the dead animal. Rubbing that spot I had touched before. "I'm sorry I couldn't help you."

"Crystal, you need to make your titan vanish. People will see it."

"It's a him."

"What?"

"Nothing." Lowering my head and calling Kit back into my heart. That rush of light and warmth telling me no one would see him.

"We should get going before it gets too dark. The

forest will be too dangerous for travelling."

"Fine." Moving past that dead titan. Hoping it would disappear into a burst of light or something but it felt so real. Having it laying there dead. My feet carrying me past its side. Seeing movement out the corner of my eye made me stop.

Looking at the smaller fins down near its tail. One of them becoming loose and dropping off to the floor. Moving over quickly out of sight. Crouching down and touching this part of the titan. One fin sticking up from a piece of shell. Dark green like an emerald.

My hand touching but pulling back quickly when a head popped out the end. Snapping at me. Then legs slipped out, along with a short stubby tail. I peered around the corpse and no one was around.

I slipped off my chequered shirt and wrapped it around the little creature. It was small enough to sit in my hands. So I bundled it up, careful not to jab that fin into my arm. Cradling it so it just looked like my shirt was rolled up.

Carrying it back to the jeep and climbing in. The president looked at me. "Hey, you got hurt."

"Huh?" Concentrating on keeping the little creature secret I almost didn't hear him. Seeing where he was looking. Peering down and seeing the gash along my arm. I hadn't even feel it happen.

"Here." Ethan leant over to the glove box. Pulling out one of three vials of green liquid. "Drink this, will make you feel much better."

"Alright." Taking it from him and gulping it back without a second thought. Handing the empty vial back then curling my arms around my shirt. Trying to stop the little thing from wriggling lose.

e

Giving my shoulder a quick look. Seeing the gash healing from that potion. "That's amazing."

"It's only good for little injuries." The jeep was turned around and we drove out of the little village. Tilting my head to watch the body of that titan moving further away. Fingers gripping the thing in my lap tighter.

People were gathered by the buildings as we drove by. Cheering that their beast had been vanquished. None of them seemed bothered that we had taken its life. No one mourned that titan except me. Knowing that I had calmed it, knowing that it wouldn't have attacked me. I could have gotten it to move somewhere else. There was no need to kill it.

Looking at the president as we drove back through the forest. The sky starting to dim as the sun headed down towards the horizon. Catching movement amongst the trees. Darkness starting to hide those monsters. Feeling a little unsure as my eyes darted about.

My heart slowing down as we left the tree line. Shifting in my seat. "You didn't have to kill it."

"That thing would have killed us both."

"No, it wouldn't have. It was calm and you crushed it."

"I did what I had to do. Your life was in danger."

Not bothering to argue with him. We got back to the school as it was starting to get dark. Mr West didn't bother defending himself any more. We parked in the garage area and I walked off without a word. He left me to it which I was very happy about.

Hearing the chatter from the cafeteria where another movie was being played. Noticing that some people had their laptops out. Headphones in as they played games or surfed the internet. I pulled that bundle close to my body. No one paying me any attention as I turned to the elevator.

Heading up to my room I came through the door. Startling D who was sitting on her bed. Noticing her bag was still packed and yet she was still here. She blew out a frustrated sigh. "You scared me."

"Sorry. I didn't mean to."

"It's fine." She took in my saliva soaked outfit. "I don't even want to know what happened." Looking down. Blowing out a breath, another load of clothes that would need some care. "Well, here's your chance. Flo told me to hear you out so I'm here to hear you out. But if I don't like it then I'm gone. I don't care if I have to bunk with Larsh."

"Look, now isn't really a good time to chat." The bundle under my arm wriggling, digging that fin into my armpit.

"I knew it. You stand up for me. Act all cool but now that you're taken care of by the president, you're too good for me."

"It's not like that at all."

"Oh please. I've heard it too many times. I'm gone."

"No, D. You don't understand."

She flung her bag over her shoulder and headed for the door. As I moved to cut her off I dropped my shirt. The thing hit the floor with a thud. Bringing both our eyes down to the now wriggling shirt. "What the hell have you got?"

"I'll explain."

D leant down and pulled back the piece of

clothing. Revealing that little baby titan. The fin sticking up, the face looking at us both. "What the hell is that?"

"I'm not entirely sure what it is. But.......it's a titan. I think."

Her eyes lifting to mine, her mouth gaping in shock. "A titan. So you are......"

"Yep. I'm half-everfae."

"Really?"

I was about to re-affirm my statement but instead I decided to show her. Breathing in and out, calling to Kit who appeared with that light from my chest. Black paws touching the ground. Then it turned around baring its teeth. Not at either of us but at that little creature I had brought back. "Kit, it's okay."

"I seem to remember something very similar almost crushing us."

"But this is just a baby. Or at least I think it is."

My kitsune calmed down, looking up to D who was staring at him. "Showing me off again?"

"This is D."

"You call it Kit?"

"It? I think I preferred being called cute."

"Sorry." They exchanged a look before Kit walked off, curling up near my bed. As he settled the new visitor waddled over to him. Growling for a moment before this thing just plopped down. Watching the two of them as my titan rested his head on his paws.

"So you're everfae."

"Half, yeah." Turning back to D. "It's why the president of the school has been giving me some help. He's half-everfae as well. I'm helping him look for titans. But it's not going so well."

"What do you mean?"

"The president, killed this titan."

"Was it dangerous?"

"It was destroying stuff but it didn't know any better. I had it calm but he killed it any way. Crushed it with earth magic right in front of me. Was horrible." Picturing that large animal laying there dead. Feeling tears suddenly falling from my eyes. D's arms wrapped me up tight. Getting really annoyed with all the crying I've been doing.

Letting my tears wash away the sadness I felt. Feeling her rough skin running across my arms as I pulled back. Wiping away the wetness on my cheeks. "Thanks."

"I shouldn't have been so quick to judge and let you explain."

"Flo explained why you reacted like that. It's alright."

"You're too sweet, you know that."

"Thanks." Giving the two animals another glance. "I'm going to pop down and get something to eat. I didn't eat much at tea."

Seeing her bashful look which had me thinking the two of them had chucked my food at tea. Deciding to ignore it since I had her back. D looked over to the little titans laying on the floor. The new visitor trying to catch Kit's tail with its mouth. "You want me to look after them?"

"Just the little one, Kit should..." Seeing how comfortable he looked. "If you could. Kit won't be a problem. He had an energetic evening. Just make sure the other one doesn't eat the furniture."

"I think I can handle it. Then you can explain

exactly what happened."

"Sure." Heading down to the cafeteria. Grabbing a plate from the counter and scanning my watch. Only it came back with a beep and a red flash. "Looks like you've used up all your credit. Sorry."

"No worries." My stomach grumbling in retaliation. The plate was taken from me so I decided to leave. The television catching my attention. A news report showing that a village was attacked recently. A little girl recounting her encounter with a monster made of black shadows. Reminding me of that titan at the back of leather book. Noticing some of the looks I was getting so I decided to leave.

Planning to head for the elevator but I heard chatter coming from the shop. Looking over and seeing the barrier was pulled across but the lights were still on. Hearing someone laughing his head off. Moving closer and peering in. Some figures moving about near the back. Remembering my clothes but they weren't down on the floor like he had threatened.

Banging on the metal gate made the chatter stop. That little goblin appearing with an annoyed look on his face. "What do you want?"

"Where are my clothes. You said you would leave them on the floor."

"Get lost. I'm busy."

My eyes going wide in horror as one of his friends came around the corner. Holding up my bra to his chest and wearing my underwear on his head. "What the hell are you doing?!"

The little goblin turned around. "You're kidding me right?" Shoving him back around the shelves. "You're going to get me into trouble, you bloody idiot."

"Tell him to take those off. Right now."

"Alright, alright. This is just between us. No need to tell anyone."

"Give me my clothes and something to eat and I'll keep it to myself."

"Yeah, yeah." He disappeared then came back a few minutes later with my clothes in his arms. Watching as he took some packets off a hook. Then piled two pintos on my clothes. He passed them through the bars. "Look, no one can hear about this."

"I thought after hours the shop is open to others."

"Yeah but they aren't supposed to interact with the students. Or mess around with their possessions."

"I won't tell anyone. I'm not that kind of person."

I reached my arms forward to take my stuff. His eyes flicking down for a second as I took them from him. "Come by tomorrow when I'm open. I'd like to apologise properly."

"It's okay, you don't need to."

"It's a culture thing. Something I need to do."

"Oh." His eyes looking into mine. "Okay, I'll be in tomorrow sometime."

"Thanks."

Taking my stuff cautiously, then heading back up to my room. Finding Kit still asleep on the floor. The other little critter was nudging against the bottom of D's bed. She was sitting on top cross legged. "Everything okay?"

"This little thing keeps trying to nibble my feet."

"Might be hungry." I sat down on the floor and it came waddling over to me. Taking one pinto I chucked it to D, "Try this, it's gorgeous." With the other I cracked it open and offered half to the baby animal. Without hesitation it chomped straight through it in seconds. Scoffing it all down so I offered it the other half.

Watching as it was devoured as well. Opening one of the packets, spilling out some of the nutty nibbles onto the floor. Letting it munch away as I looked up. Explaining everything to D about what had happened.

Munching on the nuts myself as I did. By the time I had finished this thing had crawled up onto my lap and was just sitting there. Settling it's belly after finishing off the second packet of nuts.

"Why do you think it was attacking?"

"Kit said that without everfae to look after them, some titans have gone wild." My hand resting on the green shell on my lap. Seeing how content it seemed after having a meal. "Maybe it was just hungry."

"The little one seemed to be." My eyes still on it as it sat there. Seeing a slight glow coming from its shell. Running my fingers over it as it spread. Then the baby titan started to fade from sight. Feeling that pressure against my chest right over my heart. Similar to how Kit vanished for the first time. Looking down at my forearm where the kitsune tattoo sat.

Confused since another one didn't appear. I stood up and looked around at the floor. "That's really weird. Did it die?"

"I don't think so."

"The big titan didn't vanish like that and what just happened was exactly how it went with Kit."

"Um, Crys. Look at your shoulder."

"What?" Tilting my head to look over my shoulder but I couldn't see anything. Moving to the mirror on the door for my wardrobe. Shifting my body until I saw the black fin sitting in my skin. "At least this one is easier to hide than Kit's."

"Why do you have to hide them?"

"Because people can't find out my true heritage and there isn't exactly a tattoo parlour at the school."

"Right, yeah. That would take some explaining."

"Exactly." Turning back around from the mirror. Giving Kit another look. "I'm probably going to crash now. Feel a bit battered."

"Sounds like it." I climbed into bed after a quick change into something comfy. Feeling the cover shift as Kit climbed up and curled up next to me. His black fur still giving off a bit of heat. Helping me fall asleep quickly.

The darkness coming to get me and dropping me down into a storm. Black all around me, feeling fingers rubbing against my body. Claws pricking against my skin. I batted them away, trying to see where they were coming from.

Only, they were everywhere. All around me. Those shadows a cloud of terror. With no escape. My heart pounding in my chest. Panting in fear. My whole body jumping as a spear of black came for me.

Shooting straight through my chest and out the back. Looking over my shoulder and seeing my heart on the end. Blood dripping all over the ground. My eyes dimming before shutting completely. My body going limp then feeling that black spear pulled from my chest. That pulse of pain waking me up with a gasp. "What the hell was that?"

CHAPTER 8

Kit stirred which made me yelp. The titan jumping at my noise. "Morning." A huge yawn spreading his jaws open.

"Morning." Rubbing my hands over my eyes. "Time to go back I'm afraid."

"Of course. Was nice though."

"I'm sure you can come back out tonight."

"Great." With a smile he jumped from the bed, turning into that warm light and going back to my heart. That tattoo on my wrist glowing red for a moment. My eyes lifted and looked at my photos. Remembering the locket behind them.

Turning around I saw D was still asleep. So I took my washing stuff and grabbed a shower down the hall. Coming back with damp hair but feeling very refreshed.

Getting dressed in my usual combats. Black the same as my long-sleeved top. Then I grabbed the locket. Slipping it around my neck and checking myself out in the mirror. Clumping my hair in my hands to make it even curlier.

Standing and pausing. Smiling as I thought about my mum at this age. Thinking I would look exactly like her. Hearing D shuffling in bed I turned. Watching her sleep for a moment when a tray was pushed under our door.

Turning to see the bowl's of porridge sitting on

the tray with those sachets. I placed it on the table, feeling a little like a prisoner. Giving D a little nudge to wake her up.

She looked over with a sleepy look and a smile. "Morning."

"Breakfast has arrived." I sat on my bed with my back to the wall. Rubbing my finger over the front of my locket before grabbing that book the president had given me. Flicking through. Seeing the page that described the fire kitsune. Thinking how procedural it was. Nothing about behaviour or personality. Offering me nothing I hadn't already figured out myself.

Moving further into the book I found a page with a drawing. Fins, green shading. That long snout and the stubby tail. This was the titan I fought yesterday. Reading through the mini-descriptions.

Lives underground in a labyrinth of tunnels. Comes up for food. Its babies live on its back for safety. No points of attacking humans or other animals. Nothing to indicate that it would ever do what it had done. Kitsune had said with the absence of everfae the titans could become wild. Another thing the humans have to be proud of. It didn't even have the name of the titan.

Chucking the book on my bed which brought me D's attention. "Everything okay?"

"Just learning about the titans. The humans have caused this problem. Eradicating my kind has just pushed them to act out and attack. It's all their fault."

"It's okay."

"It's not. I watched the president kill that titan. I couldn't do anything to stop it."

D came running over and pulled me into a hug.

"It is okay. It will be okay."

"I hope so. Not sure I could go through that again."

"That's because you're a protector. You protected that little baby and I'm sure you protect Kit as well."

"I guess."

"I'm being serious. You don't like violence but its okay to be violent when you're helping someone. Like you did in the showers for me."

Lifting my eyes to hers. Crying too much to argue her point. Smiling as she wiped a tear away. "Ever since being here I've been crying more. Having a go at people. The thing I did in earth magic class. I could have hurt someone."

"It was only Troy though, so it's forgivable."

Bursting out a laugh which sprayed tears over her top. "Sorry."

"Don't worry about it." She hugged me for a bit longer before getting up and getting dressed. I finished my porridge as she did. Then we headed out into the hallway when our watches buzzed.

Using the elevator to get to Holbrook's class. Our teacher waiting at the front like normal. Waiting until all of us were queued up. "Today we will be studying moves and defences like before. Go get your weapons."

We shuffled across to the wall of dangerous objects. I locked my eyes on Troy as he came around the corner. Not even rushing to my weapon. Just watching him and smiling as he grabbed something else.

Then I moved to retrieve the one that belonged to me. It feeling light in my hand. I returned, giving D a smile before heading over to where my screen was shown. Only one other person had a staff like me. Just a normal stick unlike the extendable one I had.

I pressed the middle button and the two ends shot out in a flash. Watching the screen and backing away from the other student as she started swinging her weapon. Almost getting caught a couple of times.

Once I felt safe I started mimicking the actions. Matching step by step and feeling so comfortable with this thing. Spinning it around my body. Around my hand. By the end of the lesson I had picked it up so quick. Even moving a little faster than the man on the screen. Moving a lot faster than the other student.

She seemed quite annoyed about that which made me enjoy it even more. Feeling so different from before coming here. It could have been the crystal ceremony. Or it could have been inside me all along.

Everyone put their weapons back but instead of being dismissed Holbrook told us what was happening next. "We're not heading to lunch just yet. We've got a visitor today and we need to head down into the training ground to meet him. I'll meet you down in the lobby."

We left the room and bundled into the elevator. Taking it down and grouping around the fountain. I leant against the wall and saw my brother walking by. Quickly jogging over to him and tapping his arm. "Hey, you heard anything about dad?"

"No not yet. I'm sure he'll be home before we know it."

"Yeah. How are your classes going?"

"Good. Joint first for elite points with two others."

"That's really good. I haven't got a clue where I am. But I think I'm doing good."

"You are?"

"Hey." Punching him in the arm. "Why do you sound so surprised?"

"Because you've always been against violence."

"Yeah, things are changing." Hearing Holbrook's voice and seeing him coming from the elevator. "I have to get going."

"Alright, I'll see you around." He pecked my cheek and headed off towards the cafeteria. Watching as he was quickly joined by that bully girl. Her frizzy hair bouncing as she pulled a fake smile at him.

Holbrook's voice pulling me back to the class. Arriving just as he headed through the double doors labelled training area. We followed him down the hallway of grey walls. Noticing how the architecture changed from the smooth, fancy looking building. Becoming more sturdy. A massive steel door stood in front of us.

Holbrook put in a code and we all watched as this huge mechanism turned. Like a giant cylinder, showing a path through the middle once it stopped. Following our teacher further through another door like the last. Coming to our destination.

A man was standing there, waiting for us. But my eyes weren't fixed on him. They were moving around the huge room. Massive trees reaching up high. Bushes that didn't come from this continent. Like we had walked into a jungle.

My eyes coming back to the man we were here to visit. Wearing trousers and a grey shirt. Looking like he had just come from an expedition in the wild. A few scars on his arms and face. His neck having the longest, thickest one. My eyes went back to the jungle. Worry starting to build of what could be in there.

"Thank you, Holbrook, for bringing your students here. When you're out on missions or jobs. You will come across all kinds of situations. Many of those will involve monsters. That's my job, to introduce you to your first."

He blew into a whistle which gave off a high-pitched noise. Hearing rustling coming from a distance, getting closer until a flower head came bursting into view. A long green stem leading out of sight into the foliage.

The head blossoming, bright blue petals flashing open. The middle had a big eye in it. The petals closing and opening like it was blinking. Then another came through the bushes. Blue petals opening up and showing off another eye. Bobbing back and forth as they scanned us.

They hovered looking at all of us for a moment. The guide for monsters turning his back on it. "This is called blossoming death. A very deadly creature found in jungles and woodland areas. As you can see it has two eyes that can work independently from each other. One can be looking at us and the other could be hunting for something to eat on the other side of the biome."

The bushes started moving again, bringing out a third bulb. Petals opening but this time they were red. The middle had a little hole surrounded by sharp teeth. My eyes watching it until something came shooting out towards us.

My breath getting caught in my throat before it hit an invisible wall. The whole class jumping back in shock. "Don't worry, we take safety very seriously. This barrier won't let anything through, you're perfectly safe."

The thing that had come shooting towards us hit the floor. A long pink tongue with barbs at the end slithered back towards the red flower. "It has two more flower heads just like that one. If you want to see it in action, don't look away."

He pushed a button and I heard a metal door opening with a thud. Watching the scene in front of us as the heads started moving. Sensing something in the air and then a bird came flying through the trees.

It swooped up but was suddenly caught by that barbed tongue. Getting skewered before pulled back suddenly. Like a frog's tongue grabbing a fly. It was devoured by that mouth. Watching it chew the bird until it swallowed.

"The belly of the monster burrows underground. They find a nice place to bury themselves. Using these five bulbs to hunt and eat. When they're young they have one eye and one mouth. This is in the middle of its cycle. The oldest can have up to four eyes and ten mouths. Or at least that's the highest someone has found and lived to document." A laugh erupting from his mouth. The whole class stared uneasily.

The mouth came closer to that barrier. Able to see the tunnel of teeth and that barb just sticking out. It nudged the barrier that was protecting us. Figuring it couldn't get to us and moving off into the forest.

Hearing a few rustles before it rested. No doubt just looking like a bunch of flowers that hadn't bloomed yet. "Do you have any questions?" The man standing there with his hands hanging in front of him.

One of the other students cleared her throat. "How would you escape something like that?"

"I wish I could tell you it would be simple, like standing still. Only this thing hunts, all the time. Day and night. You wander into its domain and you're unprepared? You'll have to kill it to escape being digested slowly over the span of a week."

"And how would they do that?" Holbrook pushing the conversation into a helpful direction.

"The best would be fire. Burn the body and it will die. The heads won't be a problem after that. Look for disturbed dirt or follow the stems from the flowers to the body. That would be my choice."

"And if you didn't want to kill a creature who was just living?"

His eyes looking at me as the rest of the students turned. Some making comments. "If you didn't want to kill it then I suggest you stay away from the forest just in case you stumble upon one."

"Couldn't you hide?"

"No. Did you notice how those heads came for us. It doesn't have ears. It measures the air current with tiny hairs along those stems. Even if you were breathing, it would eventually find you."

"Oh."

"Yeah. Are there any other questions?"

The class stayed silent and Holbrook thanked the man for his help. Telling us all to head for the cafeteria for lunch. Moving along the hallway, discussing what we just saw with D. Getting in line and collected a nice seafood sandwich, some fruit and a bottle of water. Both of us heading to our usual table.

Giving Flo and Larsh a soft smile as I sat but I only got one in return. "What the hell is she doing at our table again?"

"She's a friend." D stood up for me with a smile.

"She isn't my friend. She seems more friendly with the president."

"It's not like that."

Staying silent but that just brought her aggression towards me. "You don't have anything to say?"

Blowing out a sigh, thinking about defending myself. But I had had enough of people thinking they knew what's going on. I've been warned by a teacher, other students making comments. Looking at Larsh's eyes, "I don't honestly care if you like me or not. I don't like you. Not because of how you're treating me. But the way you treat Flo."

"Excuse me. You've known us for two days and you think you can talk smack about how I treat my girlfriend?"

"I didn't need two days to see it. She's incredibly sweet and lovely. You on the other hand are mean. You don't talk to her softly, you bark at her. What she sees in you I don't understand."

"You little…" She stood up hard enough to drop her chair to the floor. "You don't get to say that kind of thing to me. Either she goes or I do." Larsh shot a look at Flo.

Looking at her myself I saw the sadness in her eyes. "She's right, Larsh. You don't talk to me like I'm your girlfriend. I can't remember the last time we hugged or held hands."

"Flo? You're not serious."

"I am. I get you have issues but we all do. Including Crystal. The way you talk to her, she's one of us whether you like it or not. She's an outsider. And she needs us right now. You remember what it was like when the school turned on you. That's what she's going through."

"It's not the same. She's brought this upon herself for being with...."

"She's not with him. She didn't ask for this. None of us did. If you can't see that then you should leave."

Not able to look away from the argument. Looking like they were going to break up all because of me. Sensing D's body tensing. Looking like she was ready to jump into action. Looking at Larsh and seeing her hands balling up.

Worry hitting me even harder as she moved. My heart skipping and D jumped to her feet. But in that flash Larsh had just turned and walked away. Flo watching her with a tear falling down her cheek.

She turned to the table and let out a long breath. "I guess that's that."

"I'm really sorry." Reaching across the table and touching my hand to hers. Curling fingers around it. "It's all my fault."

"No, it's not. That was coming for a long time. She's been growing more and more distant. Maybe she's met someone else, I don't know."

"She couldn't possibly find someone cooler than you." D joined me in holding her hand. "It'll be alright, Flo."

"I know. Just hard right now."

"Then we need a new subject to talk about. Do you know what me and Crys just saw?"

Her eyes lifting. A smile being pushed to her lips with effort. "What?"

"A blossoming death."

"A what?" D explained all about. Talking about how it attacks with a tongue. Pulling Flo's curiosity out, making her forget about Larsh for a moment. Watching as she listened. Whilst she did I noticed the little goblin from the shop waving at me from the lobby. I excused myself with a mouthful of prawns.

Wondering why the little thing kept peering around. It just made him look suspicious. "I want to ask you something in private."

"Oh?"

"Come to the shop." I followed slowly since his legs were a lot shorter than mine. We moved into the shop and around to the fancy side. The little owner fiddling with things on the shelf. "I was wondering if I could ask you a favour."

"A favour?"

"Yeah. Us goblins tend to work in favours. It's like a currency for us."

"And what would I be getting in return?"

"You can have anything from this side of the shop." My eyes moving over the weird looking objects. "Like this for instance."

Turning back to him just in time to catch an object he had tossed into the air. The metal hitting my palm and giving off a soft hum. Turning it over, studying the small sphere. "What is it?"

Looking up and seeing his wide grin. "It's a sensor. It reacts to magic wielders."

"I don't think I have a need for something like that."

"True." He took it from my hand and it stopped making that noise. "But like I said you can have anything. I'll explain what things can do later tonight.

You willing to help me with something? After tea, when it's dark."

"What's the favour?"

"Just something really small but I'll make it worth your while."

"I don't think so."

"Please. I could really use the help and you're really the only person I can ask. Just a quick job. Plus I would owe you a favour. Trust me when I say that's a really big deal."

"Alright, I'll grab some food then head over here after tea."

"Thanks. Excellent."

"No worries." Turning and heading for the exit. Wondering what he was so excited about. Giving the shelves a quick look, seeing if anything looked good enough to be doing such a favour. Some of the things looked interesting but I still had no idea what they could do.

Leaving the shop and heading across the lobby when a voice called to me. Looking over to the entrance and seeing my father standing there. "Dad?" Rushing over and launching myself into a tight hug. Fingers gripping his shirt, so happy that he had been released. "You're out."

"Yeah, they had no real reason to keep me. One simple test and it was proven I'm human. They just took there time doing it."

"But you're okay?"

"Yeah, I'm fine, pumpkin. I wanted to come by and speak to you face to face." His eyes looked at my neck and worry set in. "Did you find the box, in the attic?"

"Yeah I found it. And the letters from mum. Lance read his."

"And you read yours?"

"Yes."

"Are you okay?" His hand came up and cupped my cheek.

"I'm alright. Learning new things about myself."

"It's all okay. It's been a part of you your whole life. Nothing has changed."

"I feel like I have though."

We walked over to one of the benches and sat down. "How do you mean?"

"I'm more confident. Instead of staying quiet I'm standing up for people. Standing up for myself. I won a fight in weaponry class."

"You did? But you're against violence."

"I know but I wanted to prove to everyone that I deserved to be here. That I could do it myself with no help from the president. It's hard to explain. Just feel different."

"Maybe that's a good thing. Your half me, half your mum. She was always the one to stand up for people. Defending her friends or strangers. I always leaned more towards being quiet and dealing with my own life."

"That was me until I got here. It might have something to do with the crystal ceremony. It awakens your abilities with magic and all that. Maybe it woke up this side of me."

"Perhaps. Is that a bad thing?"

"I don't know. I like being there for my friends. But I don't want to be fighting."

"You can fight and still be you. Fight to defend.

Protect people. It's not all about going to war and killing the enemy."

"I guess I've been a little close minded."

"It's all part of growing up. Opening your mind to new things. You came here and saw things you've never experienced before. I've seen some of the students in there. You hadn't seen anyone apart from humans in our little village."

"It was certainly a shock first time I met my room mate."

"Exactly. It's going to be a shock to your system. The world is huge outside of Livenbrook. Maybe it's time you started expanding with it."

"Yeah. I like the way you put it." Grabbing him for a quick hug. "You going to see Lance whilst you're here."

"Of course."

"He's in the cafeteria with his friends."

"What about you? Do you have any friends?"

"A couple. They're really great actually."

"I'm really happy to hear that. And the other stuff?"

"What do you mean?"

Lowering his voice, "Everfae stuff."

"Oh. That's taking time to get used to but you don't have anything to worry about. I've got another friend." Pulling my sleeve up and showing him the kitsune tattoo.

"Wow, a fire kitsune?"

"Yeah, how do you know about them?"

"I was with your mother for thirteen years. She never hid what she was from me. We spent many nights chatting, letting her tell me stories about these titans she knew about."

"Did she ever explain the connection she felt to the titans?"

"She said it was like having a pet that could kick arse."

Laughing, "Yeah, that sounds about right." Thinking of Kit and how powerful he was. "Thanks, for sharing."

"Just happy I can do it now. She didn't want you to ever know about it. She wanted you to have a clear future without prejudice."

"I can understand that. She must have been scared for me. Passing the genes to me."

"She was. But she was happy to give you life. You and your brother. She was a happy woman, no regret or doubt."

"A part of me feels like I took her away from you and Lance."

"Oh, darling. Don't ever think that. It was her decision to have your brother and you. I kept telling her that it was too dangerous. She just smiled and said how I was destined to be a father. Love is hard, like a battlefield. You just have to make sure you find someone who will fight by your side. That was her for me. So I did everything for her that I could."

"She sounds amazing. Wish I could have met her."

"Me to, honey." I got another hug which brought a tear to my eye. "I'll go say hey to Lance. Let him know that I'm back home."

"Alright. It was great seeing you."

"You to. Keep up the good work. I called the president to make sure it was okay to drop by. He mentioned how well you're doing in classes. Just remember, violence isn't always about hurting the other person."

"Sure, dad. I'll remember."

"You're just like her, more than you know."

Smiling as he turned and walked into the cafeteria. Hearing Lance calling out to him. I sat on the bench for a bit longer. Only moving when my watch vibrated for my next class. Waiting for D before heading up to the classroom.

Mrs Kelp led us in. Moving to my pod and standing beside it like everyone else. The teacher standing there with her clipboard. "You will go into your pods. A ceiling will cover it and the walls will come alive. You will make your way through a gauntlet, showing off your abilities. Nothing too extreme, the fire system will still come into effect. No earth magic either for obvious reasons."

As we climbed down into our pods she carried on talking. "The top three quickest times will get the elite points today. And Crystal." I paused on the rungs and looked over to her. "I want you to put some effort in. Not like before."

"Yes, Mrs Kelp."

"Good. The gauntlet will start as soon as the ceiling shuts." Stepping off the ladder. Scanning my watch and making my way to the middle, noticing that the floor was no longer stable. As I walked on it, it moved like a mini treadmill, no matter which direction I headed. "Walk, do not run or you will just hit the wall."

Standing there, waiting when I heard the teacher's voice above me. She was knelt down at the edge of my pod. "You didn't come and see me yesterday."

"Sorry, the president needed my help with

something. Didn't get back until late."

"Uh-huh." Seeing the judgemental look she expressed. "See me after class then."

"Sure, alright."

Her stare stayed on me as she stood. Finally turning and shouting to the class. "Begin!"

Hearing some of the other ceilings shutting with a whoosh of air. Watching as mine did the same. The walls of my pod coming alive, seeing that I was in a large white room. Turning on the spot and looking at it all.

An information box appeared. Watching as it explained the objective. Shoot the targets with my magic. Red is for fire, blue is for water and white is for wind. Points for hitting the target, double the points for using the right spell.

Sounded easy enough. A countdown from three and then it started. Suddenly the wall was covered in targets. Some stationary, some moving in erratic patterns. Not even able to figure where to start so I just started launching spells.

Hitting the targets, trying to make out the colour on the fast moving ones. Spinning on the spot until it was all clear. An arrow appearing on the screen so I started walking. Moving through a corridor, more targets appearing.

Keeping my movement steady despite the need to run and finish with a good time. Legs moving, arms swinging. Keeping the spells small. Projectiles hitting against the wall. Moving through the course. Starting to breath heavily as I came into a big room.

Targets up high, far away. Pinning myself in the very middle and spinning. Shooting out spells as quickly as I could. Missing some of the targets completely. Sweat building at the back of my neck, trickling down under my black top.

Breathing out a long sigh as the last target was hit and the walls went back to that usual black. My ceiling opening up above me. I dropped to my knees, sucking in air. Mrs Kelp's voice coming from above. "Very impressive. Second."

"Damn, I didn't come first?" Looking up, wiping the back of my hand across my forehead. "Who came first?"

"Your friend in the next pod over."

"D?" She nodded. "Can't be mad about that." Smiling as I stood. Still breathing heavily as I left my pod. Moving over and offering her a hand as she climbed out of hers. "Congrats. You came first."

"Elite teams here I come." She laughed and I would have joined her if I could muster up the energy.

"Why aren't you sweating?"

"Not only do I not sweat, I didn't actually do the whole course."

"What? How did you get all the targets?"

"I found a little room in the first hallway. Through a section of the wall. There was a target inside that destroyed all the others. It just took a while to destroy. It kept changing colours for the different spells."

"Oh. That sounds much easier."

"And apparently, quicker."

"Clearly." Grinning as she gave me a smile. "I'll get you on the next test."

"You're on."

I laughed with an outward burst of breath. Shaking my head. "I could do with a lie down after that."

"You won't have time." Mrs Kelp came walking over. "You've got homework."

"Homework?"

"Yes. It will be loaded to your watches. Advanced spells that you'll need for the final test."

"Sounds cool." Feeling better ever since putting my all into this program. My talk with my father helped as well. Knowing that I might be changing from my usual Crystal self. But I was also becoming more like my mother. Which couldn't be a bad thing. The villagers had always mentioned how great she was.

Mrs Kelp took her position at the front of the class. "Study your watches this evening. It's just information at this point. If you want to practice then this classroom will be left unlocked after tea. Come back if you need to. Now get going."

When I didn't head for the door D stopped and turned, "You okay?"

"Mrs Kelp wants a chat."

"Alright, I'll see you down there."

"Hopefully." Pulling a scared face which D laughed at before leaving. I walked over to where our teacher stood. She was looking at her clipboard, "What do you want to chat about?"

"What's going on with you and the president?"

"Uh. I don't know what you're on about."

"Yes you do. I don't believe the rumours, you're not one of those silly girls who swoons whenever a guy smiles at them. But I know something is going on. I take these classes very seriously. The elite teams are extremely important. You're doing great with your scores now. Happy you started to take it seriously. However."

"However?" Blowing out a sigh, feeling like I've heard this already.

"If I sense any favouritism towards you, I will ignore it. I will not be adding to your score unless you earn it. If you succeed then you will succeed by yourself. Not because of him. You got it?"

"I got it, loud and clear."

"Alright, now go get something to eat. You look bushed."

"Good idea." Giving her a smile before leaving. My stomach was grumbling but I was feeling too sticky for food right now. Grabbing a shower and changing my clothes back in my room. Grabbing another pair of black combats and putting a nice thick white jumper over my bra.

Getting to the lobby I noticed the gate to the shop was left open a little. Remembering my promise to help the owner. Grabbing something that I could eat with my hands and pocketing a drink of orange juice.

Getting a horrible look from Larsh who was sitting by herself. Flo giving me a much friendlier one. I excused myself and walked across the lobby, munching away on my hot sandwich. The strange looking pieces inside seemed to be meat but they felt crispier like pastry. However they tasted delicious so I wasn't complaining.

Sliding the gate open a little more and knocking on the wall. The little being appearing with a toothy grin. "Great, you decided to show up."

"Yeah. Figured why not." Moving into the shop and making my way around to the weird side. "So what kind of things do you have?"

"That comes after the favour. Come, I have to

grab something from the back of my wagon. You'll appreciate what I have back there."

"Alright." A little alarm bell ringing in the back of my mind but I ignored it. I was at a school, nothing was going to happen to me here. Following the little man out the back of the shop where his wagon was still parked.

He climbed up the steps and offered me his hand, getting help to climb aboard the vehicle. We moved into the back through a pair of cloth curtains. Looking around at the cramped space. Hearing the jangle of keys knocking about.

Watching as he slotted one of those gorgeous cylinders next to a doorway. As he turned there was a whoosh of power before there was a click of something being unlocked. "What is that?"

"A doorway."

"Fancy for a wagon like this."

"Us goblins are good at stealing. Gives me access."

"Access to what?"

"The goblin marketplace."

"The what?" He pulled back the door, hearing the loud noise of a market coming through the gap. Stepping forward and peering through. Seeing a locked gate separating us from the hustle and bustle.

"Come on."

"Wait, is it safe for me?"

"Of course. I wouldn't bring you here if it wasn't. I'm not crazy."

"Right." Looking ahead as we walked through the doorway. It was shut and locked again. The goblin punched in a code for the gate and we went through. Letting it lock behind us, keeping his wagon safe from random visitors.

I followed him closely as he moved betweens the stalls. The market place seemed to be inside a massive cavern. So old that the spikes rising up from the ground almost met the ones reaching down.

The stalls looked like they had been here for years. Old tattered cloth covered the woodwork. Some using rocks as tables, others having blankets on the ground. Seeing goblins of all colours and sizes. Haggling over products from food and drink to trinkets that looked like they were found on another planet.

Stopping for a moment to watch a couple of goblin children playing in one of the stalls. They giggled and played, making me smile. Then the owner of the stall caught my glimpse. "What the hell are you looking at? What are you doing here?"

"She's with me." My goblin came back and took my hand. "You shouldn't leave my side around here."

"You said it was safe."

"Safe, if you stick by my side."

Letting him lead us through the market. Heading towards a building near the back. "And what exactly am I helping you with here?"

"You'll see." Moving in step with him, eyes still looking around. Getting looks back like I didn't belong there. Passing between two massive goblins wearing silver armour over one arm. The other cradling a massive hammer each.

Getting a quick look, neither of them moving an inch to stop us. The little goblin in front of me pushed open the huge red doors. The walls inside the building were covered in antiques. Paintings, masks and weapons.

Pottery and dishes sat upon stands, dotted along

the black rug that stretched all the way across the room. The dark red of the columns that reached up to the high ceiling matched the glistening deep red tiles on the floor.

Looking ahead as we ventured further into the massive room. Seeing a couple of goblins chatting in the distance. They stood around a massive wooden table. Two guards standing close by, wearing the same kind of armour as the others by the entrance. "What am I doing here exactly?"

"Helping, let me do all the talking. Alright?"

"Yeah, yeah. Of course." Going back to being silent, wishing I hadn't agreed to this. My gut twisting with worry. Gruff voices coming from the goblins by the table. Their conversation coming to an abrupt end when they noticed our arrival. The taller of the two goblins, almost the same size as me, stared at the shop owner. Looking very unhappy.

The other gave a bow before leaving the room past us. We stopped in front of that massive table. Looking down and seeing what was like a massive board game. Pieces dotted around in different areas.

"What are you looking at?" The goblin's voice so deep it was hard to make out the words.

"Sorry?"

"I said no talking." Quickly shutting my mouth. "Senna. I've come with a proposition."

Eyes burning into mine before he blinked and turned to the much shorter goblin. "What makes you think you even have the chance for a proposition, Baldock?"

"Just hear me out."

"Why? Why should I?"

"You won't regret it."

"Regret!" His voice boomed around the vast space. Then he stepped, hearing the clink of metal as it clung around his arm. Leaving his chest bare, muscles rippling as he walked around the table. The sides of his head shaved bare, a line of hair running from forehead to the tip of a ponytail. Gold hoops keeping the strands together.

The way this goblin held himself made him look important. Almost like he was the leader of all the goblins in the land. "There are a lot of things I regret. My fifth child and my seventh wife. Eating from the vendors here. But the biggest regret is not squashing you after you betrayed your own kind."

"I didn't betray...."

His words getting cut off as a fist smashed into his face. The goblin losing his footing and hitting into the table. My whole body going rigid at the violence. "You don't talk until you are asked a question."

"Yes, sir."

"Now, the only thing that's keeping my interest is this human. Why have you brought it here?"

"I know that you've been looking for a long time. For something very particular."

"Yes?" Seeing the change in this goblins expression. No longer angry, his interest in me clearly growing. "And is this?"

"Yes."

"That is good news. But I need proof." Trying to back track as the little shop owner came for me. A hand grabbing my sleeve and pulling it up. Showing off the tattoo I got when catching Kit. "That doesn't prove anything. Humans get tattoos all the time."

"No, I swear. There are rumours."

"Putting your faith in rumours. Wasting my time." He got another fist in the face. Sending him to his back. "I won't have that regret for much longer."

The goblin stomping over to the wall. Pulling a massive saw from the wall. His muscles straining from the weight. "No, please. I'm telling you the truth."

"This is ancient. No idea how old. The price, there aren't even numbers created to explain how expensive this is. Yet, I'm going to enjoy using it to cut off that lying head of yours."

"No!"

Not sure if I was actually witnessing this or not. Watching as the bigger creature stomped across the red floor. Imagining the blood leaking out and blending right in. "There's nothing that you can say that will make me stop."

"Please, tell him the truth."

Looking down into those pleading eyes. Knowing that I shouldn't tell anyone what I truly was. But this goblin was about to be killed. With him dead, who would protect me from these savages. Taking a deep breath, no idea what this whole thing was about. However I stood between them and held up my hands. "He's telling the truth."

"What makes you think I would believe a human? You're lucky you haven't been killed already for stepping foot in our market."

"It's true, I promise."

"Your promises mean the same as his lies. Now get out of the way or I'll cut you down as well." Getting shoved aside by one of his big arms.

Taking a deep breath and letting that fire erupt

from my chest. The red light forming into Kit as he landed. "There, that's proof enough."

Kit quickly sprinted to me, standing between me and the goblin as he turned. "What are you doing with goblins?"

"It's a long story."

"It's going to be a short story when they kill us."

The being holding that massive saw stared. "All my years and I have yet to meet an actual titan. It's a little under-whelming."

"Keep talking and I'll burn this whole place to the ground."

"Somehow, I don't see that happening."

Kit flicked his tail and it split into eight more. His body growing and that fire raging harder. "Try me."

"Now this is more like it." A laugh came from his thin lips. "Excellent. Bag them."

My mind hitting confusion hard at his words. Then feeling a dull thud to the back of my head. The world going dark, not feeling the ground as I dropped to it fast.

CHAPTER 9

Feeling my body shaking from side to side. The sound of wood crunching over stone bouncing around my head made the ache pulse. Rolling onto my back, feeling the hard wood underneath me.

Opening my eyes and seeing the cage I was laying in. Not enough room to stand but I shifted into a sitting position, leaning back against the side. The room I was in was much larger than a wagon.

But those noises were undeniable. Wishing I could see through the darkness but there was no hope of that. "Kit?" Not hearing his voice coming back to me. Hopefully he had just gone back inside my heart but worry was too hard to stop. Thinking he could be in his own cage.

Moving onto my knees I reached out. Finding my boundary then pushing my arm through the hole. Feeling another cage not too far away. Fingers reaching further then touching over fur. A thought of Kit hit hard but the fur was cold, damp.

Fingers curling before this thing shifted. Hearing a hiss then a snap of teeth close to taking my fingers off. Pulling my arm, hitting the metal of my cage as I shot back. Gritting through the pain as I breathed.

Eyes scanning for movement but that darkness refused to lighten. My eyes not getting used to it which had me thinking it could be magic related. That thought igniting an idea. Rubbing my hands together and conjuring a ball of fire.

Letting it sit in my palms as it grew. Shining flickers of light around the inside of the space. Seeing the beast I had touched. It was huge, three times as big as me. The fur was thick and dark blue. White whiskers sat above a huge mouth.

The thing baring its teeth at me but it wasn't growling. Not being aggressive. Looking into those bright blue eyes. "It's okay. I don't think you'll be able to understand me but it's okay. I'm not going to hurt you."

Speaking softly. Not making any sudden movements. Seeing this animal shift in its cage. Only having enough room to lay down. Watching as it curled it's body tightly. Eyes still on me but those teeth were put away.

Growing my light and seeing the other two cages in here. One of them was empty, the second held a snake but this thing was huge. It's body the width of mine. The length unable to figure out since it was curled up in a spiral.

The body splitting in two a metre from its heads. A tongue each flicking out, tasting the air. One head hidden at the back but the other was my side of its cage. Eyes wide open and staring but they didn't move. Not reacting to the light in my hands.

"I hope that you're asleep and not staring at your next meal."

A deep voice filling the wagon. "It's been asleep for the whole journey."

My head snapping back to the blue beast. "You can talk?" Waiting a moment, trying to feel for a calling. "But you're not a titan."

"You know about titans?"

"A little."

It shuffled around, laying out towards me. "You're an everfae?"

"Half."

"Wow, never thought I would meet one of you. Even if you're only half."

"You know about us and how are you able to talk?"

"The amount of species out there. You're surprised that I'm able to talk?"

"I didn't think of it like that."

"It doesn't surprise me." My eyes running over those features. Those eyes looking beautiful. "And yes I know about everfae and titans. As well as talking, I can also read." Sarcasm clear in his words.

My eyes moving down to his paws. Massive claws stuck out from the thick fur. "How do you turn the page?"

"You find yourself in a cage and you're asking questions about how I read a book?"

"It just popped into my brain."

"Hmm." The animal rested its head on those massive paws. "I've never seen them catch something that wasn't an animal."

"Where are we going?"

"To the big show."

"Show?"

"You'll see soon enough." Feeling the rocking stop. No more noises coming from the wheels. "Here we are."

"What's going to happen?"

"I doubt they'll give you a collar."

"What!?" There was a turn of a key then one side of the room was pulled open. Clapping my hands together to extinguish my spell. The light coming in from a lantern. Seeing the goblin face of the shop owner. Topless with his left arm covered in that metal armour. "Hey, why are you doing this?"

"Shut it!" The goblin hung up the lantern and pulled open a chest. Out came a metal collar with spikes on the inside. The beast growling as it was put round it's neck. The side of the cage was opened and it left, a tail I hadn't noticed before swinging down between its legs.

Then the goblin moved to the snake. As his footsteps tapped against the wood the two heads flicked up suddenly. Big eyes staring at this green being. Tongues flicking out angrily. This time the goblin grabbed a pole.

Something pointed on the end that was shoved under the chin of the left head. The snake recoiled back, hitting the cage with a hard thud. Noticing the end of the pole had detached. Sticking out between the scales.

"Calm down or I'll give you a shock. Don't test me again." At these words the snake calmed. Lowering the two heads and the cage was opened. "I'm watching you two, no ideas or I'll cut you in half."

Then it was my turn. My cage being opened. "You don't have a collar for me?"

"I don't need to control you. You act up and I'll just feed you to one of those. We barely feed them so you won't last a second."

"Why are you doing this?"

"Come on, they're waiting on you."

"Who is?"

"Come on." A hand roughly yanked me from the

cage. We passed through the open curtain. Coming out onto the front of his wagon. He jumped down but I stayed where I was. Turning my head left and right. Taking in the busy scene.

The market had been one thing but this was on a much larger scale. Instead of stalls and vendors. There were cages of all sizes. Animals and beasts contained inside. Hearing the banging of them trying to escape over the loud noise of the crowd.

It wasn't just goblins here, all kinds of beings walked around. Some being followed by beasts like the two I saw in the back of Baldock's wagon. Watching gangs walking around, trying to understand what was happening.

But a hand grabbed my wrist and tugged me down from the wagon. "Quit staring and follow me."

Locking my eyes on his green head and moving through the crowd with him. Shouting making me jump each time. We moved past people, not seeing a single human around. Making me fear for my life even more.

We took some steps and stood behind a row of chairs on a stage. Seeing the mohawk hairstyle of that massive goblin. There we stood, waiting as the other chairs were filled by all kinds of beings. The common thing about them were their ugly looks. All looking like brutes.

Peering out I saw the groups split up around an arena. Fencing made out of pieces of wood and rubbish. A queue sitting outside it, cages waiting to come in. Once all the chairs were filled the mohawk goblin stood. Shouting out to everyone in this massive area. "Welcome to you all. Bidding will start, wait your turn and if any of you cause any trouble, you will be chucked out."

He waved an arm and the gate was opened. The first cage was wheeled in with one of those spheres at the front. We all watched as a small creature was bouncing around inside. Every now and again it stopped, long claws wrapped around the bars. It snarled at us all before trying to escape again.

It finally settled and retreated to the corner. A long tail curling around it. Huge eyes that took up most of its face. Such a little thing with a mouth full of saliva-dripping teeth.

"Council members. This is so rare that we haven't found a name for it. Fast, agile and vicious. We lost two of our men hunting this thing down. Starting bid is six months."

As soon as he was finished the bidding started. To my confusion they were bidding months and then years. Leaning down to Baldock. "What are they bidding?"

"The time they can collect their favour. The rarer the item they're selling, the more time they have."

"What, like helping them move?"

"Don't be an idiot. Serious favours. Now be quiet." Feeling the sting of a slap against my thigh.

Looking around at the whole area. Hearing calls from the crowd as well as the council. Creatures being carted in within their cages. Taking a step back as everyone was paying attention to the new creature.

Breathing in and calling to Kit, hoping that he would come out without that mouth of his. But nothing was happening. There was no release of warmth. No light and no titan. Calling again but getting the same response.

That's when worry hit me like a brick. My eyes darting around at the cages. Trying to pick out Kit amongst all those creatures. But there was no sign of him. Moving back towards Baldock. "Where's my titan?"

"We're keeping him hostage. So you do as promised."

"What am I supposed to be doing here? You haven't told me anything."

Just then a loud voice came from the cleared space in front of the crowd. "This is a titan. You all heard stories about them and here we have one for you to see."

My eyes moving to the middle, expecting a cage but instead it was just a platform on sphere wheels. Being brought to the middle where everyone stared. Nothing seeming to be there except for chains laying on the wood.

Baldock's leader stood up, grabbing a massive hammer in his hand. "What is this? Trying to fool us again, Valsteer."

"I swear. What I say is the truth. Watch." A little goblin came hobbling in, carrying some kind of electric prod. It was handed over and the presenter jammed it into something. Electricity running over an invisible body until the chains flew up. Seeing the lines of wind moving as huge wings flapped. Kicking up the dirt around the arena.

This thing was huge and powerful. Lifting two of the wheels from the ground as it flapped. More goblins running in and yanked down on those chains. Pulling until this thing gave in and floated down to the wood. As it settled those lines of air disappeared and nothing seemed to be there yet again.

Baldock's leader grinned wide and looked over his shoulder at me. Lowering his gruff voice making it sound like a growl. "Well? Is that a titan or not?"

Looking at the platform. Reaching out to the creature that was there. As I felt that call the chains shifted with a clank. Feeling the thing calling right back to me. The chains lifting, showing the creature standing.

A growl coming from that goblin. Noticing he still had his fingers wrapped around that hammer. "Yes, it's a titan. What's going to happen to it?"

"That's no concern of yours. Get her back to the wagon, Baldock. Once we have this titan we're leaving."

"Yes, sir." A hand grabbed me and I was pulled off stage. Down some steps, looking back at the platform as the chains moved. The titan watching me as I was shoved into the crowd. "What's going to happen to that titan?"

"None of your business."

"Tell me! Call it your favour to me before you return me to the school."

"Return you?" Baldock threw his head back and laughed. "You're not going back. You're our little titan detector. I'm back in with the clan, no need for my little shop now. No need to keep scraping by."

"You can't just kidnap me."

He laughed again, still tugging me through the crowds. "Kidnapping is the least of my crimes."

"Let go of me!" Struggling against his grip but it was too strong. Then I told myself to stop thinking like a human. Letting my mind fill with all the feelings raging at the moment and clicking my fingers.

Sparks flying up into flames making the goblin

jump back in terror. Pushing my hand forward and throwing a ball of fire at him. Sending him to the floor with a crack of flames. He bumped into the crowd who all turned.

Hands grabbed him and a fight quickly erupted. Spreading rapidly as the ruffians attacked each other. Backing away before turning and running. I had no idea where Kit was or the wagon.

My feet carrying me until I saw a large red tent. Bursting through the flaps. My lungs pumping air in and out of my body. Looking around I saw the cages sitting in here. Creatures laying down with their eyes shut.

Seeing one that looked so small in the large cage. Running over and running my fingers through the black fur. Not feeling any kind of heat coming from him. "Kit? Wake up."

"He can't." Turning and seeing the large blue cat from the wagon. That collar still sitting around its neck. "He's been poisoned."

"What?!"

"He's going to be fine. He's sleeping it off. Like the others."

Crouching back down and stroking Kit as he slept. "Why do you help them?"

"Does it look like I have much of a choice?"

The large animal came padding over to me. Seeing the huge claws coming out of its paws. "What are you going to do to me?"

"Nothing. I am brought here to protect these cages from thieves. I don't know if you noticed but these kind of people aren't the most honourable."

"No kidding." Still stroking my titan but looking

up at the blue panther. "Can't you escape?"

"Not with this thing around my neck. If I move too far from the wagon then these things will constrict and I'll bleed out."

"Maybe I can remove it." Standing up and grabbing the metal collar. Tugging at the lock holding it together.

"You would have to be a lot stronger."

"Maybe the collar just needs to be weaker." Holding my watch up I flicked through the spells Mrs Kelp uploaded. Seeing an ice spell and thinking about a movie I had seen a few years ago.

Holding the collar so the lock was facing up. Using my water spell to leak droplets into the mechanism. Then using the ice spell I had seen. Turning it cold, hearing those crystals being formed. The water expanding. Metal creaking then suddenly giving way with a crack.

Pulling on the collar again made it snap free. Dropping it to the floor with a huge thud. Seeing the blue fur ruffling back up as the panther turned its head to me. "You look much better."

"Not yet." He backed away and shook his body. Fur swaying with the movement. Seeing it shorten. The cat standing up on those hind legs. Becoming more human as those features changed. Still cat-like but it was a little less strange when he spoke. "There, that's much better."

"Wow. I've never seen anything like that."

"Not many people have. My name is Arnold and I'm a panseer."

"Crystal and you already know what I am." He grunted. "Now what?"

The black slits in his yellow eyes flicked from me to my titan. "I guess I could repay you for your help."

"Please, that would be amazing." A grin appeared, showing off his sharp canines. Before he could move to Kit's cage there was a sharp hiss behind us.

Before turning something swept through the air. Knocking the panseer flying into some crates. Destroying them and sending food tumbling over the floor. Arnold rolled onto his back but didn't move again.

Turning around in time to get whacked with a thick, scaly tail. The attack hitting my arms and sending me into Kit's cage. My back aching harshly as I dropped. Grunting, trying to rid myself of that pain.

The snake coming further into the tent. The long body curling underneath it as the heads lifted. Those two tongues flicking out. I pushed myself up but couldn't conjure the energy to stand. Crouching on the ground. "Kit! Now would be a great time to wake up!"

The snake hissing at my voice. Giving the panseer another look but he still wasn't moving. Leaving it up to me to take care of this monster.

CHAPTER 10

Racking through my brain about reptiles, anything that I could remember. Not able to think straight with this massive creature creeping closer. Catching the collar on the floor as it moved forwards. The reptile recoiling back as it bumped it. At first I thought it was just surprised. Then I remembered that reptiles didn't like the cold.

So I balled up my hands quickly and pulled in that icy spell. Creating what I could and launching it forwards. Seeing a sphere of ice hitting one of its heads. Like throwing a snowball at an avalanche.

It simply dropped and smashing on the ground. The snake rushing forwards with open jaws. Diving out the way just in time, the ring of metal being hit bouncing around the tent. I flipped onto my back and crawled away.

Watching as the snake shook away the pain and turned to me. Slithering forward. Feeling like a cornered mouse as my back pressed up against the tent. Eyes going wide as it attacked again. Seeing the fangs hanging down as they came closer. The rush of wind as it used those muscles to launch at me.

The last seconds going by in a blink but my body didn't get bitten. getting yanked to the side so the snake crashed into more boxes. A massive paw pulled me to my feet. Looking up into those bright eyes. "Thanks."

"Know how to use one of these?"

A sword was offered to me but I shook my head. "Not a clue." Then I noticed the crates the snake had smashed were filled with spears. Grabbing one quickly, "This on the other hand I know very well."

The snake's body shifting around in the space. Hearing it's tail slithering behind us. So as the heads attacked I jumped back over it. The panseer launched forward, a sword in each hand. Swiping and swinging. Seeing blood spilling through scales as the heads tried to dodge and bite.

I was taking the spear and jamming it into the body before me. It didn't seem to be doing much until I rammed it in as hard as I could. The tail whipping out and knocking me on my arse. Then I felt the muscly body curling around me. Pulling me in a spiral until I was completely wrapped up. My head poking out the top of the coil.

Not able to call for help as the squeeze took my breath away. Shutting my eyes and thinking about the ice spell again. Only this time I willed it all over my body. Wanting to be encased in the stuff.

The cold starting at my hands but I could feel it spreading. My lungs burning as I tried to suck air in. Watching as the two slaves fought. Seeing the head coming around Arnold. Wanting to warn him but I couldn't.

The cold becoming unbearable but I kept pushing myself. My whole body feeling the cool spell until the snake finally let go of me. Pushing and shoving at the body until I was able to slip free.

As I shot my arms out I saw the blue of my skin. Then it suddenly faded as the spell burst out in a stream of ice. Hitting the snakes head, freezing it in that position just before it could attack.

Keeping up the spell until there was a layer all over it. The head too much weight to hold, the neck cracking then snapped. Ice shooting everywhere as it crashed into the ground.

Panseer seized the slight delay in the other heads next attack and jammed the sword up under its jaw. Piercing through the top, eyes going dark before the whole reptile went limp and dropped. Rolling out across the floor until the whole thing was lifeless.

I sucked in air whilst I could. Filling my lungs with a happy sigh each time. Arnold turned, placing a huge paw on my shoulder. "You handled yourself really well."

"Thanks."

"Who taught you?"

"I go to school."

"Some school."

"Yes and I'd love to get back there."

"The best bet is the wagon but we'll need Baldock's keys to use the portal."

"What about my titan? Is there any way to wake him up?"

"No, the snake's venom will keep him sedated for a while. I can carry him to the wagon but it would leave it to you to retrieve the keys."

"You're kidding."

"Can you carry your pet?"

I looked over to him laying there. He was in his smallest form but I still wouldn't be able to carry him. Not for long enough. "Alright, any suggestions on how to do this?"

We moved to the exit and opened the flap enough to see. The whole place had turned into a fighting ring. Weapons being swung, the sounds of blood being spilled filling my ears. "Don't get killed."

"That's just great."

"You're an everfae, don't you have another titan you can call upon?"

"I do but I don't think it'll be much help."

"It's worth a try."

"If you say so." Turning away from the opening I crouched. Thinking about the tattoo on my shoulder and that little baby titan. Breathing out as I called to it. The light shining before the tiny creature appeared on the ground.

It spun around a couple of times, sniffing the dirt until it looked up into my eyes. Taking a deep breath. "I have no idea if you can understand me. But we could do with some help. In any way you can give it."

"That's it?"

"I tried to warn you." Giving him a quick look before cupping the little titan in my hands. "We need your help." Thinking about how Kit grows bigger, fiercer. Hoping that this was the same. Only all I got was a sudden high-pitched screech.

A growl coming over my shoulder. "Shut it up."

"It's not that easy." Telling the little thing to shush but it kept calling out like that. Thinking my life was about to be finished when the ground started shaking. Something moving through it, something big. Remembering how it felt at the little farming village. The little critter lighting up green before disappearing. "We might be getting some help after all."

Rushing to the opening just as the ground

started to give way. Fins slicing through the ground and smashing wagons to pieces. The screams and yells of all those men as the destruction ran riot. The fighting stopping and everyone running for their lives.

"Now is our time. Let's go. You get the keys and I'll take care of your friend."

"You make it sound so simple."

"Get moving. Meet you at the wagon."

"How do I find it amongst all this?"

"On the keys will be a blue ball. Squeeze it and it'll pulse. The closer you get the quicker it'll pulse. Now move."

His words making me run out into the mayhem. Dodging as bigger beings rushed around. I started running towards the arena, hoping that Baldock was still there. As I ran I saw the fins running through the ground. As they neared, the titan popped up to the surface.

Looking up into those black eyes. The titan looking down, feeling that link between us like I do Kit. "Keep moving, protect yourself." It nodded and jumped in the opposite direction. Balling up so that hard shell protected it. Rolling about like a ball. Destroying even more. Seeing how everyone was so terrified by it. Any attack just bouncing off of that green shell.

Coming up to the arena where there was still fighting. Baldock was screaming at the top of his lungs as he bashed a club into someone's head. Seeing the keys attached to his belt I ran towards him.

Using my earth spell I gathered up a ball from the ground and launched it. Cracking his head, dropping him to the floor. He rolled around, screaming, holding his hands up to his face.

My hands fumbled around his belt, trying to yank those keys free. I took too long and hands grabbed my arms. "You. I'm going to kill you for that." His strength beyond human. My feet leaving the ground and being flung into the air.

Hitting hard. Pain pushing through my whole body as I laid there. Baldock gathered his footing and picked up his club. In the distance I could hear my titan rolling over wagons and cages.

Seeing that creatures had been let lose, creating just as much havoc. Calling out as loud as I could. "Over here!" The ground rumbling harder as Baldock ran at me. Feeling my connection growing stronger as my titan grew nearer.

Baldock attacked I pulled up a wall of earth. He hit it hard enough to send him stumbling back, dropping him to the floor. Just in time as the ball of fins came rolling over him. Crushing his little body easily with a scream that was suddenly cut short.

Not wanting to look at the mess that was left behind as my titan carried on. But I had to look for those keys. Finding a mashed arm and a missing leg as I unhooked the keyring from his belt. Turning to leave when I noticed that platform was missing. The one holding the wind titan.

No pieces of wood on the floor but I noticed tracks leading out of the arena. They must have taken it away. Which meant it wasn't my problem. I needed to save myself. So I ran. People were too busy trying to save themselves to worry about a human running amongst them.

My fingers gripping that little ball tightly. Feeling the pulses as I neared the wagon. My heart sinking as

I found it smashed to pieces. The wheels crushed, the whole thing tilted to one side. Hearing a voice coming from within. "Are you just going to stand there?"

Crouching down and seeing Kit laying on the wood, the panseer in its cat form. "I thought the thing was destroyed."

"The wagon yes, the portal, no. Get in."

"Alright." I straightened up and stepped a leg through the gap. That's when I heard chains clanging. Looking over as goblins held onto the titan like they were flying a kite. Senna ordering his little goblins to hurry up.

"What's taking you so long?"

"I just."

"Get in!" Blowing out a frustrated breath I gave the scene a quick look. Still seeing that massive ball of titan rolling around. Breathing in and bringing that titan back inside my heart. Ducking through the hole to join Arnold and my sleeping Kitsune inside. Holding up the key ring. Normal keys were mixed with those weird cylinders. "The purple one. Slide it into the hole and turn."

"Where will it take us?"

"The warehouse. We can figure it out from there."

"Do they take their purchases there?"

"The leader? He'll take anything he has back to his palace. He likes to use them for fights."

"What? Which one takes us there?"

"I'm not going back there."

"Fine, you can use the purple one after I've gone."

"What about your titan here. He's not awake yet."

"Take him with you, please. I need to help that

titan they were bidding on."

The panseer growled at me, eyes flicking around the messed up wagon. "Fine. You've got thirty minutes then I'll leave your titan in the warehouse."

"Fine, I won't need that long."

"Use the red one to get back to the market. Be careful and good luck."

"Thanks." Pulling off the red cylinder and handing the rest to Arnold. Pushing the short pole into the hole and turning it. Hearing the soft hum of the portal working. The door had been destroyed so all I saw was a shimmering curtain.

Giving Arnold a quick smile then stepping through. The sound of the panicking auction giving way to the goblin market. Most of the stalls from earlier were still open like it continued day and night.

Getting a few looks as I entered the cavern. Punching in the same code Baldock had before. Moving into the market quickly, hoping no one paid me any attention. I grabbed a rag from the floor. Wrapping it around my shoulders and over my face. Covering my hair up I tried to blend in the best I knew how. Making my way through the little maze, not able to spot the wooden platform anywhere. No chains floating through the air.

So I headed for that big building near the back. Knowing I needed to hurry otherwise Kit would be left defenceless. Keeping clear of the front entrance we had used before. Dodging those massive guards and slipping in through the side.

Finding an open window and shimmying through, dropping quietly onto the red tiled flooring. Hearing the clanking of chains in the distance. Making my way through the main hall. Fear building inside. My brain telling me to turn around. But I kept going.

The noise of those chains getting louder. Moving down a corridor, following the sound until I came to a large room. A dome of metal grating sat above, letting the sun filter down through a funnel of rock.

The leader of the goblins was standing there, marvelling at his latest purchase. The titan still chained, locked to the floor now. Wings flapped but it wasn't going anywhere. A second and third goblin came into the room, holding poles with electric prods on the end.

"How have the others settled in?"

"They know who's boss."

"Excellent. Now it's time to teach this titan who it belongs to." He stepped forwards, waving his big arms in the air. "Hey, you up there. There's no escape. You're mine and if you don't do what you're told. You'll keep getting pain until you do. Do you understand?"

The winged air slowing it's wings. Dropping to the floor softly. Seeing the shape of a head moving down at the goblin. Then it lifted, looking in my direction. That tug of it calling to me hit a little firmer.

Wind gently brushing over my ears. Hearing a voice coming with it. "Help me. Please."

Clearing my throat as my eyes looked at the titan. Giving a gentle nod. After all, that was why I was here. Racking through my brain for ideas.

My own titans were out because Kit was asleep and I doubt the other would be able to get through the floor in here. So it was just me and my magic and weaponry skills. One of those electric prods would be perfect for me.

Getting a plan set in my head and I attacked as they were all still staring at their capture. The first goblin turning at the sound of my feet hitting those tiles. Building up my emotions and throwing out a huge ball of fire.

It hit his chest and burst into flames, engulfing him. The scream he made as he ran in circles brought the attention of the other two. Throwing another fireball at the leader but he turned. My attack hitting the armour on his back.

Ignoring that failure and looking at the smaller goblin. Eyes on that weapon that he held in my direction. Chanting to myself that I can do this. He jabbed forwards with it and I slipped to the side.

Hitting my fist to his left hand, making him cry out in pain. As he let go of the prod I let it fall to my foot. Kicking it up and over the goblin's head. Catching and jamming it into the back of his neck. The body jolting as the electricity incapacitated him.

Bringing the pole back and spinning it around my arm. Fingers clutched the wood as I held it vertical. My body ready to attack again. Looking at the leader. A grin full of teeth showed. "You're impressive for someone so young."

"I'm not here to talk." Knowing that it would waste time, increasing my chances of getting caught by other goblins. My fingers gripped the pole and I shot forwards. Planning my steps, my hands. Knowing what I was going to do.

Only when a massive hammer came swinging towards me I couldn't do anything but leap to the side. Rolling to my feet but he was already there, swinging again. I held up the pole but it just snapped in two.

A third swing slammed into my shoulder. My body tumbled over the tiles. Crying out, feeling my eyes filling with tears. Looking up from my back as he came to me. Not able to tower over me with his height but he still looked terrifying.

I was still a sixteen year old girl. What was I thinking about doing all this. "What are you going to do?"

"You're hoping I'll say something other than kill you?" A laugh rolled through his lips. "So hopeful but yes, I'm going to kill you. I'd love to keep you. Use you but sadly you're unreliable. So you must die."

Up came that hammer but my eyes weren't watching him. They moved past him to where the titan was swinging its wings. Lifting itself from the floor until it gave a huge push. Feeling the gale force air hitting against my body, sending the leader hurtling into the wall head first. Bringing his life to a sudden close.

Seeing how mashed up his skull was and not feeling any remorse. Knowing he would have killed me if the titan hadn't helped. So I moved over to it as it settled. Fingers running over the metal that was holding it down.

Unclipping the creature and releasing it. Feeling the air kick up as it stretched out. The wing span even larger than before. Almost filling up the whole room. That soft voice coming again as a breeze brushed over my ears. "Thank you."

"Thank you as well. If it wasn't for you I would be dead."

"We are in debt to each other. I am yours to command, forever." Feeling the power of the titan slipping inside my body like the others had. Seeing the lines of air is it moved. Filling my heart with that wind power.

Wind kicking all around me like I was trapped inside a tornado. Only, I wasn't scared. The power of it felt like it channelled from my body. Feeling the tattoos appearing on my back, one either side just inside my shoulder blades. Flexing my arms as the titan settled within my body. With it safe I needed to keep myself that way.

The wind dying as I moved back to the main hall. Luckily it was still empty so I went back out the way I came in. Only when I saw the market it was busier. More armed guards walking around. There was no way I could slip out of here, not even with my face covered.

So I slipped back to where they had been keeping the titan chained up. Remembering the open dome in the ceiling. The light coming from above. Getting under it and looking up. Seeing the blue sky up high. Taking a few deep breaths, thinking through my idea.

Calling to my new titan. Feeling the air rushing around me as it appeared wisp by wisp. Seeing the wings flicking out and a gentle gust hitting my body. "You have called upon me."

"Yes, would you be able to take me up there?" Pointing with my finger towards the sky.

The head lifted and dropped back down. Feeling invisible eyes staring at me. "But of course. All you had to do was ask." Feeling the air moving around me. Like being wrapped up by fingers. Feeling it all over my body until those wings flapped behind me.

My feet leaving the floor as the titan carried me up. Feeling like it was actually me flying as those wings kept us climbing. My body slipping through the bars easily. The titan's body getting disrupted by the metal. Quickly feeling it forming again, those wings still moving.

My stare falling to the market below. Seeing goblins looking up as I left the massive cavern. Following the funnel of rock until we hit out into the open air. The sun washing over my face, feeling so warm and inviting. Wings slowing, tipping forwards and using the rush of air to glide. Wings stretched out as we zoomed through the air.

Dropping so close to the grass I could reach out and run my fingers through it. My smile so big it hurt my cheeks. Amazed how it felt flying like this. The wings behind me flapping every once in a while.

We neared the edge of a cliff, the goblin market inside. Hidden down in the harsh rock whereas the outside world was bright and soft. Fields were deep green. Stretching for miles ahead of us.

The rush of air feeling so powerful as we soared over the edge. Surprised I wasn't scared as the ground came zooming closer. Knowing the titan had me. Getting proven right as the wings flicked out.

Gliding us over the ground. My body stretched out with the titan. Arms like they controlled those wings. "This is amazing."

"I remember my first flight. Much like you, I was amazed."

"As amazing as it is, I have no clue where we're going?"

"That poses a slight problem."

"I don't even know where we are." Watching the world whizzing underneath us. Not seeing a single settlement in sight. "Do you?"

"I do not. One moment." My body tipped back and we soared up into the air. Pushing through clouds and coming to a stop. Wings beating to keep us in that position. Looking around the large land mass below. "Do you recognise anything?"

For a moment I was dumbstruck by the view. Eyes following the shoreline in the distance. "Not sure." Spotting a city far away. The buildings looking so small at this distance. "Is that, Whitestone?"

"If it is?"

"Then I'm no longer in Mythoria." Looking around like there would be a glint on the horizon to aim me in the right direction. "I don't know. I just want to be back, check on Kit."

"Who is this, Kit?"

"Another titan."

"This titan isn't with you, right now?"

"No. He was put to sleep and held in a cage. To make sure I did what I was told. I need to meet them at a warehouse. Stupid me, didn't ask where it actually was."

"Call to him. He'll hear it and call back. That gives us a direction."

"Okay, I just hope he's awake." Taking a deep breath and reaching out for that fire kitsune. Calling his name a few times. Hoping he heard it. My breath catching in my throat as I felt a tug. That calling from Kit pulled me towards him. "That way." Nodding with me head.

"That way it is." The titan swooping down through the clouds and we flew. All my thoughts lost to the rush I experienced. Wind running over my body, the clouds whizzing past. The lands changing underneath.

Being flown over the massive body of water that split the two continents. Seeing the one I needed coming into the distance. Directing the flyer and spotting the massive warehouse coming into view. We swooped down to the ground around the back.

Breathing heavily like it had been me who had done all the flying. Looking up as it stood there. "Thanks, for flying me here."

"Of course. Call for me if you need me."

"Wait, what do I call you?"

"I don't understand the question."

"Do you have a name?"

"Oh." The head moved from left to right. "No one has ever asked me that question." The wisps looking down at me. "You may call me, Fujin. Origin of the wind."

"My name is Crystal."

"A pleasure to meet you."

"You to. See you around." I called the titan into my heart. Feeling the wind kicking up around me as it vanished. Feeling the last hit slip into my heart. Leaving me alone I turned and checked for guards.

CHAPTER 11

It seemed to be clear so I walked up the side of the warehouse. Looking through the massive shutter. Rows of racking held crates of all sizes. Arnold was standing there like he was waiting for a bus.

His dark blue fur bristled up along the back of his neck. Seeing Kit standing in front of him. Seeing his lips moving, knowing how much he loved to talk. Walking into view and giving them a wave.

The little fire fox came bounding over to me. Crouching so he could leap into my arms. Fingers stroking that warm fur. "So glad you're okay."

"You to. When I woke up I was scared. And between you and me, that guy isn't much of a talker."

Laughing as I looked over at the panseer. "He helped us."

"He said." I let Kit jump down and I walked over to Arnold. "She's here, looks like you don't need to listen to my voice any longer."

"Not a moment too soon." The panseer turned to me with a friendlier look. "Did you retrieve what you wanted?"

"I did. Thank you for helping us escape and for looking after him."

"You're lucky I didn't walk away as soon as he opened that mouth."

"It's very much appreciated." Looking around at

the warehouse. Not a single person working here. "I thought this place would be crawling with goblins."

"They're not the only people who house things here. Each collection have their own codes and keys. You try to take something that doesn't belong to you....well, you won't be walking away."

"Oh." Looking around like I would see cameras or guns. But there was nothing. "What will you do now?" Looking back as Arnold looked off into the distance.

"I've been a slave for over three decades. The world might have changed since the last time I explored it. It's about time I do that again."

"Honestly, would be great to see you again in the future."

"You're a very strange girl. I like you. Make sure you stay safe." As he stepped he gave Kit one last look. A growl as a way of saying goodbye. Kit just smiled the way he does. Then he walked out of the warehouse.

With us alone I crouched down and gave him another hug. Thinking I could have lost him was the worse feeling. Stroking down over his fur. Those eyes looking up into mine. His voice out soft. "I think we should stay away from trouble. That was far too scary."

"Agreed. School is looking much better."

"Let's get back before someone comes looking for their stuff."

"Let's put you back where you're safe then." His lips curled into a smile before he shifted into that light. Pulsing warmth through my body as he disappeared. Suddenly being alone in this place worried me even more.

Looking around I saw those portals, knowing that someone or something could appear at any moment. Leaving by the big shutter door and walking across the courtyard. Through a pair of gates and out onto the open road.

My feet carrying me slowly as I thought about my options. I could use the flying titan and get there quicker. However I didn't know exactly where the school was. So I kept walking, my hand out, thumb sticking up.

Hearing a screech as I walked. Peering over to see a monster with wings swooping down for its prey. Small critters running around in circles trying to avoid those talons. One getting snatched and gutted before it had even flown back up to the sky. Happy that it wasn't dark otherwise I would have to contend with larger monster.

The soft rumble of an engine making me turn. Holding my thumb up higher, smiling as the vehicle slowed to a stop. Two old ladies sitting in the front of their van. Speaking with friendly tones. "What are you doing all the way out here, young girl?"

"You could say I got lost. Would you know where Fawkes Institute of Training is?"

"We heard it had come to a nearby sector."

"Know where it is exactly?"

"It's over by that ranch isn't it?"

"Oh, you mean Elling Ranch. They have those funny creatures."

"That's the one."

I remembered spotting the ranch they were on about. "Elling Ranch? Which direction would that be?"

"Oh darling. Along this road then a left. We can give you a lift."

"No, that's fine. Thank you for your help. It's

greatly appreciated."

"Are you sure you don't want a lift? It's quite a walk."

"We wouldn't feel right leaving you out here on your own."

"It's okay, I'll be fine. Honestly. You carry on and thank you again."

"If you're sure." I nodded. "Alright, safe walking." The van carried on its journey along the road.

Giving my surroundings a quick look then calling to the wind titan. Feeling Fujin moving around my body before it appeared in front of me. At least if anyone drove by they would barely see the titan. "You called, Crystal."

"Yes, we have some more flying to do. Is that okay?"

"Of course it is. Ready?" Nodding, feeling the wind catching around my body and taking me up. Flying once again. Still amazed how great it felt as we moved. Following the road and turning left just like the ladies had said.

After some time my heart filled with hope when I saw the tall tower at the centre of the school. Never having thought I would be so happy to see the place. Letting the titan drop me down on the grass gently. Dismissing Fujin as I walked with a thank you.

Entering the school entrance, walking across the lobby. I hadn't known how long I had been gone until I saw what they were serving in the lunch hall. I had missed breakfast completely including the morning lesson.

I hadn't even felt my watch vibrate to notify me of my class. As I stood there my name was called out.

Turning in time to have Flo launching herself at me. Hugging her back and feeling her lips moving against my cheek. "Where the hell have you been?"

"I second that question." Seeing D standing there with her arms crossed over her chest. She didn't seem too happy with me. "Where have you been?"

"Honestly." Pulling back, looking into Flo's eyes. "You wouldn't believe me if I told you."

"I'm up for a story."

"Could I grab some food first? I haven't eaten since last night."

"Food, then story." Happy that Flo just seemed happy to see me.

"And it better be a good one." Looking into D's eyes. Seeing that her reaction was due to worry more than actually being angry. The three of us walked in. The two heading to their table and I joined the queue. Managing to get through with no problems. Until I came to sit down.

My eyes finding the president standing in the doorway to the lobby. Only I didn't care about his angry face. Standing beside him was my brother. I ran across the cafeteria and hugged him tight. So happy to see his face again. "You disappeared, I was so worried about you."

"I'm alright."

The president cleared his throat. "Come find me in my office once you're done with your reunion."

The man left us for the elevator, feeling dread filling my heart. But then my brother hugged me again. "Come sit down with us. I'll explain what happened to everyone at once." And I did just that. Having my voice low so people didn't overhear us. Telling them everything that had happened, all three on the edge of their seats the entire time.

Finishing my story and looking at them in turn. "That's insane." My brother laughed. "That's completely insane."

"I know."

"I'm just happy you're okay." Flo reached forward and touched her fingers to mine. When I noticed Lance's look I pulled my hand free. "I've never even seen a creature like you've described let alone killed one."

"You were really lucky."

"I know." Giving D a quick smile. "Honestly, I'm more scared about the president being mad at me than what I had gone through." The three of them laughed. As I stood my brother came around and hugged me again, so tight. "I'm alright."

"I can see that. You're stronger than I've ever noticed."

I pulled back and looked into his eyes. "Thank you."

"Don't worry about the president. He needs you more than you need him."

"Maybe. I best get going." Pecking his cheek and walking out the cafeteria after putting my plates away.

Moving into the elevator and climbing up the floors, making sure my eyes stayed away from the glass. Walking out and coming face to face with Holbrook. He almost seemed happy to see me. "You had the whole school worried."

"Even you?"

"I wouldn't go that far." His face was grumpy but his words sounded soft. "Just happy to see you're still in one piece."

"Me to."

His hand came out and touched my arm. "Don't let him bully you like the others. You have a decision in whatever he's getting you to do."

"What do you mean?"

"Just remember that. I'll see you in class."

"Um...yeah." Watching as he got into the elevator and left me alone with the president. Pushing through the door. Walking over the floor, trying not to look at the massive window. But as I neared his desk I couldn't help it.

Seeing the massive space of nothingness. The wobbly legs had disappeared. Even more so, I had the urge to leap out into those clouds. Smiling to myself as I mentally thanked the wind titan that had imprinted tattoos on my back.

Looking at the president as I arrived at the desk. "You wanted to see me."

"Yes. You need to be more careful. Going off with that goblin was a mistake."

"No kidding."

"This isn't a laughing matter. What if you had been killed or kidnapped for good. What then?"

"Then I would have to live through it, not you."

"Don't get snippy with me. We made a deal and you can't help me if you're dead or in prison. You need to do better."

"What would you have me do?"

"Currently, just concentrate on your lessons. Once you're part of the team you will be sent on missions. I'll tag along, each team gets an advisor for the first three months. Just to make sure everything goes smoothly. From there, we will venture further across the continent."

"Alright." Agreeing so I could get out of here and back with my friends.

"So far you don't seem to be having a problem in your classes. However missing your morning class with Mrs Kelp knocked you down a little." He turned his computer screen, showing me my scores. At the top of my class with Holbrook. Sitting fifth with Mrs Kelp. "Get that score up and you will be fine. I've managed to get you a one-on-one class with her this evening. After tea."

"Alright. I'll do my best."

"Good." He pulled out a thumb drive from the monitor as he turned it back. Watching as it was put inside the drawer in his huge desk. "You're dismissed now."

"Yes, sir." Turning and heading back to the elevator. As I descended down I didn't bother returning to the cafeteria. Getting off and heading to Holbrook's classroom. The door was shut so I knocked, hearing his voice come from the other side.

Entering like he asked and seeing him standing by one of the screens. Watching my fight with Troy. A smile appearing as it showed me knocking him back onto his arse. "If you're coming in, come in and shut the door. Don't hover."

Closing the door and making my way over to him. The screen playing the fight from the beginning. "I wanted to ask you something."

"You see your form here. No training and yet you managed to beat him. With ease."

"Sir."

"Don't call me, sir. What happened?"

"What do you mean?"

"Whilst you were gone. Did you get into any danger?"

"Yes."

"With?"

"Some goblins and a two headed snake."

Feeling his eyes shooting to me. "A two headed snake?"

"I had some help from a panseer."

"You met a panseer?" Suddenly he turned. His face filled with joy which had me pulling a weird face. "You actually met one?"

"Yes. He helped me escape."

"That's wild. I've wanted to meet one of them since I was a kid. Read all about them. Did you see both forms?"

"I did."

"Wild, absolutely wild. It's so rare to meet one. Lucky you."

"I didn't feel so lucky at the time."

"Of course not. No." His eyes went back to the screen. His expression returning to his default annoyed look.

"What did you mean earlier? You mentioned about there being others before. Is there something I should know?"

"I'm sure there is plenty you should know. As far as the president goes." Eyes flicking to me again. "There were others, in the other sectors. Just like you. Getting special treatment, just like you have."

"And what happened to them?"

"I would love to tell you, only no one knows. The story is that they went off. Getting on with their lives."

"You don't believe that?"

"Just seems too neat. I always thought that the president was doing something he should be put in jail for. Only you don't seem that kind of girl."

"I'm not. The others weren't like that either."

Holbrook turned to face me. Crossing his chest with his good arm. "Sounds like you know something I don't. Fancy sharing."

"I'm not allowed to share."

"I've heard the rumours you know. Why the police were sent around your father's place. Of course, everyone believes it's all non-sense. Helped by the president's quick actions."

"What do you believe?"

"I've faced many foes, experienced battles, not all on the battlefield. I've learnt to trust my instincts and never take anything at face value. Make my own decisions. My own beliefs. Essentially to be my own man."

"What do your instincts tell you about me?"

A laugh came from his lips, making me jump out of surprise. "They tell me that despite your size and your age. It wouldn't be a good idea to get in a fight with you."

I laughed with him. "That feels like a huge compliment coming from someone like you."

"It truly is." I heard his deep sigh. "Look. I may be wrong about the president and the others he's given special treatment to. I'm a big boy and I can admit when I'm wrong. But I believe that I'm right."

"Did you tell any of the others this?"

"No."

"Why just me?"

"Because you have something the others never

had. Not any of the other students."

"Oh?"

Eyes moved to mine and a genuine smile came through his features. Giving his eyes those wrinkles. "My respect." I stood there shocked at what he had just said. Feeling my watch vibrating on my wrist. He noticed the soft hum. "I'm really looking forward to this class today."

"Why is that?"

"Because we're doing fights again. Only this time you students are going up against the teachers." His teeth flashing through his grin. "And I'm looking forward to seeing you up against the other teacher. She wears socks with sandals for gods sake."

Smiling wide. "I'll try not to disappoint."

"I'm sure you won't." The classroom started to fill upon both sides. Holbrook held up his hands as we stood there. He explained what was going to happen and the stage was surrounded by us like before.

Both teachers jumping up there. Looking down at the woman's feet and seeing the socks and sandals combination. Giggling to myself as I listened. "We're doing fights again today. But against us teachers. No protection spells since we're more trained than you kids. First up is Mrs Grey. When your name is called, come up. The aim is to not get knocked down. Good luck." He stepped down with a grin. Instead of watching from where he stood before. He came over to stand beside me. Calling over a couple of other students including D to watch with us.

As the fights proceeded Holbrook gave us tips. Told us what to watch out for. Tactics to take up. The fights not lasting that long before the student was sent to the floor. D was called for. She went to retrieve her nunchucks and stood across from the brightly track suited teacher.

The tips we received were helpful and D survived longer than the others before. But she was still sent to the floor with a thud. D however was smiling as she came off the stage. Then my name was called out. Holbrook giving me a tap on the shoulder. "Remember all the things I told you."

"Sure." I grabbed the retractable staff and stepped up onto the stage. Not only did I have Holbrook's tips in my head, I also observed a few things myself. Mrs Grey liked to attack first but not always right away. More like a counter-attack before the student even knows what is going on.

Knowing my capabilities with my weapon. Watching her as she spun her wooden sword in her hands. Switching from left to right, knowing she was waiting for my attack. But I didn't do what she wanted. Standing there, my staff still in it's shortest position. My thumb rubbing over that middle button.

The seconds ticking by slowly, the two of us watching and waiting. A cough coming from the side. Holbrook's voice travelling over the crowd. "Sometime today would be great."

"You've got a smart one here."

"Then you'll have to be smarter."

"Indeed I will." The teacher brought the sword in front of her and bowed. Not sure if it was a sign of respect or something to distract me. Keeping my body tensed and ready. Watching the point of her sword, having noticed she enjoyed a lot of stabbing movements. My eyes studying until she moved.

CHAPTER 12

Expecting the sword to come down to then be thrust forwards. Only it came at me swinging. My thumb pushed the button on my staff. The end shooting out and as I moved my arm it hit against the sword. Knocking it back, the staff extending fully and I spun around.

Swinging it down towards her feet. Knowing she would back step. Fingers lightly turning that piece of wood as I spun around again. One more swing towards her foot then bringing the other end round towards her head quickly.

Hearing wood on wood as she deflected it. Needing to keep on the attack unlike the others. Swinging my weapon. Thrusting it forwards, making her retreat all the way to the edge of the stage.

Then she jumped, kicking one foot out to defend against my staff, the second hitting my chest. I stumbled back but would have recovered if she wasn't so quick. Throwing her wooden sword like a spear between my legs.

Tripping over it and dropping through the air. Shooting my staff back and stopping my motion. My arm muscles straining against the effort. My arm aching where that big hammer had hit me, making it impossible to keep a tight grip.

My arm giving way and I fell to the soft flooring.

Huffing and puffing as I laid there. "Holbrook, this one isn't bad. Top marks?"

"Top marks so far. Perhaps there's someone who can actually get a hit in."

I rolled off the stage and placed my weapon back in its place. Taking up my position next to D. Blowing out a long frustrated breath. Hooking one of my long curls behind me ear. "That was annoying."

"You got closer than anyone else."

"I guess."

I got a look from her. "What's gotten into you? What happened to being against violence."

"That was before I was taken." A couple of the other girls looked over their shoulders. I just stared at them until they turned back. Lowering my voice. "The training seemed silly before. Now however learning this stuff helped me survive. Now it seems more of a necessity. If I want to stay alive."

"I've got your back whenever you need it. I think your brother would as well."

"Of course he would. I'm his little sister."

Laughing together as another student was sent to the floor. The teacher barely breaking a sweat. "What about Flo? I reckon she'd be willing to lend a hand."

Looking sideways, seeing the big grin. "What are you getting at?"

"Please tell me you've noticed it."

"Flo? She's just a friendly person."

"Yeah, right. She never held my hand like that."

Feeling my cheeks flushing red, the heat making me look away. "Her and Larsh have only just broken up."

"Oh please. That's been ending for years. They were both too stubborn to actually do it. She's all yours."

"Shut it." Biting my bottom lip as I thought about Flo. Never having felt like that about a girl before. It had always been boys but then it had always been books over them any way.

Once our class had all been defeated. It was Holbrook's turn to take the stage. Looking so comfortable even with one arm. The fights were started and over within seconds. Unlike Mrs Grey, Holbrook favoured attacking with speed. Getting in before the students could even swing their weapons.

Sending each one down harder and harder. Enjoying the view when Troy was sent to the floor. Looking like he really hurt himself as he landed. Once everyone had finished their fight the two teachers took to the stage. They ran through tips and pointers they had made for each student.

Most of them weren't good since most hadn't lasted more than a few seconds. Until Holbrook came to me. "Good instinct, you watched Mrs Grey and made mental notes. The only thing that betrayed your performance was your upper body strength. The gym isn't usually open to students outside of the fighting class. But I'll load one up to your watch."

"Thanks."

A voice coming from the crowd, knowing exactly who it was. "Special treatment again."

Holbrook shot him a glance. "If you think it's special treatment. Would you like to go one-on-one with her again? You remember what happened last time."

"No, sir."

"Perhaps you'll meet her in the tournament tomorrow to see who is at the top of their classes. Both weaponry and magic will be involved. The final test before the elite scores are released."

I looked over and saw Troy staring at me. Giving him a huge grin back because I would love to face against him again. To be able to launch a fireball at that face of his. As the class was brought to a finish I walked up to Holbrook. "About the others that had special treatment. What do you think happened to them?"

"Maybe that's something you should ask the president of the school."

"He's not very happy with me at the moment."

"He's the one who will know the full truth. You should get something to eat. Keep up your strength for tomorrow."

"Yeah. Looking forward to my fight with Troy."

"It's not just a fight with Troy or the others. There are other tests as well."

"Like what?"

"I'm not allowed to say. Just be ready for anything."

"Thanks."

"Go on, get something to eat."

I left the classroom, able to get onto the elevator before it descended down. Heading into the cafeteria with D. As we waited in line I looked over to where my brother was sitting. With his usual group of friends only there were a few additions.

One in particular I didn't approve of was Alesha. And she was looking very friendly with my brother. Happily, he didn't seem as interested in return. I sat down with my food, having something that resembled a roast dinner. But I wasn't too sure what the meat actually was.

Munching away as Flo came and sat with us, seeing the tears on her cheeks. "What's up?"

"Just Larsh. Saying some......I don't want to talk about it." I reached across and touched her hand. Getting a soft smile back but she didn't let her eyes meet mine. "How's your classes going?"

"Crystal here is topping them both."

"D isn't too far behind. What about yours?"

"Good, I'm near the top. Tournament will determine if I make the elite teams I think."

"Do these tournaments happen at the same time?"

"Some do, ours and Flo's will so we won't be able to cheer her on."

"That sucks."

Flo lifted her eyes to meet mine. A smile pushing through her sadness. "Would you be my cheerleader then?"

Blushing, feeling D's eyes on me as well. Taking a deep breath and smiling back. "I would."

Flo bit her bottom lip softly before looking down at her plate. Seeing her smile growing so wide. "Then it is a shame."

"Why do I feel like a gooseberry all of a sudden?"

My cheeks going red. Flo flicking a pea at her. "Shut it, D."

"Food warfare, that's something they don't teach here." Laughing as a spoonful of peas were launched back.

We carried on chatting and eating. My eyes darting over to my brother and Alesha. Annoyed that she was still there. So focused on her I jumped when someone spoke to me. Turning in my chair and finding

William standing there. "Did you say something to me?"

"Yes, I was wondering if I could talk to you. Alone."

"What for?"

"I can explain that when we're alone."

"Anything you want to say to Crystal, you can say in front of us."

Seeing his eyes moving from D, then to Flo. Pulling my lips together to stop from smiling at his vulnerable look. "Alright then. Crystal, I want to apologise."

"For your behaviour?"

"Not completely. I still stand by the things I've said."

"I think you need to read up on what an apology is." I gave D a quick look but it was fun seeing William looking so squirmy.

"I'm apologising for hurting your feelings. I should have been more empathetic to your emotions."

Watching his face, waiting for the sudden change in attitude. Waiting for the cruel punchline. But it didn't come. D cutting in again. "So now you've apologised you want to be friends? Take her on a moonlit walk across the grass outside."

William's eyes leaving mine and locking onto D's. "Look, I get that you don't like me. However I'm not here apologising to you. I'm speaking to Crystal." His eyes coming back to mine. "I'm saying sorry because it's the right thing to do. I'm not looking for something in return. Now that I've said my piece I'll leave you three to your food."

A simple nod and he walked off. Turning back

around. "That almost sounded genuine."

"Crystal, I think it was." Giving Flo a smile. "That doesn't mean you have to like him for it."

Our table laughed loudly. "Don't worry. He's still an arse. But it was nice for him to apologise. That's something."

"It was."

D blew out a sigh. "Alright, I'll agree with you two."

My watch vibrated bringing D's attention to it. "I've got an extra class to make up the morning I missed. Catch up with you two later."

"Sure, have fun." Enjoying Flo's sweet smile before leaving. Heading up into the elevator and walking to Mrs Kelp's class. The door was open but she wasn't inside. The screen at the back was operational with a note sitting on the desk.

Walking over and giving it a read. *The screen is set up for your next spells. Work through them as many time as you like. See you in the morning for the tournament.*

Looking around the empty classroom. Then giving a slight smile. It was just me and how quick I could learn these spells. So I went back and shut the door.

Taking up my position in front of that screen and setting it in motion. Bringing up the first spell. Working through it and once happy with my progress moving on. During my time in the classroom I learnt how to use lightning, shadows and spirit spells. Brushing up on how I could use the ice spell.

Enjoying that not all are to be used as a way of destruction. Getting some information at the end what is used best for which creatures. The weaknesses they have like plant based monsters being weak to fire. All good information which I took in with a smile.

I checked my watch for the time, seeing that I had only been at it for a couple of hours. Not sure how long this extra lesson was supposed to last. So I descended down into my pod that I had been using so far.

Not bothering to scan my watch since what I had planned had nothing to do with spells. Sitting crossed legged in the very middle and unhooking my silver necklace. Holding the pendant in my palms, looking at it. Knowing what it held.

It was dangerous and I knew what it said in my mother's letter. Only I felt like I knew myself. Being more comfortable with you I truly am. Both the human side and the everfae side. Taking a deep breath and speaking the titan's name in a whisper, "Belemoth."

Feeling the sudden absence of the classroom. Opening my eyes, finding myself sitting on some thick grass. My eyes picking out a massive mountain in the distance, fog rolling around it like miserable tinsel on a terrible Christmas tree.

Hearing a voice coming from behind me. "Who are you?"

I stood and turned, finding a scruffy looking monkey standing in front of me. Black fur with a white patch on his chest. Seeing a symbol burnt into his fur. The same shape on my mum's locket.

Belemoth shifting from one foot to the other as he stood upright. Looking into those dark eyes, watching as they shifted colour like a river running past. "Um." My words getting lost at the shock of meeting him. "My name is, Crystal."

"Crystal? I haven't heard that name in a long time."

"What do you mean?"

"I should have known as soon as I saw you. Short. Curly blonde hair. You're Narla's daughter aren't you?"

"Yeah. I guess you knew her really well."

"More than anyone."

His eyes studying me. "So how does this work?"

"I look into your mind and see if you're worthy."

"Oh." Looking at him as he stared. Not able to feel him prodding around in my brain. Letting my eyes run over his fur. Seeing a brand burnt on his chest. The shape the same as on that locket.

His voice coming through those sharp canines. "I sense a little conflict in you. The shy, quiet girl and the more recent personality that has come forth."

"You make it sound like I have two personalities."

"Oh, you have more than two. Everyone does. All little variations but they're there. What do you think about it?"

"I was conflicted before. But lately, I feel like I'm coming to know who I am. A mix of my father and my mother." Remembering my father's word. What D had said to me. "I'm a protector. I'm still against violence but I understand that others won't feel the same. And they hurt people, creatures, titans. So someone needs to protect them and I know that this is my purpose now."

"I see." His stare still locked on my eyes, using it's ability to read my mind. Looking right back at him. "You're certain about this?"

"I am."

"So be it. But first…." The titan took a deep breath and slowly exhaled. Feeling the breeze rubbing against my body as a mist started to appear around me. The world blocked, seeing the inside of my home appearing through the fog. The little kitchen table and chairs.

The blue walls covered in colourful fishes, feeling like I was actually standing there. Looking over my shoulder when I heard a cupboard being shut. Seeing a short blonde standing there with an apron on. The smell of cookies wafting into the air as she plated some up.

My fingers rising up and twirling the end of my curly hair, seeing how it matched hers. "Is this a dream?"

Instead of the fear titan replying the woman turned around. Seeing the face that I had studied in those photos. A huge smile appearing, her eyes shining bright like they twinkled when they saw me.

"Mum?"

"Yes, dear. It's me."

CHAPTER 13

"But, how?"

"Because this isn't real. Belemoth is doing this. We knew each other very well and he promised me that if you were ever ready, he would show you....well, me."

"I still don't understand."

"Come sit down, I wanted to make you cookies since I haven't been able to for the last sixteen years." I walked forwards with a shaky leg. Seeing how delighted she was at doing such a simple thing. "As you know Belemoth can see into your mind. We spent some time together, letting him map mine. My thoughts and behaviours, memories. So you could me when the time was right."

"Mum?" My hand moving out and brushing hers. The touch making a tear fall from my eye and I chucked my body forwards. Hugging her tight as the tears kept coming. Sobbing against her, my heart filled with joy and sadness at the same time. "I never knew you and yet I miss you so much."

"I know, darling." My body getting squeezed just as tight back. Never wanting to be let go. "I want you to know how proud I am of you."

"You are?"

"Of course. You've grown up into such an amazing woman. And I agree with you completely. Titans need protecting." My mum pulled back enough to rub her thumbs over my cheeks, wiping away those tears. Sucking in big gulps of air to try and stop from crying. Her rubbing touch not resting until I had. "Now that our numbers are so low, there aren't enough everfae to protect the titans."

"The stuff I've read about them sound like hunting guides. They're much more than that. Their personalities are so pure."

"Not all but I know what you mean. They're just as varied as all the species in the world. I remember my first." Looking down as she ran a thumb over the back of her hand. "It was such a cute little thing. Like a caterpillar. But it transformed every time I called into a huge butterfly. So beautiful and friendly."

My fingers tracing where hers ran. "Why don't you have your tattoos?"

"When I changed into a human, the tattoos went away. Otherwise we would be too easy to find. And they hunted for so many years. And over time, I lost that connection with the titans. I couldn't let them loose because they would be spotted and killed."

"What about Belemoth then?"

"I couldn't let him go. He was like a close friend. But when I knew, I could feel it, that you would gain my genes. I had to do something so I found a mage. He created a prison for him so he would survive past my death."

"You knew you would die?"

"Yes."

"I'm so sorry."

"Hey, now." She cupped my cheeks before I could start crying again. "You have nothing to say sorry about. It was my decision and I would make the same one again. Over and over."

"But you're not here to see me grow up. I didn't have a mum to do my pigtails or plait my hair."

"I'm sorry but that's the way it was." Feeling the soft touch of her finger running across my wrist. Looking down and seeing Kit's tattoo. "Tell me."

"His name is Kit. He's a fire Kitsune. Has a cheeky personality."

"I remember Kitsunes. They're great titans. What about this one?" She got up out of her chair and walked around behind me. "Two of them?"

"I haven't actually seen what they look like." Looking over my shoulder I saw her expression. "And you can't tell me. Can you?" A gloomy look came over her face and she shook her head. "Because you're not really here. Because we're inside my head."

"Yes, dear."

Moving away from her touch, climbing to my feet. Facing her, "You're not my mum."

"I'm as close as you're going to get."

Sniffing as my eyes filled with tears. "Is this even what my mum sounded like?"

"Completely. Think of it as a three dimensional video recording that you can interact with. This is exactly how it would feel if she was truly here."

"Right." Looking back at this blonde woman. Chewing at the side of my cheek as I thought.

"Is there anything you want to talk about? Or ask?"

"No. All I want is a hug."

"Of course, darling." Arms were extended and I crashed myself into them. Breathing in her scent, telling my mind that this was real. Her embrace bringing tears to my eyes. Holding on until the world started slipping away. The last thing to go were those arms around me. That tightness there until the last second and my mum disappeared. Opening my eyes to find that mountain in the distance again. On the grass with that monkey-like being.

"Sorry that it had to come to an end."

"If it didn't, I would never have left."

"Understandable."

"You knew her quite well then." The titan nodded. "What was she like?"

"The best person of any species I've met in over a century. She was one of a kind. She actually saved my life."

"By locking you in a necklace?"

"That's exactly how she did it. When an everfae dies, the titans bound to them die as well. She knew what was coming so she bound me to this pendant." His paw reaching up to the burnt fur. "She saved my life."

"Don't you get lonely?"

"I can conjure anything I want. Part of my power. So I've kept myself occupied."

"Oh." The thought of him having a party in the pendant made me smile. "I'm Crystal."

"I know. I can see inside your mind, remember."

"Right."

There was a moment of silence before he smiled, showing off those dangerous canines. "I'm a satori."

"Huh?"

"I can see the question floating around in your thoughts. I'm a satori. You know I can read people's minds but what I get attracted to is their fear. Once I know someone's fear I can play on it, push it to the front of their thoughts or even conjure it in the real world."

"Wow, that's impressive."

"Thank you. Your mum was right, she always insisted that you would be just like her. Sweet and kind. Your titans are in good hands, including myself." He gave a bow before the world around me started to fade with a shimmer.

Finding myself back in my pod, feeling a soft tickle against my collar bone. Pulling down my top enough to see the new tattoo. The black pattern making up a skull with cracks. Not my favourite tattoo but I was too happy about having a chat with my mum. Even if it was Belemoth.

Rubbing my cheeks and feeling the tears that had fallen during my conversation. I stood up and climbed out of the pod. My heart jumping into my throat when I saw a figure by the door.

Eyes focusing and noticing it was the president of the school. "Are you okay?"

Rubbing my face with my sleeve quickly. "Yeah, I'm fine."

"Are you sure?"

"Yep, just thinking about my mum. Had a moment by myself so didn't see the harm."

"It's good. Sorry to have disturbed you."

"I was finished."

"And the spells?"

"Done some good progress."

"That's great." I climbed out the rest of the way. Hooking my necklace around my neck. Making sure my cheeks were dry before walking over to him. "Think you'll be ready for the tournament tomorrow?"

"As ready as I can be."

"I would love to share what you'll face but that would be cheating."

"I think I'll be able to handle it." My eyes picking up the fancy suit he was wearing. Seeing a pin attached to his collar. A skull with two spears making a cross behind it. "Off out?"

"Yes, I have a meeting with a donor. Needing to lock in some more money so wining and dining is the mission for tonight." He turned as I got to him and we walked to the elevator. "The horrible things I have to endure for this place."

"Yeah, it sounds terrible."

"Oh it is. The conversation isn't the best."

"Just have a drink or five. I'm sure you'll survive." My emotions still high from meeting my mother for the first time. Plus his attitude change from earlier in the day giving my mind whiplash. As we came down to the lobby I noticed the shop was open. "Who's running the shop?"

"No one. The place was cleared of all those antiques and contraptions. You walk in, take what you want and scan your watch on the way out. Had to get an expensive machine in to keep track of the inventory. Pain in the arse."

"Who hired the goblin in the first place?"

Giving him a look as he turned away. "Whoever it was will be getting reported."

"Good." Watching him as he kept looking off into the distance. Stopping my feet when he suddenly turned. "Not going to have another go at me are you?"

"No. I may have been a little short with you before but I only do it for your own safety."

"And for the titans."

"How so?"

"If I die then they die as well. Right?"

He made his confirmation with a noise. "Titans? Plural?"

I bit my cheek for being so stupid. Nodding as I turned. Pulling down my top to show off the wings on my skin. "Picked it up whilst being held captive."

"What is it?"

"A fujin. Basically a big wind eagle. As far as I can tell."

"Sounds beautiful. You'll have to show me some time." I kept quiet as I turned back around. Seeing a car waiting outside the entrance. The driver standing by the back door. "That reminds me. During the tournament, don't use your titans. There will be people watching at all times."

"Got it."

"I'll be sending good vibes tomorrow."

"Thanks. Have a good night."

"I will if he donates."

Just as he left me, Flo and D came walking up. The three of us looking out as the car door was opened. Seeing the man sitting there waiting. The suit looking three times as expensive as the president's. Black hair peppered with white strands. Nice and short and very well kept.

"Who's that?"

D nudged me and nodded towards the cafeteria, seeing William walking by the entrance. "That's his father."

"His dad? The president said he's going to be donating towards the school."

"I wouldn't be surprised. He owns a whole street

in Collstar."

"The capital city? A whole street."

"Yep. And the humongous mansion that sits outside the city limits."

"And the rumour is he doesn't do it legally. Who knows where the money comes from."

Giving them both a look each. "Nice to rub elbows with the son of a criminal." Watching as the car left, taking the president with it. My mind going to his office. To the others that he had given special treatment to. Remembering that he had my reports on a flash drive in his desk. Wondering if he still had them for the others.

"How easy do you think it is to get into the presidents computer?"

"I don't think he keeps the office locked but I bet he's got at least a password for his computer. What are you thinking?"

"Don't look worried, Flo."

"She's not the only one worried."

"You shouldn't be either, I'm not inviting you two to come along."

Turning to head for the elevator when D grabbed my elbow. "We didn't say we weren't coming."

"We didn't?" Smirking at Flo. "What? I don't do trouble."

"Then stay here and keep an eye on D."

"Screw that, I'm coming."

She laughed as we moved up to the elevator. Hearing footsteps coming up behind us. Turning with a smile. "I'm not going to be left down here by myself. Larsh might come along and want to.....talk." Laughing as she did air quotations with her fingers.

"Don't worry. Crystal will hold your hand the whole time."

"Huh?" Before I knew it I felt her long fingers entwining with mine. Feeling the two palms kissing together, trying to stop my cheeks from going red. My confidence being chased away by that sudden connection.

We moved into the elevator and up to the top floor. Happy the door wasn't locked, gaining entry to his personal office. Flo's eyes going wide as she took in all the paintings. Her fingers leaving mine as she walked off. "How the hell did he get an original?"

"You like paintings?"

"Flo does her own paintings."

"Nothing like this. I can't even think how much it would have cost him."

Looking over to her as she admired the brush strokes. "What do you think the password will be?"

D gave me a funny look. "You going to sit there and guess it? Won't it say, you tried your password a bunch of times and failed, you're locked out."

"I'm hoping not." Leaning over his desk and wiggling the mouse. The screen coming to life and to my surprise went straight to the desktop. "Huh, no password needed."

"In that case I doubt he's got anything of value on there."

"Maybe I don't need something of value." Pulling open the drawer. Seeing the flash drives sitting all neat. Seeing my name written on one. The others having the sticky residue where a label once sat. Picking one up at random I plugged it into the computer.

A window popping up. A file just like the one he

had shown about me. Filled up with information about a girl. She had been sixteen years of age. Scrolling down I found a list. Three titans she had gotten control of.

A moment of joy that there were others out there like me. But it was quickly destroyed by the red lettering along the bottom. She was dead. It didn't say how but that meant that the three titans had died as well.

Switching out the flash drive for another, checking all of them. Coming up with the same results. All five of them both male and female were dead. In total there had been fourteen titans lost with them. My mind worried about what had gotten to them.

Was a titan responsible or did someone find out what they were? These thoughts had me wondering about my own file. He had shown me my results from my classes but nothing else. Plugging it in I scrolled down. Finding the fire Kitsune written at the top of the list. To my surprise he had another already written in.

There was no name just a description that fit the titan we came up against in that farming village. How did he know a baby one had come back with me? Flo's sudden scream of excitement made me jump. Looking up and seeing her touching one of those old looking books. "Hey, careful. If you destroy something he'll know someone was in here."

"Alright. Oh, it's one of those crystals."

"Huh?"

"From the ceremony on the first day. The one that changes colours."

"Yeah, it's part of his collection."

"Woah. What's going on?"

D turned and walked closer to her. "What have you done now?"

"I'm an everfae."

Watching her as she chucked the crystal to D. "Guys, what are you talking about?"

"So am I."

Feeling utterly confused as I stared at the dinoser. "Want to explain your bad jokes?"

"The crystal. It turned black." She spun around and showed me. Seeing the black smoke moving around the inside.

Flo came down to stand next to D. "Did for me as well."

"Wait, what?" Watching it, staring like it would change back at any second. "That can't be right."

"I'm definitely not an everfae."

"Me neither."

"No kidding. It's a fake."

"What does that mean?" D turned back around and gave it to Flo who put it back where she found it.

"It means that he was lying. He's not an everfae either. So that means his whole story is made up." My mind filling with so many questions. My eyes lowering to the computer screen. "I haven't got a clue what's really going on but we have to get out of here."

CHAPTER 14

I pulled the flash drive from the computer and put it back into the drawer. My eyes moving over the screen, spotting a symbol in the bottom left corner. Finding it very familiar. Clicking on it just brought up a login box. Asking for a password.

I ignored the blinking cursor and focused on the symbol in the background. A black skull with two spears behind it. It was the exact same symbol that the president was wearing on his jacket collar.

"The president was wearing this symbol."

"What is it?" Both of them coming to stand either side of me.

"Not a clue. I've never spotted it before until tonight. And he's wearing it whilst out with William's dad. They could be part of the same group."

"It's probably just a boys club. Hang out drinking and smoking cigars or something."

"Flo is right. I dread to think the kind of things he's got locked behind this password."

"I guess." I could understand what they were saying but something deep down was nagging me not to believe it. If he was such a stand up man why did he lie about being everfae. It could be innocent but I've been getting told I can't trust people.

I left the screen to turn off by itself and we exited the office. Calling the elevator and heading back down to the cafeteria. D and Flo took up a couple of chairs to watch the huge television. Noticing that it was the news \ running but I had other things on my mind.

Looking around and spotting William sitting near the back playing some kind of board game with his friends. Heading over and putting on the friendliest smile I could muster. "Hey, William. Could I have a chat with you?"

"What about?" He didn't bother looking at me, noticing that he was too busy moving his pieces around the board.

"Just want to ask a question. Won't take very long."

"Alright." William got up out of his chair. "No moving my men about. I know exactly where they are." We took a few steps away from the table. William's attention was still on the board game. "What is it?"

"Do you know why your father was here picking up the president?"

My question making him look at me with a confused look. "You want to ask me about my father? Why the sudden interest in my family?"

"Don't worry, I'm not going to ask him for your hand in marriage."

"You know, you were so quiet and shy when I first met you."

"Amazing what finding yourself can do."

"Why do you want to know about my father?"

"Just a theory that I haven't quite thought through yet. Have you ever seen a symbol before?"

"A symbol?"

"Uh-huh. It's a skull with two spears crossed behind it."

"Yeah, I've seen it a couple of times."

"Any idea what it stands for?"

"Not a clue. My father is a member of loads of groups and programs. I doubt he knows what they all do, it's just a great look for a public figure."

"I see you've already met my son." Spinning around to find two men standing there. The president of the school and the man that he had gone out to dinner with. William's dad standing there. His suit looked even more expensive up close.

Noticing the pin attached to the collar just like the president's. "I'm sorry?"

"My son. I hope he's been making a good impression."

"Of course." Looking up into this eyes. His skin wrinkled with age but those eyes were so bright blue. "He's been the perfect gentleman."

"I doubt that very much but it's sweet of you to say. Ethan here was telling me all about his students. He had high praise for you."

"Mister Kilroy is a huge donor for the school. I've told him all about you and your time here."

"Have you? I'm no one special." Giving a fake smile.

"Nonsense young lady. You're the future of Mythoria. You never know what the future holds for you." A hand came out and squeezed my shoulder. "Who knows who you might save."

My eyes falling to that pin, seeing letters engraved around the outside but they were too warn to make out. "It was nice to meet you. I best get to bed. I've got some studying to do before the tournament tomorrow."

"Of course. Get a good nights sleep. I'll be watching."

"You're going to be here for the tournament?"

William asked the question but his father was still looking at me when he replied. "Of course I will. It's an important day for so many of you. Plus I can see what my money gets me." His laugh came out weak and forced.

"Good night to you all." Giving each one a smile before heading for the exit. As I walked I noticed my brother getting cosy with Alesha. Feeling myself changing course without thinking. Making my way to stand right in front of them.

Lance smiled but the look I got from the girl was much less friendly. "Can we help you? You're standing in the way." Simply keeping my mouth shut as I stared at her. Knowing that she wouldn't be able to help herself. Seeing it boiling up behind those eyes. "Get out the way you freak."

Breathing in slowly as my brother stood. Coming next to me and wrapping an arm around my shoulder. "I think you owe my little sister an apology."

"What!?" The realisation dawning on her. She almost looked like she was going to say sorry. Then her hostility won out. "I'm not going to apologise to someone like her."

"Then you can find somewhere else to sit."

Grinning as she pulled a face. Jaw gaping open, looking back and forth between us. "Your loss, you moron."

She stood and stormed off. Being joined by her two friends. "Thanks for sticking up for me."

"Of course. I've always protected you from the

popular girls."

"Yeah you have." Giving him a quick hug but finding it went on longer once I had the embrace. Finally letting go, faking a yawn. "I'm going to get an early night. If I don't see you in the morning, good luck with the tournament."

"We have ours the day after, so I might see you around. And the only real competition I have is William. And there are three teams. So no worries." Laughing at his cocky behaviour. Giving the rest of the gang a quick wave before heading towards the exit. Spotting the news report on the screen.

Seeing the destruction of buildings in a small town. Not really listening to the reporter. More focused on the map it was showing. A direct line from one point to the other. A path of demolition smashing through villages and towns. What was more worrying was the school was in that direction.

Thinking about the nightmare I had. The black shadowy creature pulling apart the world around me. Could it be linked? Could a titan hear me calling to it from that distance? Shaking away the worries when I noticed the president edging closer. Wanting to get away from both him and William's father until I figured out what that symbol was for.

It could be completely innocent but the fact he lied about being an everfae had me rattled. The trust was no longer there and for a species that had been eradicated by humans. I needed that trust.

Riding the elevator by myself and heading up to my room. Getting in and sitting on the edge of my bed. Touching my fingers to my necklace. I knew Belemoth wasn't in there but I still kept it on. A piece of my mother came with it, just like those photos on my shelf.

Reaching back and grabbing that book the president had lent me. Flicking through to the back. My eyes seeing that black figure. Wishing that there was something written about it. If this thing was in my dreams and the real world. I had to figure out what it was.

Thinking about the wake of broken lives it was leaving behind, I stood no chance against such a thing. Chucking the book back on the shelf. Taking a few deep breaths as I placed my face in my hands. Breathing in and out steadily. Trying not to worry about something that could have nothing to do with me.

Only at the back of my mind was that nagging feeling. It was no use to try and get rid of it. So I decided to get some answers a different way. Calling to Belemoth, feeling that tattoo against my chest before he appeared in front of me. Shimmering into existence like he didn't belong to this world.

"Crystal."

"Belemoth. I was wondering if my mum had spoken to you about a symbol. A skull with two spears behind it."

"That doesn't ring a bell but I know she was making investigations into a few groups. Your typical radicals that are causing a lot of noise but no actual action. Why do you ask?"

"Something is feeling a little off. You know all my memories don't you."

"You're on about the president. The fact he lied about being an everfae."

"Exactly. What do you think?"

"I think you can't trust anyone. Your mother only

trusted your father. People will hate you just because you pulled half your genes from your mother. They will do experiments on you. Anything to gain control of the titans. They'll rip yours from you, to steal them. When that doesn't work they will keep you sedated. Pull you out and force you to destroy a town or kill someone."

Seeing the horror in his eyes, the tears gathering but he blinked and they vanished. "How do you know all this?"

"I can see people's memories and I've been around for a very long time. When I see those memories I adopt them. The feelings and emotions. I've lived through many more things than I should have."

"That must be horrible."

"Incredibly so but that's the life I have. Nothing can change that now. I hope this conversation was helpful."

"It was, thank you. Gives me more to think about but yes. Sorry to just pull you out for a single question."

"Don't. Me and your mother would sit and chat for hours. I guess for her, I was the closest thing she had as a friend beyond your father." There was a short pause before he added, "I miss her as well." His long arms coming around me, feeling the fur brushing over my skin. "Feel free to call on me any time."

"Thank you." Brushing fingers through his fur. "Best get out of here before my room mate comes up. Think you might give her a little fright."

"That's always fun to do but I understand. See you around, Crystal." Seeing him shimmer like he did before. Disappearing and leaving me in my room alone. My eyes flicked over to where the book sat.

Feeling that I knew more about titans than was

written inside it. Perhaps that was the president's idea. To keep me blind to what it was all about. To think titans are like those monsters that will attack you without a moments notice. But they were more than that. They felt like companions that lived inside my heart.

Curling up onto my bed, I leant back against the wall. Closing my eyes and calling to Kit. Feeling the light and then his fur sitting over my lap.

Stroking my touch through that coat as it heated up. Opening my eyes and seeing it turning from black to orange, giving off a slight glow. "This is nice."

Laughing, "I'm not surprised you like being stroked."

"Everyone likes being stroked." Those eyes looking up at me. "Glad this time we don't have something to attack."

"I guess it's hard to remember that titans are just like other animals. The way people have chatted about them, it's like they're there to be controlled and used."

"It would be the same as having a dog and making it fight to the death."

"Well I don't ever plan on putting you into a fight to the death."

"I'm very happy to hear that." Smiling as Kit rubbing his head against my hand, scratching through that heated fur.

"I gotta go grab a shower. You okay here?"

"If I'm allowed."

"Of course. Only D should be coming up to the room and she already knows about you." I grabbed a thick towel from the cupboard and some pyjamas. Heading to the showers and taking a cubicle. Happy that I was the only one there.

I washed using the toiletries they supplied. Once I was all clean I stood there, letting the water run down my hair and down my spine. Feeling so nice as I took a few deep breaths. Then I concentrated on the liquid.

Thinking about my magic and stopping it, keeping my eyes closed. The sensation of the water hitting my body stopped. I looked up and smiled, seeing the growing ball of water at the shower head.

Then I shut my eyes and let it drop. The ball hitting my head and splashing everywhere. Gasping in air as the shower started again. Staying there for a bit longer before turning it off and getting into my pyjamas.

Heading back to the room, still finding D hadn't returned yet. Kit was snuggled up by my pillow asleep. I climbed into bed, feeling his body rubbing my skin as he repositioned himself. Letting him lay across one of my arms.

Resting my hand on the pillow, my eyes peering over to my shelf where my little light shone. Seeing my mother looking back at me. "Night, mum." Shutting the light off then laying back, feeling myself drift until sleep took me.

Getting torn from that peaceful slumber by the thought of black and shadows. My skin being ripped into by claws. The rumble inside that cloud, the growling thunder all around me. Screaming as pain flared through my body like I was dipped in fire.

Fingers wrapping around my wrist making me pull it free. Eyes opening suddenly and I shot my hand out. Feeling the heat of fire erupting into my room. Hitting against the figure in the dark. The flames lighting him up for a moment. Seeing Holbrook hitting the wall with a grunt.

My fingers quickly switched the shelf light on. My teacher sitting against the wall holding his chest. Panic pushed me to my feet. Crouching down in front of him. "Are you okay?"

"I'm fine. It was more the force of the fireball than the burning. Good reflexes."

"I was having a nightmare."

"Figured, you were tossing and turning." Then my eyes went wide, looking over my shoulder but Kit was no longer there. Wondering at which point he had disappeared. Turning back to Holbrook. "Help me up will you?"

"Yeah, of course." Standing and tugging him to his feet. "What are you doing in my room?"

"I've come to collect you for your first test in the tournament."

"I don't feel like I've had much sleep."

"It's two in the morning." Looking over to see D's bed empty. "She's doing hers now. I'll be outside whilst you get dressed."

"Thanks." Sleepily chucking on some black combats and a long sleeved black top. Tying my hair back into a ponytail. Now ready Holbrook took me down to the training area. Remembering the exotic plant we were shown.

Feeling my heart pounding at the thought of what I was about to be asked to do. Finding the teacher who taught defensive magic standing by the last turning door. Scruffy, curly hair sticking up at all angles. His beard looking unkempt. He was wrapped up in a robe looking just as tired as I felt.

"Holbrook."

"Stevens."

"I'm Crystal."

I got a sleepy smile. "I know." A hand moved and grabbed a vial from a trolley sitting behind him. "This will protect you from any long-term damage. You will not die and you will be monitored at all times. You will still feel pain and are likely to black out if you endure too much. Please take this and step up to the line."

"Alright." Feeling like I was being shoved into the lion's den. Drinking down that liquid which gave off a horrible after taste. Not able to detect the spell doing its work, just hoping that it would.

Waiting for another five minutes before the massive door started turning. Smiling as D came walking through. Then spotting the cuts and bruises already showing up on her skin. My heart beating even harder. "What happened to you?"

A voice coming from behind me. "No discussing the test." D gave me a smile and a nod. A soft touch to my arm before walking to the two men. She took another vial which immediately started healing those cuts and bruises. Then Holbrook escorted her out of here.

Looking at Mr Stevens as he spoke again. "Inside there are three creatures. Different kinds, all needing different ways of killing them. Your weapon has been deposited inside, search it out if you want. Or go at it without. Cameras will track your progress and there are people inside who will jump in if needed. Got it?"

"I think so."

"Great. Off you go." The conversation coming to an abrupt end. Making me feel like I was being forced in. Taking a few steps past that massive door, hearing it close with a thud. Shutting me off inside this exotic area.

Looking around, left and right. Eyes darting with every rustle or movement. My heart ready to burst from fear. Silence stretching out for so long as I just stood there. Swallowing past the lump growing in my throat.

Shaking my head and breathing out. "This is silly, I'm capable of defending myself. I've killed goblins and two-headed snakes. This will be easy." Stepping forward when there was a burst of speed. Seeing the colour green before I felt something stabbing into my chest.

Looking down and surprised I hadn't been skewered. My feet leaving the ground as this thing lifted me up. Staring into large black eyes, a bug face looking up at me as pincers snapped together over its mouth. A second arm swinging through the air. Ending in a point, barbs of some kind lining the underneath. It was these that dug into my arm. Crying out in pain.

CHAPTER 15

Again when I looked they only cut through my skin, not venturing further into my body for more damage. Glad that the protection potion was doing its job. Bleeding still but I was able to move and ignore that pain.

Shoving my hand against its face. Not even thinking and bringing forth that easiest magic. Flames engulfing my fingers. Making it screech and stumble back. It's limb tugging from my body and I dropped. Hitting the floor hard.

Keeping my hands there connected to the earth. Bringing up that magic and building a dome piece by piece around that thing. Doing exactly what the president did in Vinnerston. Pulling it in until that thing started screeching again.

Ignoring the pain it must feel and pulling down that rubble until there was nothing left underneath. Leaving the bundle of rocks there, covering the destroyed body of that monster. Checking my wounds, happy they were no deeper than I first thought. Rubbing the blood from my fingertips onto my combats. Seeing the rips in my top. Annoyed I didn't wear something I didn't mind getting ruined.

Taking a deep breath and looking at that jungle. It couldn't be that deep but it was thick. And my gut was telling me that flower monster we got shown the other day was still in here. Otherwise, why would it have been brought in for show and tell.

I needed my weapon and I needed to be on high alert. Doing it in the fastest time was not on the table right now. I just wanted to get it done. Pushing forwards into the thick foliage. Pushing by large leaves that stroked me.

The deeper I went the less I could see. Soon completely forgetting the way out and getting lost. Hoping that I would stumble across my weapon. Something that I could use to defend myself. Only the next thing I found confused me.

Moving to the edge of a little clearing I found a little creature. It was scurrying around on all fours. Low to the ground with its long body and short legs. A small head whipping left and right in unison with the scaly tail.

The thing was like a little dog but that face was all screwed up. Nose at an angle, eyes bulging out. It looked rabid and I wanted nothing to do with it. It didn't matter if it was food or just a critter that lived here.

I backed away but typically my foot snapped something as I did. The little thing raised beady eyes at me. Foaming at the mouth as it breathed heavily. My whole body jumping as it dived at the ground. Clawing it's way out of sight.

Laughing to myself at how silly I had been. Relief about to set in fully when I heard the scratching of claws. Then the ground was disturbed. One head popping up, then another. Soon the little clearing was full of those heads.

Those eyes all staring at me. Making my blood run cold. My heart beating like a loud drum. My whole body frozen until they attacked. Shooting into a sprint. Hearing weird noises coming from behind.

My feet carrying me, feeling like I was outrunning those little legs until I felt something hit my shoulder. Claws digging in then that bite. Screaming as the pain blacked out my vision for a moment.

Blinking until it came back. My hand wrapping around the little critter and launched it. My step stumbling and my shoulder cracked into wood. Spinning sideways and hitting the ground. My hands flinging up, my mind running through the spells.

Flexing my fingers and pushing out that time magic. Watching as the little things practically stopped in mid-air. Those disfigured faces twisted as they gave off deep drawn out noises. Little tiny teeth baring and snarling.

My brain started to pulse pain under the pressure of the time spell. Looking around at my surroundings. Not able to see anything, not even a stick or branch to use as a staff. Thinking about my spells. Fire would work like any other creature.

Only the thought of burning these things alive was not on my to-do list today. My ears picking up the rushing noise of water and it made my decision for me. Reaching out with my left hand. Allowing those things to move through the air quicker as my time spell faded. Coming towards me.

Pulling on that water magic, feeling my headache coming harder. Clenching my eyes shut and willing the liquid to come to me. Feeling the pull taking hold. Changing the direction of the river and hearing it come rushing towards us.

Feeling a soft splash of it against my skin as it

crashed against tree trunks. Then it came, pushing into those little animals and taking them away in a rush of power. Letting go of both spells as they were took off. The water carrying on with its own momentum.

Letting my head rest back against the ground, breathing heavily as I tried to not pass out. Ignoring that pain, telling myself I wasn't finished yet. Climbing to my feet. Trying to catch my bearings which didn't help matters.

Picking a direction and I walked. Pushing through the jungle as it seemed to wrap around me. Making distance until I spotted a black window up high on the wall. Finding myself almost back to the door, seeing the metal through the trees.

Looking back up at the window I remembered the president and his friend saying they would be watching. Feeling their eyes on me. My curiosity blocking out the worry of the third creature.

Pushing back through the greenery I stopped. Breathing out slowly and pulling at the wind titan. The eagle appearing before me in those lines of movement before disappearing from the naked eye. That whispery voice speaking to me. "You called upon me."

"Yes, there's a blacked out window that way." Nodding with my head. "Are you able to get behind it, without being spotted?"

"Quite possibly. To what end?"

"I need to know what the people behind it are saying. What they're talking about."

"Alright. Call me when you need me to return."

Surprised it was so willing to do what it was asked. "Thanks. Make sure you're not spotted."

"I will do my best." Then it drifted off. Seeing

the lines but it didn't disturb the leafs, not even a leaf moved. Turning back to the deeper part of the jungle. Taking a deep breath and moving again.

Thinking about those flower heads that had been described before. The main part of it was what I needed to attack. To kill it. Remembering that it hunted with the vibrations in the air. So noise was no issue, it already knew I was here.

Stomping through, eyes darting, my ears on high alert. Hearing movement to my right. Turning, thinking about the plant based monster. Fire would be perfect to burn it up just like the animal guy said.

Bringing a ball of flames in my palm. The heat of it flickering against my face as I watched and waited. As soon as that thing came bursting through the jungle I launched my spell. But my face dropped as I saw what was attacking me.

The fireball hitting against metal and doing no damage. My eyes going wide as this things feet dug through the ground. Steaming towards me and I was frozen. This beast was twice as tall as me.

A long tail whipping behind it. A massive head lowered down and metal jaws opened up. Teeth lining upper and lower. The ground shaking as it stomped right in front of me. Spinning around and I didn't know what happened next.

Only feeling pain as I was smashed flying through the air. The metal tail had created all kinds of havoc on my body. Hoping that the defensive spell meant my insides wouldn't get crushed from the impact.

When my eyes finally opened up I was staring up at a grey ceiling. Breathing in was hard to do with the pain threatening to drop me back unconscious. Keeping my breaths shallow. Blinking a few times, straightening out the world around me.

Tilting my head made my neck ache. Seeing D sitting there in a small chair. Flo next to her, both fast asleep with their bodies at odd angles. Thinking they would ache as much as I do if they're not careful.

My laughter bringing a cough which pushed that pain to every nerve in my body in waves. The sound of my groaning waking my friends. D was about to speak when a male's voice came from the doorway. "You're finally awake."

My eyes moving without my head. Seeing it was the president standing there. He had changed out of his nice suit and the pin was missing as well. Still looking smart in a shirt and trousers. "Yeah." My voice weak and croaky. No idea how long I had been out for. The room was lit up by the window above my head.

"Why didn't you defend yourself?"

My memory flashing back to that metal monster. It looked like some kind of dinosaur. Strong legs, little arms and those teeth. "I was attacked. Am I okay?"

"You're fine." Flo interjected herself into our conversation. "The spell protected you for the most part. You'll ache for a bit though."

"Glad nothing was broken."

D sighed as she came to the bed. "It could have easily been that way. You need to be more careful."

"I thought that plant thing would be in there."

"That was just so we were prepared for it. Was a nice surprise when that metal thing came bursting out at me." Smiling as D explained. "I got a couple of hits in before I was knocked down." Her stare dropping to the floor. "I ran for the door."

"I would have preferred that option." Pulling myself up a little. Resting back on the hard pillows. "I guess I didn't do so well with the elite scores."

The president rubbed his forehead, looking annoyed. "No you didn't. Luckily you should be well enough for the next test."

"Right now, that's not what I'm thinking about."

"And you shouldn't." Flo stood and confronted the president. "She needs her rest. Perhaps you could come back another time."

His lips moved to speak but then he caught her stare. Giggling as he made his goodbye and left. She gave me a wink that had me smiling even more. "He was out of line."

"I guess. One sec, girls." Shifting again and then calling to Fujin. The breeze of his entrance cooling my body. "Hey, did you find out anything good?"

Flo's and D's eyes fixated on the barely visible titan. "They were chatting about you. Discussing how many titans you had. If you would be ready for the elite teams or not. The younger of the two was confident you would be. The other wasn't so sure. Even more so when you were knocked out."

"And after that?"

"I don't know. I sensed that you were in trouble. I came to you but the thing that attacked you was no longer there."

"The test was over as soon as I was knocked out."

"That would explain it. Is there anything else?"

"No, thank you." Breathing in that wind. Letting the titan move back into my heart, the tattoos on my back feeling cool as it disappeared. Seeing the looks on my friend's faces. "What?"

"Nothing. That one is different."

"I think they're all different, D."

"I know that."

"I think she means, that was really cool."

Laughing but stopping as my side hurt. "Thanks. I got another one but I don't think you would show the same appreciation."

"Why not?"

"We're not animals."

About to laugh but controlling it, "He looks very different to the others. Kinda like a monkey walking on its hind legs."

Flo suddenly burst out laughing. A high-pitched giggle that was extremely adorable. "I'm so sorry, that image just hit my funny bone."

"We could tell." D gave her a nudge.

"What is the next test?"

"We've had no information about it."

"Plus, mine are different. I didn't have to go in the jungle and kill monsters."

"No?" Looking into her eyes. "What did you have to do?"

"Defeat four versions of myself at the same time."

"Huh?" My brain trying to comprehend what she was on about.

"Holograms. We've been getting recorded through our training sessions. These holograms know exactly what I do. Was quite hard. Managed to take three of them out before being hit."

"Remind me not to ever get in a fight with you then."

"You better believe it." Giggling together.

Noticing D rolling her eyes.

"Why don't you two give me some time to relax."

"Sounds like a good idea. God knows what they'll have us doing next." D leant over my bed and hugged me. Flo was about to leave when she stopped. Confused until she suddenly turned. Seeing her cheeks going red as she leant over as well.

At first I thought it was just for a hug. Then I felt her lips kissing my cheek and then it was my turn to blush. Not because I was embarrassed. Just that it was a nice surprise and I liked it. Looking into her eyes as she backed away. "Thanks." Biting my lip because I said something so stupid.

Flo giggled and went for the door. My mind going a little fuzzy as I watched her leave. Wanting her to come back if only to spend time with her. Watching the open doorway just in case she did. When I heard footsteps my heart filled with joy. Then I watched as a nurse came walking in, wearing white scrubs. "How are you feeling?"

"I ache all over."

"Not to worry, this will help with that in seconds." She placed a potion on the side table. The liquid a green colour like the one the president had given me. Popping the lid I drank it down. Feeling it work its magic quickly.

My body starting to mend in the next few seconds. Tilting my head brought no flare of pain. Checking the bruise on my arm from the goblin's hammer showed that too had been healed. Slowly swinging my legs over the side of the bed. Standing and despite being a little dizzy, I felt fine. "Thanks for the potion."

"Of course. You will be back to full strength in a few minutes."

"I'm free to go then?"

"Yes. Feel faint just take a rest and you should be fine."

"Thank you." Leaving the infirmary and coming out into the lobby behind the shaft the elevator took. Making my way around the large circle before coming to the cafeteria. My brother spotted me and ran over.

His eyes looking at the rips in my top. "D told me what happened to you."

"I'm fine. Don't worry."

"If it wasn't for the potion they gave you, you would be dead."

"It's a school test. They're not going to put us in danger."

"Maybe."

"I'm sure yours will be similar."

"I've heard rumours that they're taking us weaponry lot out to the forest. But you know gossip in a place like this."

"Far too well." Seeing that Ayesha was sitting with her usual followers. Then I saw Troy giving me the evils. I couldn't wait to face him again. "I'm going to get changed into something with less holes."

"Alright." Receiving a sudden hug. "If I don't see you before your next test, good luck. Give them hell."

"I plan to." I got a kiss to my forehead before I moved back into the lobby. Seeing the shops gates open, the self-service machine operational. Grabbing a quick snack before heading up the elevator.

Changing into a white vest top with a thin hoody over the top. The murky green going well with the camo combats. About to exit when there was a knock to the door. Freezing for a moment. "Who is it?"

"It's me, Mister Kilroy."

"Oh." My thoughts getting muddled with confusion. Moving to the door making it open up. Seeing him standing there, looking important in his clothing. "Can I help you?"

"I just wanted to stop by and wish you luck in your next test. Your scores in the last left much to be desired. However, Ethan insists that you will prove me wrong."

"I hope so to. My aim is to get on one of the elite teams."

"Yes, so I've been told. There have been many before you with that thought. Many of whom failed. I do hope that you will succeed where they didn't."

"Thank you, Mister Kilroy."

"Please, call me Godfrey."

"Godfrey Kilroy? That's a hell of a name."

"A family name. My ancestors were part of the first to land on this continent. My lineage goes way back. I'm sure you know what it's like to live through a relatives legacy."

"A little." Hearing his words and the way he looked at me. His relationship with the president hinted at his knowledge of my everfae ancestry. But I didn't mention it. I wasn't trusting the president completely right now and this man's presence here made it twice as bad.

Feeling my watch vibrating. The screen showing that I was needed outside the school for my test. "Your next test?"

"Yes. I should get going. Was nice chatting with

you."

"Likewise." Happy that he didn't come down in the elevator with me. Before heading outside I grabbed a sandwich from the canteen. Munching on it as I came outside. The fancy train sitting on the tracks, waiting for us.

Walking up beside D, "Hey, any clue where we're heading?"

"Nope." We fell in line with the rest. Spotting Holbrook and Mrs Grey standing there. Her tracksuit a bright red colour today. I grabbed a seat by the window and the train shot off using those magnets underneath.

Not saying a word to D, my mind still thinking about William's father and the president. Who knows who else was part of this group of theirs. I didn't even have a clue what it was. Mister Kilroy's interest in me was worrying.

Had he met all the others? What was their plan with me and why hadn't it worked before? All those deaths, I didn't want my file to have that red writing printed over it.

My worries hitting free from my thoughts as the train came to a sudden stop. Looking out into the little train station. Not a single person to be seen, not a worker or pedestrian. The two teachers climbing off.

We joined them on the platform, none of us being allowed to walk into the small town. Listening as Holbrook raised his voice above the chatter. "Welcome to Huxton. A little place that we have been allowed to take over. The whole town has been locked down and abandoned for the day. Buildings have been set up for our test."

Mrs Grey taking over. "Inside each building there

are red and blue markers. Holograms in the form of zombies. They will move and attack but they can't touch you. They react to your spells, use whichever you want, it will have the same result."

"We have five buildings set up, you will be sent in four teams. And you will have someone to go up against. The most holograms tagged by the end of the time limit wins. Red or blue, the whole team wins once all the scores have been added up. No elite scores for the losing team. So remember, it's not just you who counts this time. You have your team to think about."

Holbrook pulled a scanner out of his pocket, playing around with the buttons before calling out names. One of which was mine. Stepping forwards, joined by D. She got given the school and I was given the police station.

Thinking about what I needed to do until I heard Troy's name as well. Smiling as he was given the same building. Once the first set of teams were called, our watches were scanned. A time limit of ten minutes popping up.

My teacher's voice coming out loud. "This is a test against the holograms. You will not attack each other. If we see any of this behaviour you will be punished as well as your team. Is that clear?"

He might have been talking to the whole class but he was looking at me. Seeing how his eyes flicked to Troy. I could keep to the rule as long as that bully did as well. There was no way I would not defend myself if he came after me.

The call being sent out from our watches and the time started ticking. The teams running from the train station and seeing the town for the first time. All homes were terraced houses. Rows and rows of them ran off to the right. A small square outside the train station held a notice board.

Moving down the metal steps a bunch of us stopped there. Checking the route through the rows of buildings to find my police station. Giving Troy a check over my shoulder. He wasn't too far behind but I hoped he was slower.

Dodging through the roads, the whole place feeling eerie with no one here. Cars parked on the side. No noise apart from Huxton's new visitors. Coming up to the police station I moved through the front doors.

Hearing a horrible gargling noise as I came face to face with two zombies. Letting out a yelp of horror as dead eyes moved to me. The red one having his jaw hanging to one side. Teeth dropping out as it swung.

My stomach groaning at the horrible sight. Then the door was shoved open and an out of breath Troy nudged into my back. "Why are you standing in the way?"

"Shut it."

"Oh wow, these look grotesque. Amazing."

"You think this is cool?"

I saw the grin he pulled. "You can always wait outside if you're scared." Then he shot off a lightning bolt at the blue zombie. Bursting it into digital dust. Troy gave me a wink before running through the next set of doors.

Sending out a fireball at that disfigured zombie and joining him. Moving from the reception area and into a long hallway that came to a crossroad. Hearing spells being cast. Light flashing around the corner.

Before I could move any further forward a figure

came out of a doorway to my right. The sound of moaning putting the hairs on the back of my neck on end. Throwing up my hands and seeing the dead person bursting and disappearing with flames.

Steadying my breathing as I walked to the crossroads. Hearing my heart pounding in my ears. "Why the hell did they have to use zombies?"

"To weed out the scaredy cats. Can't be part of the elite team if you're scared of some dead holograms." His laugh making me clench my teeth, tempted to launch a fireball at him and say I simply missed a zombie.

But a different idea came to mind as I watched him move into a room. The flash of lightning shining out of the doorway. I moved into an empty room. Whispering to myself and that titan that lived deep down. "Belemoth."

The monkey figure appearing in front of me with a shimmer. "Could you pull out a fear in Troy?"

"I certainly can. Anything you want particularly?"

"They can't know that I used you, so just keep it zombie based. Scare him out of here and if possible, can you manage it without him spotting you?"

"When I'm hunting a fear, no one can see me."

"Alright, don't make it permanent. Just for the next..." Bringing my watch up. "Six minutes."

"Got it. I'll return to my resting place in your heart once it's finished."

"Great." The monkey nodding his head before shimmering out of existence. Listening for his footsteps but there was nothing. Happy that Troy wouldn't understand what was going on. Now I could concentrate on doing what I was here for.

Coming out of the room and moving in the opposite direction of Troy. Heading up the stairs and coming to some zombies in the hallway. Shooting out fireballs and lightning. Ignoring the blue and destroying the red.

Coming into a large room, standing above the pit of desks and cubicles. Zombies stumbling about until I started using magic. Sending out my lightning like a whip. Hitting each red hologram I saw in turn.

Emptying the room by half and leaving the blues to carry on their shuffling. Sending out spells as I needed. After clearing the cells I moved back down stairs. Hearing a cry of terror then footsteps.

Troy came running down the crossroads. His eyes wide and full of fear. He spotted me. "Hey, Troy."

"Stay away from me. All of you, don't touch me." The chubby kid speeding past me. Up one crossroad and turning back around when a zombie came out of a room. Giggling as he screamed at them to leave him alone. Troy truly looked terrified of them and it had me in stitches.

Biting my lip to stop from bawling out with laughter. "Do you have a problem with the zombies now?"

"Please, don't let them get me."

"The exit is that way." Pointing and he took the direction quickly. Screaming at the top of his lungs. Doors being barged open. Feeling a presence to my right, thinking it was a zombie I shot out a lightning bolt. My heart jumping as I realised it was Belemoth.

Unable to stop the spell but it didn't matter. The monkey-being lifted up a palm and the shot of lightning hit with a sizzle. The fur getting singed but within the next second it was back to normal. "Wow, can't you be hurt?"

"You can't hurt fear."

"Will he be alright?"

"It'll wear off in a few minutes."

"Perfect, everyone will just think he got scared."

"That's the idea. Happy hunting." Belemoth nodded to the holograms walking around. Then he shimmered out of sight. Giving that space he left a smile before checking my watch. I only had two minutes left so I moved quickly.

Jogging through the police station and throwing out spells as I went. All the way until the last seconds ticked away. As soon as it happened the zombies disappeared. Happy that there were plenty of blue left after Troy's sudden exit from the building.

Taking a slow stroll back to the train station. Seeing Troy looking confused rather than afraid. Calling over to him, "Was it a little scary for you?"

He stuck his middle finger up in reply which made me laugh. I sat down next to D. We chatted whilst the other teams made their runs. Finding it nice to relax for a moment. Not to worry about the president and his plans. Or worry about elite scores.

The topic of me and Flo coming up with a cheeky grin from D. "So what's going on between you two?"

"I haven't got a clue. It's always been boys for as long as I can remember. There's something about her. Can't place it."

"Sounds like you've got it bad."

"Not entirely sure about that but I like her. Just hard to ignore that little voice in the back of my head."

"What's the voice saying?"

Looking across to her, "That it's wrong and a bad idea."

"Don't worry. That voice doesn't last very long. I remember my first kiss with a girl. They're much softer than boys. Much more enjoyable as well."

"I might be looking forward to the first kiss, just a little bit."

"I'm sure Flo is as well. She's very forthcoming with her emotions. You'll never be guessing how she feels."

"That's good because this is all new territory for me."

"You mean liking a girl?"

"Yeah, it never crossed my mind before. Not until I met Flo."

"She's quite a girl. Been friends for many years."

Turning my head to look into her eyes. "You're not about to do that threatening thing, are you?"

D burst out laughing. "No, believe it or not, Flo can handle herself. Even more so now she's had lessons in fighting. She once knocked a boy's tooth out for touching her arse."

"Did she get into trouble for it?"

"Not as much as the boy. His father yelled at him, in front of the whole school because of it. Put him in his place."

"Sounds like a good father."

"Yeah. We need more men who agree unwanted touching is out of order."

"And yet we get more kids like Troy." Looking over to him, remembering that look of fear he had. I leant in close to D and told her about what I did. How I used my titan to scare him out of the building.

She couldn't stop laughing the whole story. "I can imagine how funny that was. His face would have been perfect for a photo."

"I'll think of that next time."

"You planning on doing it again?"

"Well, Holbrook is making sure we meet each other when the fights start."

"I'll get the camera ready then." We sat there laughing.

Waiting for the other teams to finish and the final scores were called out by Holbrook. "Red team wins by six. Elite scores will be updated before the fights start tonight. Everyone back on the train and they can have their town back."

The whole group of us bundling back on our transport. On my way to grab a seat with D I felt a hand grabbing my arm. Getting tugged around to face Troy. The anger would have been steaming out of his nose if he was a cartoon. "I don't know what happened in there. But I know it was you."

"I haven't got a clue what you're on about. You ran out of there looking so scared. Maybe those zombies just jumped out at you at the wrong time."

"You can say you don't know anything. Plea that you're innocent. But I know it was you."

"You can think whatever you want. Nothing will change that you ran out of there like a little mouse. And you're going to lose our fight."

"I wouldn't be so sure about that. The president won't be able to help you. I'm going to destroy you."

"Like you did last time?" He was about to speak again when I turned my back to him. Sitting down next to D. The only reaction he got was a laugh as he stormed off. I wasn't worried in the slightest.

The train journey felt shorter going back to the school. As it pulled up the whole car switched to one side. Looking out the window at the stage that had been erected on the grass. A few metres up in the air with crash mats surrounding it.

This wasn't a simple stage like in class. Even though it was still daylight lights were starting to come on, shining down upon it brightly. We were all pulled off and the two teachers lined us up. Feeling the excitement starting to build as they explained the rules.

Mister Stevens was standing there with a trolley covered in potions. Looking more awake than last time. Wearing a pair of jeans and a band t-shirt instead of his robe. His hair and beard looking much better. Protective spells ready to be swallowed.

We were allowed to use magic and weapons. Hand to hand if we felt up to it. Once the end of the fight was called, that was it. No do-overs or late attacks. The rules would need to be followed or we would be expelled from the school.

Names were called out. Some fights involving members of the same sex, unlike the classroom fights. Seeing that it was based on skill level. Seeing D go up against one of the other girls.

Standing there, ready to cheer her on. Hearing the whistle getting blown and they both launched into attacks. D swinging her nunchucks around. The metal end missing the opponents head by centimetres.

They dodged, seeing spells being chucked. Each one getting a good amount of hits in. The fight seeming even until D got cracked on the side of the head. She dropped down hard. Seeing that Holbrook was about to blow the whistle. "Come on, D. You can do it, get back up."

The dinoser let out a growl and jumped from her downed position. The other girl didn't expect it, having lowered her guard completely. D wrapped arms around her body and spun the girl over her hip. She hit the stage harder than my friend had.

The whistling stopping the fight. Giving D a wink as she climbed back down from the stage. "Thanks, I needed that."

"Always here to cheer you on."

"Your turn now."

"I can't wait." Hearing my name getting called out. Heading over to Mr Stevens to get that protection potion. Retrieving my weapon from the racking they had assembled out here. Taking the ladder up to the stage. Stretching once I was up there. Spinning my staff around my hand effortlessly.

Watching Troy coming into view. Seeing that he had two daggers in his hands. A ring at the bottom of the handle for a finger. Watching as he spun them around. The blades moving so fast they made that whistling noise.

Troy looked determined, staring at me. I on the other hand was studying him. The weapons were grasped in a closed fist. Meaning he wouldn't be able to use most of his spells. I also had the reach with my weapon. Keeping him at bay would be my best bet. The whistle being blown and the fight began.

CHAPTER 16

Troy running straight for me. Pushing that middle button, the staff shot out as I extended my arm quickly. Troy swiped it out of his way. Shifting in close to my body so I back stepped.

Bringing my staff across my chest and stopping his stabbing motion. Kicking out my feet to sweep him down but he jumped. Blocking his downward swipe with my staff but that other hand was free and quick.

Feeling his blade slicing through my hoody and top. The blade cutting across my stomach. The potion protecting me from any further damage but I could feel the blood trickling from the wound. Troy didn't follow it up with another attack. Just stepping back and grinning.

Blowing out a frustrated breath. He was quick and those daggers were dangerous. Standing up, rolling my shoulders. Bringing my staff upright. My hand coming out and conjuring a fireball. Letting it roll around in my palm.

"You think a little fire is going to win you the fight?"

"It's not the only spell I know."

"Me neither and I've been training." Troy flicked his wrists. His daggers becoming covered in fire.

Wondering how he managed it but I had no time as he came for me. Swinging his arms, the fire erupting out from the daggers. Balls coming towards me. Dodging out the way of two. Swatting the third with my staff but Troy was already there.

Swinging those blades at my head. Ducking and jamming my weapon into the inside of his knee. He cried out but he was ready for the next swing of the staff. Backing off and shooting out a fireball.

It hit my shoulder and spun me to the floor. Fingers letting go of my weapon, hearing it thud onto the stage. My opponent stood over me, his weapons still on fire. "See, I told you, you're not anything special after all."

"Shut it."

"What can you expect from someone like you. Your mum couldn't survive in this world and neither can you."

"Shut it!" Jumping to my feet and shoving him. "You don't know what you're talking about."

"I actually thought you were going to beat me. That's why I trained so hard. But I didn't really need to bother. You thought you were going to walk it. Like you did last time. You under-estimate me. Now I'm going to finish this fight."

"No you're not." Launching myself at him. Getting an arm around him but he just turned and flung me to the side. Rolling across the stage until it fell away from underneath me. Fingers gripping the edge. Holding on. Looking down at those crash mats.

The fall wouldn't be as bad as losing to this bully. Pulling myself up but falling back, fingers aching as they clung on. Troy came walking over with an annoying grin. "You can just fall off and lose."

"I'm not going to lose."

"Come on, give it up. You're just like your mother. Not fit for this world. People like me are the winners in life."

"Stop talking about my mum!"

"Make me then." Feeling wind kicking up underneath me. Lifting me, helping me to climb back up. "Last chance." My feet touched the stage. Troy even chucked me my staff. "This time I won't go easy on you."

Looking down at the crowd. Spotting D's face, looking worried as she watched. Then I noticed Holbrook staring up at me. Giving me a gentle nod. Feeling his support. Giving Troy a little smile. "You want to humiliate me by beating me in a fight. However, I want to be on the elite team. I want to protect people because that is who I am. Good versus evil. Good always wins."

"This isn't a book or a movie. You're going down." Those daggers of his were erupted into fire again. So I called down to my soul. Thinking about the spells I could conjure. My eyes coming to his daggers. How his spell covered them in flames.

He was clearly proficient with fire. However, I was able to use a varied amount of spells with talent. Thinking about the lightning. Thinking with a bit more theatrics than needed. Pulling my lightning magic and bringing a bolt down from the sky.

As it hit my weapon I watched as it spread over the staff. Wrapping around it like a snake, even slipping up my arm to my elbow. Feeling the surge of it but no pain. "You're not the only one who is well versed with magic."

"It's not going to be enough to beat me."

"We'll see about that." Jabbing the staff forwards

and sending a bolt out of the end. He dodged it and I didn't follow it up with another. Watching as Troy rolled and was ready for another. Daggers up. Giving him a funny face.

Watching as he stood upright. Building up the lightning in my staff, seeing how it ran over the wood, getting faster. Pushing my weapon forwards as I ran. The bolt much larger than the last time.

Troy rolled out of the way and I was right there. Swinging my staff like a bat for his head. He ducked like I thought he would. Bringing my foot up into his jaw. As he fell back I put my foot forwards and followed him. Jabbing with the end of my staff as he kept rolling. Hitting the stage over and over.

Stopping as Troy got to the edge. Staying down but he didn't give up. Hands coming at me and feeling the wind hitting my body, sending me back. Laying my body flat to the stage, fingers trying to dig into the surface.

As I looked up he kept the wind coming. Stepping towards me whilst I was pinned down. Taking a deep breath and feeling for my own wind magic. Trying to push away his attacking gale but it was too strong.

So I scooped it around behind me and then chucked my staff in that direction. Directed my spell to catch it. Swinging it around the stage. Pushing harder with my magic until it cracked into Troy's head.

He dropped hard and released me from my position. Running over to him and jumping. Pinning him down. Forgetting about my staff and my magic. Slamming my fist into his jaw. Two more times until my hand hurt so much I couldn't wriggle my fingers.

Letting out a long breath, gritting my teeth

through the pain. "That's it, such a perfect little teacher's pet."

"Shut it. You lost, fair and square."

"Not yet." Feeling his fingers wrapping around my wrist. The world around me suddenly shifting down a gear. The sounds being drawn out. My mind still moving at its normal rate but my body refused to listen.

Feeling so slow, the world around me moving even slower. Knowing that he had used the time spell. I didn't even know you could use it through touch. Gritting my teeth and pushing my muscles but it was no good.

He pushed me off of him then hit me with a gust of wind. Sending me flying from the stage. Only that wasn't enough for Troy. Eyes picking up his hands, remembering the little tornados I had created in class. Only this one was huge.

Seeing the wind gusting around me, trapping me in the eye. My body spinning, able to see it in slow-motion. Trapped there for ages until it suddenly disappeared. Finding myself even further from the stage and plummeting down as the time spell was released.

Knowing that the impact would kill me, not even the protection potion could stop that. Trying to point my arms down but I was spinning so much. Throwing out the wind to try and stop the descent but it just pushed me around, feeling like a bag caught in the wind.

My breath getting caught in my throat. Finally hitting down, my body feeling the impact. Trying to suck my breath in hard but it was no good. My eyes seeing the grass underneath me only it was still moving. Zooming past me, so close the blades touched against my hanging hands. The wind underneath me felt solid.

Slowing down before it was suddenly gone. Skidding and rolling until coming to a stop. It would have been much more painful to drop straight to the ground. Only right now my body protested against the pain pulsing through it.

Looking up as Holbrook came running over to me. He crouched and touched a hand to my cheek. "You okay?"

"What was that?"

"You can thank your friend for that. She was the one who saved you."

D came and joined Holbrook. The rest of the class standing and staring. "You okay?"

"Yeah. You saved me."

"You helped me with the spells. You saved yourself in a way."

"Trying to get out of a hug?" Sitting up but the pain kept me from doing what I wanted. "Thank you."

"It was nothing."

Holbrook looked shocked. "Nothing? You saved someone's life. None of the others moved an inch and she would have died if it wasn't for you. I'm going to make sure you make the elite teams."

His eyes coming to mine, feeling a pain in my chest that wasn't from the drop. "What about me?"

"Despite Troy's actions. Which he'll be expelled for. You still lost the fight."

"Can't I have another fight? With someone who follows the rules?"

"I'm afraid not. One fight per student. That's the

rule. I'm sorry."

"You got enough elite points from the classes though. And today's other tests."

Giving D a smile as she tried to cheer me up. "I didn't complete the one this morning."

"She's right. These tests are where the majority of your scores come from."

"So I'm not going to make it." Looking into his eyes. Holbrook simply shaking his head. "Right." Sitting up on my knees. Looking down at the grass and dirt. Nodding my head. "It's alright. I'm alright. Just a few aches and pains. Think I'll go grab something from the cafeteria and head up to my room."

"I can take you."

"D, it's okay. Think some time alone will be best right now." Pushing myself up and walking. My whole body protesting against the action but I ignored it. Just needing to be by myself. Looking away from the class as they all stared.

Hearing Mr Stevens yelling at Troy. Saying how he was out of order. The consequences of his actions will go beyond being expelled. I couldn't even enjoy him getting ripped a new one because of how sad I felt.

Getting onto one of those elite teams was my best option to help people. To travel the world and help titans. They were being hunted and killed like monsters but they were just misunderstood. I could have helped them.

Now my options were to stay here and keep training or head back home. Sit in school and be a good girl. Not having anyone pay me any attention. That might have worked before. Now there was a half of me that had woken up.

I had seen parts of the world in the last few days that I had never dreamt I would see. Been in situations I had only read in novels. My life was alive now and I could never go back to being quiet, little me.

Heading into the lobby. Moving into the shop and grabbing something that looked relatively healthy. But also grabbing a bag of sugary sweets. Comfort food my dad always called it. Wiping a tear from my cheek, refusing to cry until I was alone in my room.

Heading out and hearing some chatter coming from the cafeteria. Walking closer I saw my brother sitting at one of the tables watching the television. Poking my head around the corner and noticing William sitting right next to him.

"What's going on here?" Sniffing back my sadness.

Their eyes watching as I limped towards them. "What happened to you?"

William got a look from my brother before he stood and walked to me. "What did happen?"

Lowering my voice. "If I talk about it, I'll cry. So just for now. Don't." Lifting my look to his. Lance nodded and smiled, giving me a soft hug. "Why are you two sitting in here?"

"You could call it a timeout."

A laugh shot out of my mouth which had me clinging a hand to my ribs. "What are you talking about?"

"Hot shot here didn't want to listen to me. Thought his plan would work better."

William shooting an annoyed look at my brother. "It was, better. You would have had the whole team caught."

"Not if you followed my orders."

"I don't follow yours or anyone's orders. I'm the one that's in charge."

Lance walking from me, turning towards William. "With that attitude no one is going to follow you."

"We'll see about that, won't we."

"Yeah."

"I can see why you two were chucked out of class. Why didn't you ask to be on different teams?"

"Because William here is fourth in class. The top three got to be team leaders. And my plan would have worked. No casualties with all side-objectives complete. Minimal fighting. If this idiot had followed his orders."

"It wouldn't have worked."

My brother turned his back to the argument. "Our tests are tomorrow and I need these points."

"I'm sure you will do great. Don't worry."

"As long as I don't have William on my team."

Smiling, holding back my laugh. Hearing the television speak louder. A news report interrupting the program they had been watching. Turning to watch. Seeing the pictures being shown of destruction.

A town completely demolished. Not a single building standing. The reporter standing in front of a big white tent. People sitting on chairs, some laying on beds. All their homes and possessions gone. The course of devastation was getting worse with each night.

Seeing a few drawings, sights of the monster. Close to the one drawn at the back of the titan book in my room. The reporter explaining eye-witness accounts. Saying that it came from the east. Not moving on until it had attacked everything.

The map of the attacks being brought up again. Seeing the line getting even longer. "That thing is going to keep going. Nothing will stop it."

We both looked at William after his comment. Lance leaning in, "Is that a titan or just a monster?"

"I have no idea. But I think I know someone who could stop all this." Thinking about what it would accomplish. Stopping the devastation but also proving to everyone that I deserved to be on an elite team. This would prove to them. "Do you still have access to that hover bike?"

"Why?"

"To take me out there."

"That's insane. You're not going out there." Lance's loud remark had William come walking over. "You don't know what that thing is."

"I know that there isn't anyone else out there that can stop it like I can."

"What are you two talking about?"

"This doesn't concern you." My brother blocking him from the conversation with his body. "I won't let you go out there."

"Maybe she should be allowed to make her own decisions."

"I said it doesn't concern you." Lance turned and shoved him back. To my surprise William left it alone and sat back down.

"Look, this thing will keep going. If it is a titan then it needs my protection."

"This thing doesn't need protecting. It's dangerous."

"Maybe it's just misunderstood." Pleading with my eyes, hoping he would change his mind. "Please,

Lance. I need this."

"You need to have your head checked." He stormed off towards the counter where the food was being prepared for tea.

Watching him, hoping he would turn around. Only it wasn't him who spoke next. William stood from his chair and came to stand next to me. "I don't know what you're on about. But I've got a bike in the garage."

"You do?" Looking up, his blue eyes staring right back. "Why would you offer your help?"

"Because it will greatly annoy your brother."

He was right and I would hate to cause that. Only this was more important. "Alright. I want to go now though."

"Let's go then." Giving my brother one last look before following William to the garage. Finding his bike parked up in it's own little room. Looking much more powerful than the last one I rode. Bright blue body with red decals on the engines. The bike whirring with power. I was given a second helmet and we shot off.

Coming out into the open air and curling around the school. Shooting off so fast the class I had left didn't even notice. The engine for the bike so silent. I couldn't hear anything inside my helmet until William's voice came through the speaker. "I'm guessing we're heading to the last town that got hit."

"Yeah. The attacks are heading this way. Shouldn't be hard to find something like that."

"Let's hope it doesn't just attack us."

"It won't."

"You sure about that?"

"Completely." Feeling my heart pounding in my chest. My conscience asking what I was thinking. This was reckless and stupid. Putting my life and William's in danger. But I ignored it. Telling myself it was the right thing to do. Something I needed to do right now.

Curling my arms around William's waist and holding on. The world shifting around us. Not paying any attention until the hover bike slowed down. Coming to a stop at the side of the road we had found. "What's wrong?"

"Something is moving ahead?"

"Where?" He pointed and I looked. Seeing in the distance a shadowy figure walking along the road. We watched as it plodded. Stumbling left and right. "It looks like a kid."

"Out in the middle of nowhere? You don't think that monster.....is a kid?"

If a kid managed to gain a titan. Perhaps they couldn't control it. It would explain the attacks. "We should go see what it is."

"Are you insane?"

"It could be a kid from that town, looking for help."

"Or it could be a monster disguised as a kid."

"Fine. I'll get off and go see by myself. You stay here and piss your pants."

"There's no need for that."

"It's fine." Climbing off the bike. Chucking the helmet at him and stomping off. Coming up to that figure. The moonlight not giving me much sight at the face but it was definitely a kid. More than likely human.

Crouching down a few metres away. "Do you need some help?" My voice made it stop. Head still angled down, long black hair covering the face. Noticing it was a little girl from the dress she was wearing. She must be so cold.

Licking my lips as the kid stood there. Fingers curling into fists. "Are you hurt?"

The kid's arms started to shake. Waving back and forth before it screamed. Black erupting from the little body. Covering it and growing further. The scream turning into a roar. Something that I had heard before. Standing outside the school on my first day. In my dreams.

This was the monster. My eyes going wide as it grew and grew. Like a black cloud, a storm of anger raging inside. Hearing William calling to me but it was lost to the noise. It filled my ears and my head. That roar shaking my body.

I knew I had made a terrible mistake. This wasn't a titan. This was a kid and god knows what else it had inside. Were there monsters out there that could take hosts? Was it a spell? My experience was extremely lacking.

The thing finally stopped growing, understanding how it could destroy a whole town. My body shaking from fear. Glowing eyes looking down at me. That yellow light boring holes through the darkness. A mouth opening up, that glow coming from within. I called up, voice shaking. "I can help you."

Those eyes stared back. The little kid hadn't replied and this thing wasn't either. Feeling a rush of air coming from behind me. The hover bike skidding around my body. William had his arm out, fingers reaching for me.

Only he was the one in danger now. The monster saw the bike and brought down a huge black fist. I grabbed William's arm and yanked him from the bike.

Clearing his legs just in time for the machine to be crushed.

An explosion sending us both back onto the grass. The shadow monster roared as it recoiled. Then it came forwards. The glow growing brighter, seeming more angry as it shook the ground with each step. I through out a fireball which did nothing. Hitting against the dark body but getting swallowed by it.

Then wind but that was like swatting smoke with your hand. The thing just wavering before coming back together. I stood and pulled William to his feet. Using my earth magic and pulling up a massive piece of rock. Launching it with all my might but it was like throwing a pebble at an aircraft.

This thing rushed forward, firing out a missile of shadow. It hit the floor and exploded in blackness. Getting knocked down yet again. Breathing in and coughing out as I looked. We had been sent back even further from the road.

The monster looking left and right. Eyes pulsing with light as they spotted us. "William. I'm about to do something and you can't tell any one. You promise?"

"Is it going to save us?"

"That's the plan."

"Do it. I won't tell a soul." It wasn't a promise but it would have to do. Jumping up to my feet, surprised I wasn't passing out from the pain. Hoping I still had some protection from that potion.

Calling to the titans within my heart. Those tattoos glowing. My creatures coming out into the world. Leaving Belemoth inside because this was a physical fight.

Kit jumping out looking happy until he saw this

thing. Fujin gusting up beside me. The little critter cowering by my legs. Wondering if I had made the right decision. Blowing out a breath. "This thing is destroying homes and lives. We stop it here. Got it?"

I got two confirmations, the little creature by my legs walked forwards. "You run, we've got this."

Looking up to the wind eagle to my right. "Thank you but I'm staying. We fight together or not at all."

Kit gave me an unsure look before whipping his tail. Seeing the fiery appendage splitting into multiple tails. The fox creature growing in size. Feeling the heat of his body. "Let's go!" As the little spiky thing disappeared the other two rushed forwards.

I joined them, feeling the ground shaking as the bigger, shelled titan came up to fight. It screeched and stomped forwards. The four of us getting to our enemy and attacking. Fireballs being thrown, gusts of wind. Claws being swung.

I brought lightning down from the sky above. The crack of it sounding deafening. Only none of it was any good. Anything we threw at it didn't phase it one bit. The beast attacking back. Knocking the fin covered titan up into the air.

My mouth dropping as the huge titan came crashing down. Cratering the ground underneath and kicking up chunks of grass and dirt everywhere. My heart breaking as Kit was the next to be hit. Hearing a whimper of pain as it skidding over the ground.

Flames dimming as he just laid there. I threw up a wall of rock as I was being focused on next. The attack knocking it down with ease, getting hit in the arm by my own debris. Rock ripping through my skin but not going deeper. But I felt the weakness of my form.

Knowing that protection had just been stripped.

Fujin swooped up into the air. Turning and flying down. Wings tucked back, like a meteor falling to earth. So much power and speed. Talons flicking open only they didn't rip into the monster. Fujin flew straight through it. Hitting the floor with all that momentum.

Bouncing like a ball. Each hit sounding worse than the last. My team of titans were beaten so easily. None of us could hit this thing. The only one I had left was Belemoth. Could he be the key to our success?

Calling to him but I wasn't quick enough. The monster throwing itself at me. Force knocking me back to the ground, cracking my head hard enough to make my vision blurry. Not wanting anyone to get more hurt I called them back.

Feeling the rush of them pushing into my heart. The rush of warmth from Kit was the last thing I felt before I passed out. Black taking me in and drowning my mind. Pain filling my every thought as I tried to surface back up to the light. Only it was no good and I sunk deeper.

CHAPTER 17

Before my eyes opened I could feel my body swaying. Arms dangling down, hearing footsteps underneath me. A soft breeze running over my face. Feeling a painful throb at the back of my head. Feeling cool liquid running down my neck.

My face scrunching up as pain hit my thoughts. Hearing a voice from above. "Easy, don't wriggle or I'll drop you."

"William?"

"Yeah."

Opening my eyes, looking up into his bright blues. Seeing the red scratches down his face. A bruise on the side of his neck. "Are you alright?"

"I'm not the one being carried here. At least I can walk."

"I would punch you for that but I don't want to be dropped. I'm in enough pain."

"Down you get, then you can punch me." I felt my body being tilted. My feet touching the grass. My fingers clutching onto his shoulder. My legs aching but they were stable. "Just don't punch me in the face. Hurts like hell right now."

Looking at those cuts and bruises. Seeing the blood on his skin, marking his face. "Maybe I'll save that punch for another time. Looks like I've got you battered enough already."

"Not to mention my bike."

"Oh." Remembering the sight of it all smashed up. "How much does one of those cost?"

"You would have to save for a very long time. Don't worry about it though. I'll just say I got into a crash and my father will buy me another. The next model is out so it's a good time for it."

"Looks like I did you a favour."

"The bike I can forgive. My head is killing me and it could have been a lot worse."

With my hand still on his shoulder I turned and we started walking back. "What happened after I blacked out?"

"The monster just disappeared. Shot off into the distance."

"In this direction?" Both of us stopping on the road. "Didn't any cars come by?"

"At this time in the morning?" Looking over to where the sun was starting to poke over the horizon. "Nice of the school to send someone out to find us."

"Think of the amount of trouble we're going to be in."

"Please. The president will sort it out for you and my father will just donate a bunch of money to the school." Feeling his hand wrapping around my elbow. "Come on. We should keep walking, perhaps we'll get back before my tests start."

"Oh my god. I'm so sorry."

"We're not late yet. Don't apologise until we are." His hand supporting me as I limped. "There's something I need to ask."

"I know what you're going to ask. And yes, clearly the rumours are true."

"I know that. Pretty bloody obvious."

"Oh. So what's the question?"

"If you were so willing to throw yourself at a monster like that, with your titan friends." Finding it so weird how casual he was about me having everfae blood in me. Clearly he knew about them but he didn't seem phased about that or the titans. "How come you let that chubb beat you in your fight?"

"You were watching?"

"Uh-huh, through the window. You're clearly up for a fight, so why let him beat you?"

"It's not that simple. Did you not notice how good he was?"

"True, he was good. I doubt you're any worse. Like I said, you throw yourself up against that thing. Seemed like you could have done better in the fight."

"I guess." Looking off into the distance as we walked. Knowing that the reason I came after this thing was because I lost. Trying to prove myself and again I failed. Maybe I didn't deserve a place on the elite team.

Did I even deserve my mother's genes. To have the ability to control these titans. Not only did I put William's life's in danger. They were there as well. Getting attacked and hurt. I just hoped they would forgive me for doing that to them.

Coming up to the school around lunch time. Heading in through the lobby. D coming running out of the cafeteria. "Disappearing again? And with him?" She gave him an evil stare.

William smiled back. "I'm going to go grab something to eat. Hopefully my score won't be affected much by my tardiness."

"Thanks and sorry again."

"Don't worry about it. It was my decision to take you."

He left and Flo came walking up. Looking like she was upset with me. "What were you doing with him?"

"He was helping me with something."

"All night?"

"Yeah. I made a stupid decision."

"You sure did." Then she stormed back into the cafeteria.

Turning to D who looked just as upset with me. "What's going on?"

"She thinks you were with him all night."

"I was."

"No, together."

"Oh, god no. Not him. I went off to stop that monster that has been destroying towns and villages."

"Are you that stupid?"

"You sound like my brother."

"He's right though."

"Look, I'm done with this place. All I want to do is go home and figure out what to do with my life. I don't want to go back being the shy girl but I can't be this. The elite team isn't for me. I need to find my own path in life."

"You sure?"

"Yeah. I lost to Troy. The only way I beat him in the police station was because I used my titan. The elite team isn't a good fit for me. It won't let me be my true self. Having to hide that everfae part of me. It wouldn't be what my mum or dad want."

"Alright, only if you're sure. Going to be strange without you around."

"You'll be busy training wih your elite team."

"Only because of you. Maybe you can come back as a teacher."

"No thanks. Dealing with kids at this age is bad enough. I'm going to tell the president that it's over. He'll have to find another everfae to help."

"How do you think he'll take it?"

"He'll just have to except it. This is my life."

D laughed and gave me a tight hug. "It was nice knowing you. Hopefully see you around."

"I plan on it. You're the closest friend I've ever had. That will never go away. You're stuck with me."

"Sounds good to me. I'll explain everything to Flo."

"No, don't do that." Looking over to where she sat. Smiling as she even looked pretty with that sad look in her eyes. "It'll be easier for her. I'm gone either way."

"Don't you want to say goodbye to her?"

"I do. I never even got to kiss her. To see what it was like."

"It's not too late."

"No, no. It'll be easier on me as well. Could you talk to my brother though. I want to see him before I leave."

"Of course. He seems in good spirits at lunch so his morning test must have gone well."

"That's good. I'll be back down in a moment."

"I want another hug before you leave."

"Count on it." Talking about my decision made it seem even more like a good idea. Like I was finally taking my first step in the direction I was supposed to go. Heading up in the elevator to the top floor. Moving into that huge office, the president wasn't behind his desk.

Checking up in his little library but there was no one here at all. Finding myself looking at his books. The one he had shown me on my first day. Pulling a couple off. Some of them filled with even more titans. Others were history books. Reference books about cities and towns.

A map was hanging up on the wall showing all the continents. Marks left here and there. A book at the edge of the shelf in front of me caught my eye. The cover seeming to shine unlike the others. Like the dust couldn't touch it.

I tucked my finger into the top and pulled. It angled down until there was a click. My eyes going wide as the whole book shelf opened up like a door. Finding one of those portals I had seen in the goblin's wagon.

The cylinder hole to the right had a key stuck in it. The shine from the portal working in front of me. This must be where the president had gone. God knows where it would lead me. But my suspicions of the president forced me forward.

Pushing my body through and coming out the other side. The portal spitting me out into a little room. The wall lined with more portal doors. Names above each one like reserved parking spaces.

I moved out into a hallway. The place looking like a government facility. Walls all white, blacked out windows. The names of scientists on plaques by keypaded doors. Moving along, hoping I didn't get spotted since a young girl did not belong in a place like this.

A door opening up so I ducked into a little alcove in the wall. People walking by talking about subjects and experiments. Hearing the door shutting so I quickly moved. Pushing my body between the gap. Finding myself in a room with a large window.

Showing another room on the other side. Looking inside and seeing a young lad asleep on a bed. Cameras showed the room from all angles. A monitor tracking his vital signs. A bunch of papers were scattered across the desk.

Picking up a few I read the information. My mind racing as I took it in. Holding my hand over my mouth. Unable to believe what they were doing to this boy. He was half-everfae just like me. Using his blood to try and control titans. To see if they can replicate our natural ability to adopt them.

He didn't look in good health. Seeing the track marks of syringes in his arms. Turning around for the door, unable to look at him any longer. Pausing as I noticed a white lab coat hanging on a hook.

Putting it on and leaving. Walking further down the hallway. Wondering if each door I walked past had the same set up behind it. Coming around the corner to some normal windows. Looking down at a big room. A large, round, black table sat in the middle. The symbol of the skull and the two spears etched in white. Letters around the edge spelt out, DEATH. Validating my worry about this group.

Sitting around it were men and woman. Nicely dressed in black. Spotting the president and William's father sitting next to each other. Carrying on walking as the hallway curved above the room. Coming to a little booth with seats inside. Taking one, pulling the collar of the lab coat up, trying to hide my face from the others in here.

But they were too busy listening to the meeting

through the small speaker underneath the window. Feeling my heart pounding as I listened. "It was your idea to release that subject, Mr West."

"Yes it was, I have this girl at the school. She's had very little guidance from me and has been able to retrieve a bunch of titans. She managed to survive being kidnapped by goblins. Managing to kill a two headed snake whilst gaining a new titan at the same time."

Wondering how he knew all that. I had never told him the finer details. Especially not about the titan. "That may be. But this thing has created so much havoc. The amount of damage it has caused."

A blonde haired woman joining in. "Not to mention if the government found out about our part in all this. The damage would be the least of our troubles." Many of the people didn't seem happy with the president.

He leant forwards. "Gentlemen and ladies. If we don't remind them that titans are out of control monsters. Who will? More and more groups are popping up in aid of them. Claiming that with proper treatment they can become part of our lives."

"We know all about those groups. They never gain traction."

"Because of us. If we stop then people will start to listen to them. Fear is the weapon of choice right now. Keep the public in fear of these things. This will keep them under our control and we can keep pushing forwards with our plans."

Another member coughing for attention. "We've also been discussing about that. We gave you time to create your school. To look for remnants of the everfae species. So far each one has died before bringing real results. This wasn't what you officially said would happen."

"They've been unfortunate deaths. But you all know that people will do anything to get their hands on an everfae. Just look what happened with our shop owner. People will kill for an everfae. To be able to control a titan brings big money to the equation."

"Exactly. This is bringing attention to us."

"It brings attention to me and I can handle that. This isn't the time to retract your trust in this project. With your titan killers out there, how many monsters have they killed? Not titans, actual monsters."

"Numbers are high."

"Now, how many titans? I'm guessing its in single digits. They've been out there for years. I on the other hand, just one man. Have dispatched more than all your killers put together. This last everfae I found is even better than the rest. So far she has three titans. God knows how many when I return."

"What is your point?"

The president speaking to the whole group. "My point is. My project is the one yielding results. Not Mister Wilson's titan killers. When those other everfae died. Their titans went with them. It's easier to kill a young kid than it is a monster. Plus these kids can seek out titans. Titans even come to them. If anything you should be pouring more money into my side of the business rather than yours."

William's father leant forwards next to the president. "I'm calling a vote for a shift in funds. In favour of Ethan West. All those in favour."

Mister Wilson calling out, "You can't do this." But the man objecting was already losing. Hands going up around the table. Winning by four votes and giving him more funds. More money to create more schools. To help him find more everfae.

He was getting them killed just to get rid of their titans. My heart feeling like it was going to burst with worry. A loud bang coming as a gavel was hit against the table. The oldest of the members speaking louder than I expected. "Motion has been carried. Now onto your immediate business."

"Yes, sir."

"This thing we released. You're calling it to your home, Mr Kilroy. Am I correct?"

Godfrey leant forwards. "Yes, you are."

"You live on the outskirts of Collstar."

"Yes I do."

"Do you two think it is wise to bring such a terrible force that close to our capital city?"

"We have done our research on this thing. We are ready for it. Nothing will get past my land. We have defences in place."

Ethan West adding, "The idea is to put someone of high profile in danger. To bring more sympathy to our cause. But Mister Kilroy nor his guests will be in any danger."

"Guests?" The old man leant forwards, a shaking hand pointing a finger. "You will have guests?"

"Like I said, nothing will happen. We're completely ready for it. The guests are students from the school Mister West runs. We're throwing it to announce the elite scores for the teams."

"Ah yes, your government funded scam."

The president looked a little hurt at this comment. "It's not a scam. We've helped government forces all around the planet with our elite teams. Integrated them into all departments of defence. We've helped thousands of people over the years."

"That may be. Just don't lose focus of our true plan. The titans are the problem here."

"I haven't."

"Meeting adjourned."

They all stood up and called out. "Destruction, Extermination and Annihilation of the Titan Horde." The gavel being slammed on the table again. Making me jump into action. Heading out of the little room and back around the curve. Only voices were coming from that direction. Recognising them from the meeting room. Seeing the stairs that would lead them straight up into my path.

Spinning on my heel and heading the other way. Following the curve. Lowering my head so no one passing me would notice my young age. Coming up to some barriers, a fence blocking off the path. The facility beyond was ripped apart. Seeing the bright sky high above.

The walls were laying about like something had smashed its way out. That shadow thing that was on a path of chaos. Being led by some kind of calling. These people did this. All to make sure the public kept hating titans.

Feeling my sadness growing as I noticed black body bags sitting by the wall. Five of them. They had killed their own workers just to release this thing. I doubt the government even knew about this place.

Turning my back to the destroyed room and slowly making my way back around the curve. Not hearing any chatter so I pushed forwards. Making my way back to the room with all the portal doors. Walking up to the one I had used.

Pushing my hand forward, ready to slip back into the president's office but my palm touched the wall. My forehead creasing as I looked ahead. Expecting to shift from one place to another but I was still here.

Taking a step back and studying the portal. Not seeing the glint of magic being used. Cursing under my breath. The president must have gone back already and turned it off from the other side. Recalling my memory. Not seeing a single door marked exit and there was no way for me to get through that fenced-off area.

So the only way out of here was through one of these portals. The sound of chatter coming closer had my decision making halved. Without a clue which one would lead me where, I just picked. Rushing for it and pushing through that magic. Coming out the other side. My hand pushing at something that shifted outwards.

As my head came through the portal I saw what I had touched. A shelving unit sat in front of the secret doorway. I looked around it and found the room void of life. Eyes shooting left and right. Taking in the desks, the machines and cabinets.

Seeing tubes of blood and other fluids. Computer screens running programs that I didn't understand. Recognising machines only from medical programs on the tele. Moving out and sliding the shelves back in front of the portal.

I walked up to the closest desk. A machine spinning tubes around rapidly. The computer bringing up lists. Finding a clipboard and reading through the notes quickly. The person who works in this lab must work with the group trying to eradicate titans. This scientist was using these facilities to carry out their work.

Something about splicing two types of DNA together. This particular subject had failed the initial process. Dying from the experiment but they were still analysing the blood. To see what went wrong.

Perhaps that's why the shadow titan was so out of control. Why the kid couldn't handle the power. They were experimenting on normal kids. Their bodies can't handle what they're doing to them. Which makes them even more dangerous.

That explained why they had the half-everfae locked up. They were decoding his and other's DNA. Finding out how to put that ability into other species. Shuddering at the thought I dropped the papers back on the desk.

Turning for the door I saw those vials of blood. Taking a closer look and seeing that they've got brain matter and spinal fluid among other samples. Feeling my stomach churning at the thought of it. Little kids being torn apart for their cause.

I thought about unplugging the refrigerated cabinets. Only, they would just get more samples. Which meant more kids would suffer. My stomach doing back-flips as I left the room. Wanting to forget everything I had found.

My white lab coat helping me blend in with the other hospital staff. Ignoring patients moaning at me about something that hurt. Moving down the hallway, barging past people. Needing to leave this place.

Coming into the massive waiting room. It was so loud with all the voices, making me feel even worse. The need to throw up was growing quickly. Trying to think of anything else. The nicest things possible but it was no good. Rushing to a bin and hurling my guts down into the bag. Hearing it make that horrible noise. The smell of my stomach matching the horrible taste in my mouth.

A second fountain of insides came out. Breathing in, shutting my eyes so I didn't have to look at the mess. Holding my head back and sucking in air. Happy that my stomach didn't rebel again.

No longer feeling queasy. Hearing a soft voice coming from behind me. "Are you okay?"

Turning and seeing a little girl there. Looking up at me with huge blue eyes. Looking so sweet and innocent. Crouching down and giving her a soft smile. "Yeah. I'm alright. Thank you for asking."

"Here." Out came this little hand holding a tissue.

I took it and dabbed my mouth and chin. "Did I get it all?"

"Yep." I offered it back but she pulled a funny face. Laughing at my mistake and chucking it into the bin. "Are you a doctor?"

I chuckled then remembered the white coat I wore. Looking down at the badge hanging from the pocket. Seeing the name was Doctor Cole and the picture was of a bald guy. Putting my hand over it. "Sure am. You visiting with your parents?"

"No. I don't have any parents. I come from the Collstar orphanage. They have to do some tests."

"Oh. Sorry to hear that. You seem in a good mood for it."

"No point in being sad. It never accomplishes anything."

Her optimism making me smile. "You have such

a good spirit. Never ever lose that."

"I won't. I'll keep it tight in my hands." She clutched those little hands together like she physically held her spirit.

A voice in the background catching my attention. Hearing it again as it called for Doctor Cole. Looking up and seeing the man from the badge I wore. His bald head shining under the hospital lights.

Noticing that he wore a light blue shirt and trousers. No white coat since I was wearing it. The little girl noticed where I was looking. "Oh, that's my doctor."

"That's your doctor?"

"Yeah. He was busy with some forms when I saw you needed a tissue." We both saw the doctor suddenly looking around. Then he spotted the little girl. "I should get going."

Wanting to grab the her, to take her away from that doctor. She could easily be a normal patient of his. Here for routine tests for the orphanage. Only, it was too good to be true. A girl with no family to worry about her. Young just like the others.

The doctor walked over and took her hand. Starting to lead her away. My mind shouting at myself to do something. Only what could I do. One way to stop him would be to kill him. I may have gotten more used to violence but I wasn't about to do that.

Next would be to knock him out and take the girl away from him. Law enforcement would class that as kidnapping and I would be hunted down and arrested. I couldn't help any one from jail. So despite my gut twisting as that happy girl was taken away. I needed to turn around and get out of there.

Passing through the automatic doors as tears

trickled from my eyes. The change in the air a welcome breath. The city around me loud and noisy. Cars whizzing past on the streets. So many people it looked like a herd of animals walking by.

Moving further away from the building of healing and out into the city. Even I knew where I was just from what I could see. Recognising the radio building that broadcasted across the sector. The massive antenna on top with those satellite dishes aimed in different directions.

Then there was the monorail. Transport that would take you to all sections of the city in minutes. Hearing it shoot past with that whizz of electrics, too fast to follow.

I walked along the path, taking off the white coat and dumping it in a bin. Thinking of my plan. I had no idea how I was going to stop that monster. But I also had to stop the president and William's father. That group they were a part of.

My head hurting as I tried to figure it all out. One master plan to bring everything to a close. So I went back to the beginning and started small. The party was tonight, at Godfrey Kilroy's house. My friends would be there. That kid will attack the place when she arrives. So first things first. I needed to stop them from going. Them and my brother.

I looked to the sky. The quickest way would be Fujin. Fly out of here and back to the school. Only that wasn't an option with all these people around. Not to mention the security cameras that seemed to be on every building.

So I moved up the stairs when I came to a monorail stop. Climbing on as it came to a stop at the platform. Lucky for me it didn't cost a thing to ride. Letting it ship me around the city. Taking this opportunity to watch the buildings go by.

Huge skyscrapers near the centre held things like the police force, the courts and the council. The city was so large that it had it's own government, it's own laws and policies. It was also a democracy so they held votes for the people living here. They had a choice in the things money was spent on. They passed new laws or by-laws. They had control over their own city and it was flourishing. A shame the rest of the governments didn't agree. Keeping their hands on the steering wheel. Sending most places into debt.

The monorail finally came to my stop. Getting off just opposite the train station. This was one of the few buildings that still looked the same from before the city grew so large. Made up of red brick. Not a fancy, futuristic building. The kind we still had back home. There, it was because the village couldn't afford to renovate it. Here, it was classed as a historic building.

I moved through the entrance and surveyed the area. Seeing the ticket booths which I didn't have the money for. The turnstiles in a row, scanners for tickets to gain entrance to the platforms.

Slowly moving forwards I picked out the staff. Since the introduction of self-service ticket machines, the number of workers had dropped considerably. Now it was mainly to keep an eye on passengers.

Bringing the wind to my fingertips I sent out a small gust. Just enough to knock over a stand holding pamphlets. The crash making the staff and most of the passengers look. Taking this opportunity to duck under the turnstile.

Moving out onto the platforms. My feet keeping me going. It didn't matter where the train was going. As soon as I was off at the first stop I could use Fujin and fly back to the school. Just hoped I wasn't too late to warn my friends and my brother.

Jumping on the closest train and ducking into one of the cabins inside. Sliding the door across and going to lock it when I found there wasn't a knob. Sliding it enough to check the other side. No knob but there was a strange keyhole.

I shut the door again and called to Fujin. Feeling the wind building around me as he came out. Wings tucked away in the cramped space. "You called?"

"Yeah, are you able to slip to the other side and lock the door?"

"Not a problem." Seeing the wisps of wind shifting against the door. Slipping through the little gap where it met the wood. Waiting and hearing the slide of the lock. Then Fujin came back through. "Done. Is there anything else?"

"Not for now, thank you very much."

"As you wish." Feeling the power slipping inside my body. My wing tattoos going cold for a second. Now alone I slumped back onto the comfy seat. Breathing in and out. Thinking about the little kid that I needed to stop.

Thoughts of how to stop her weren't coming fast. None at all in fact. Blowing out a frustrated breath. Thinking about my own titans. Some of them took some big hits. Fujin seemed okay and there was no talking to the fin covered titan.

Thinking about the fire within and calling to Kit. The warmth flooding the air as the light appeared. The fur being conjured into a body. He plopped onto the chair opposite me. Eyes peering to me before he turned around. Curling up into a small ball.

"Kit?"

"You told me you would never put me in a life or death position."

My heart twinging with that promise. "Yeah, I did. But I didn't have a choice. We needed to stop that kid and that titan. They're out of control."

"That didn't work out so well, did it?"

"No it didn't but we needed to try."

"It wasn't we. It was you. You're in charge but you promised." Reaching over Kit flinched as my fingers touched his warm fur. Curling up even more, then his tail came out and flicked against my hand. "You broke your promise." His head was lifted. Seeing a bright white ember trickling down from his eye.

"I'm sorry."

"That's not good enough."

"I don't know what else to say."

"Then there isn't anything more to talk about. Please, send me back. I don't want to be out here."

"Fine." Bringing Kit back into my heart. That flush of heat reminding me of the first time we had met and talked. Felt so long ago despite only being earlier this week. Finding myself alone in the cabin.

The train giving off a soft puff of steam as it pulled out of the station. Watching the city out of the window. Changing to some nice scenery. The land stretching for miles around. Fields with hills in the distance.

Watching as we passed barns and farmland. Footsteps coming from the little corridor. Then the door was tugged, rattling as the lock kept it from being opened. A mumble came from the other side before the steps moved on. Hearing something about tickets as the next compartment was opened.

Happy that my plan had worked, even more so when we pulled into the first stop. A platform just outside a little town. A big wooden sign with the name in white, Nufftown. Calling to Fujin again I was released from the compartment and I quickly jumped off to the platform.

No turnstiles or anything to stop me. Walking with the minimal foot traffic and stopping just outside the town. A small cafe sitting close by which had the smell of freshly baked goods. My stomach grumbling which I had to ignore.

About to start a little walk until I was alone. But a calling to my heart had me stopping in my tracks. Holding there for a moment as I listened for it again. Like those tugs I felt before. Looking into town. The street heading all the way between the two rows of buildings. Stopping at a large tavern with a wooden sign hanging above the door.

But it wasn't coming from there. Somewhere down on the right. Walking, shifting past market stalls outside of houses. Ignoring the way they called to me. Trying to shift their goods at "amazing" prices.

Coming to stop in front of a pharmacy run by a doctor if the sign in the window was anything to go by. Instead of joining the end of the queue I headed down the alleyway between buildings.

Hearing some people chatting out the back. Pressing my ear to the wooden slats that made up the fence. The chatter coming to a close, a door opening and closing. Then there was silence. Trying the knob I found the gate was locked.

So I built up my wind magic, thinking about how D had saved me. Thrusting my palms down and shooting it out like jets. Lifting up, my heart catching in my throat as my foot caught the top of the fence.

Rolling over in the air and hitting the ground hard. Dirt all sloppy and thick splashed into my face. Groaning as I rolled over. Wiping it away and spitting some of it out. "Great, just what I need."

Climbing onto my feet, looking at the mess I was covered in. Annoyed that my clothes were going through some rough patches this week. Flicking the thick slop from my hands. Then I looked up, seeing the cages piled on top of cages.

Animals and monsters of all kinds being held. Looking closely I could see pieces had been cut out. Tufts of fir missing. The one that was calling to me was in the corner by the back door. Crouching down to the little cage.

A small ball of fluff sat in the middle. It seemed to be intact unlike the others. "Excuse me."

As soon as I spoke it jumped into the air. The ball coming open and revealing the titan within. A small little creature no longer than my forearm. Looking like a weasel but with softer features.

The fur looking rough to touch like a hedgehog, all brown apart from the strip of black running down from the back of its head to the tip of its slick tail. The little paws looked like they should end in a long claw. Only all four had been snipped off, leaving a little bump of nail.

Dark eyes watched me, as my fingers neared

the cage. The thing let out a bark like a dog. A cute little animal but I've learnt recently that looks aren't everything. Swallowing past that lump growing in my throat. Those little eyes studying me. It snarled and barked again, this time I didn't move.

For a moment it tilted its head left, then right. The little creature moving forwards cautiously. Sniffing the air before raising its head. Feeling that call to my heart so strongly I couldn't be mistaken. My whole body jumped when the door to the shop suddenly swung open. Cracking against the brick work with a loud thud.

Turning to see a man standing there. A dirty vest top that used to be white clung to his obese body. So much sweat covering his face that his moustache was glistening with it. A voice came out of his mouth that had me wishing I had access to a shower. "What's a young girl doing sniffing around our stuff?"

I took a step back from the cages, noticing the little animal had its teeth bared towards this man. "You shouldn't have all these animals caged up like this."

"And what are you going to do about it?"

"You shouldn't judge a book by its cover." Bringing the lightning magic to my hands. Balling it up between them before letting it fly. The bolt pinging off towards the man who just stood there. Laughing as I shot that spell at him.

CHAPTER 18

Thinking this was too easy until it struck him. Seeming to hit him but it bounced off, coming straight for me. Having to dive sideways. The bolt hitting the fence with a crack, wood being exploded in all directions.

I looked at the man from the dirt. Not a single mark on him. Thinking it was just a fluke I pulled on my fire. Getting up and launching a ball at him. This time when the spell struck it burst out into flames. Erupting up into the air, the brightness making me shield my eyes. "How is that possible?"

"We're not as thick as we look." The man was joined by similarly dressed friends. Looking as dirty as he did. "We've been studying creatures our whole lives. Even some titans when we can get our hands on them." He kicked the little cage with that weasel creature inside. The thing barking back. "Do you think it believes its a dog? Or is it just some kind of weird titan thing." The man kicked the cage again.

"Hey, stop that!"

A grin showed off gaps in his yellow teeth. "Make me." His foot smacking against the cage for a third time. I blew out a breath, looking down at the ground. Noticing a piece of the fence that had been struck by lightning sitting by my foot. A length of wood that I could easily wrap my fingers around.

Bending over I picked it up, testing the weight in my palm and liking it. "Is the little girl going to hit us with her stick?" Another of the men speaking up, sounding just as horrible as the first.

"She says we shouldn't judge a book by its cover."

"Damn straight you shouldn't." Bursting into a run, heading for them. Each one looking surprised but none of them looking worried. That was until I rammed the end of my stick into the throat of the closest man. Dropping him to the floor. Carrying on with my attack as he coughed and sucked down air.

The middle man swung a knife at me. I ducked back, hitting him twice in the ribs with each end of my weapon. The third I swung up into his jaw. The man falling back with a grumble. The knife being dropped to the floor.

As the third came for me, I kicked the knife across the mud. Feeling fingers clutching through my hair, yanking my head at an odd angle. A fist crashing into my face. Feeling blood shooting out of my nose.

Gritting my teeth I tried to ignore the pain, my vision darkening from the hit. Using the stick I jabbed it up into his armpit. Two more times before he let go. One end smacking his jaw, then swinging around the other to hit him in the neck.

A third strike in the next second, bringing it up between his legs so hard the wood snapped in half. His face screwing up. Teetering back and forth for a moment before dropping down to his knees.

Happy that whatever it was protecting them didn't stop physical attacks or pain. They wouldn't be down for long and they could be joined by more men. Quickly moving to the cages and unlocking them.

Some of the animals attacking the three men who couldn't do much to stop them. Teeth and claws ripping into clothing. Coming up to that little cage, the weasel creature watching me. As my fingers went to the latch I was surprised the thing didn't bark or try and bite me.

In fact, once the cage was opened it quickly scampered up my arm. I danced back watching it, feeling its feet climbing over my sleeve. Coming to stop on my shoulder.

Standing weirdly to keep an eye on it. "Um.....can I help you?"

"You're one of them, aren't you? Me and my brothers talked about being found by one of you."

"Your brothers?"

"They killed them." The black eyes glistening like it was about to cry. "They cut off my claws and then tested things on me. Quickly they found out what I was capable of. That I was a titan."

"What are you capable off?"

"This." It shut its eyes and rubbed its nose against mine. Pain pulsing all over my face but I didn't move. Feeling the bristly fur of this creature on my neck. When it pulled back I still felt the pain. Up until those eyes opened. A flash of yellow in that black and my nose snapped back into place.

Wriggling it and stretching my mouth. No more pain like it had never happened. "That's amazing. Thank you."

"You don't have to thank me. You freed all of us. I'm yours now, your titan." Those eyes closed again but this time the creature started to vanish. Having seen this a few times already now I waited. Watching a yellow light running over that stripe on his back.

Feeling tattoos marking the side of my neck as the titan vanished. Feeling it being printed in my skin. Running my fingers over it and thinking about the titan. Having it come back with a flash of that same light I saw in its eyes.

The titan appearing on the floor but quickly coming back up my body to sit on my shoulder. "I'm Crystal, or Crys."

"I don't really have a name. I'm a Kama Itachi."

"Then I'll call you Kam."

"What should we do with these men?"

Watching as two of them started to climb to their feet. Swiping their fists at the animals attacking them. "Can you knock them out?"

"A physical attack. That I can do." Kam leapt from my shoulder towards the ground. Before its paws touched dirt a yellow light ran down that black stripe. Then he split into three. Him and his brothers landing and running towards our enemies.

Seeing the claws that had been clipped were back. Two inches long on each paw. Twelve in total all ready to attack. Watching for the first few seconds as they arrived at their targets. Leaping through the air and then blood was being spilt.

Turning my back on the scene as I didn't want to watch. Seeing the fence that had been hit with my spell. A big enough gap for us and the animals to escape. Moving to it, crouching and slipping through.

Whistling to attract their attention. Waving them over and out to freedom. Animals running in all directions as they fled. Giving another whistle, "Kam!"

"Coming." The three weasels jumped from the

men. Seeing that the cuts looked bad but none of them were seriously injured. They stayed on the floor groaning, not moving a single inch. Happy that my order to hurt them hadn't been done in a bad way.

Kam jumped into the air, bodies shifting into one before he got to me. His body shifting out of sight with the yellow glow, the tattoo giving off a little itch. Rubbing my fingers over my neck, smiling as I fled the scene as well.

The place didn't look like it had a presence of law. Which meant these guys could exact their revenge. So I ran up the hill. Coming out into the vast land of fields my feet kept me moving.

Not stopping until I was a safe distance from town. One last look then I called to Fujin. That kick of air before I felt the wisps wrapping around my body. Letting my titan take me up into the air and we journeyed.

Using the elevation to navigate back to the school. Coming down outside, the breeze had knocked most of the dirt from my clothes. Feeling Fujin disappear into those wing tattoos as I walked into the lobby. Not a clue what time it was. Peering into the cafeteria but it was empty. No lights were on, no food being prepared. Turning back around, not hearing a single noise from anywhere. Moving up towards the elevator and making my way back to my room. The door sliding open and finding D and Flo there.

Stopping as my eyes took in Flo wearing a gorgeous black dress. The hem just above her knee. Cleavage on display. She spotted my look and posed, sticking out her hip with her hand on it. "Like what you see?"

"Yeah. You could say that." She came walking over, swaying her hips seductively. "The mud is an interesting look."

Blowing out a frustrated breath. "I'm getting really annoyed at the situations I'm getting in." Trying to clean my hands a little but it just spread it more. "Look, about earlier, with William. There isn't anything going on."

"I may have over-reacted. In the past there were other girls, with Larsh. She swore nothing was going on. It's just a trust thing."

"I get it."

"Good."

D turning around after clipping the front of her dress up to her cleavage. Seeing the line of scaly skin on show all the way to her belly button. "You're just in time. Get a dress on."

"Ready for what?"

"The party."

Flo ran her hands through her short black hair. "Yeah, was thinking of asking you to be my plus one."

Smiling at Flo who was flashing her teeth. "That sounds amazing except for one thing. There's going to be an attack on the party. You guys can't go."

"It's mandatory. They're going to give out the results for the elite teams there."

"You need to stay here. It's too dangerous."

"What are you going to do?" Flo touched her hand to my arm. "You're going aren't you?"

"I have to stop that thing."

"Then you'll need help."

"No."

"Yes." Both of them replying. Looking from D to

Flo. Both pulling an unmovable expression. "You can't change our minds. If you're going, we're going with you. To help."

My mouth opening to object but my eyes kept flicking between them. Seeing those expressions. "But….it's dangerous."

"You're not very good at arguing, are you?" Pulling a face at D.

"D's right, you're extremely bad at it."

"You to?" Annoyed at them both but Flo pulled a cute smile, rolling my eyes at her. "God, you two. So annoying."

"Friends can be quite annoying."

"Fine, alright. Since there's no changing your minds."

"Great. Now, pick out a dress. I'll help you get changed if you like."

Biting my lip as I listened to Flo's words. Looking into her eyes. They seemed to sparkle when she smiled. "I don't actually own a dress."

"I would offer one of mine but we're not exactly the same build."

Looking over to D, seeing her broader shoulders. "Not exactly."

"But we are. I'll go grab one, it'll fit you perfectly. Wait here." Off Flo ran in her dress. Looking so excited at the prospect of me dressing up.

D laughing as she kept making sure her dress looked good. "Never seen her so excited."

"It's cute."

"It certainly is. Be interesting when we get to the party and Larsh sees the two of you."

"Not like I have enough to worry about. I need to

warn my brother about the party."

"I'm sure he's getting ready as well. He passed all his tests with high scores. He's expecting to hear great news tonight."

Watching her as she spoke. Seeing the little smile she was pulling as she checked her dress. "Why are you smiling like that?"

"Huh?"

"Smiling, when you talk about my brother."

"Flo has her plus one. I have mine."

"You and my brother?"

"Is that a problem?" Getting a worried look.

"Why the hell would it be a problem.? You two would make a great couple. He needs someone who can kick as much arse as he can."

D giggled. "I'm really happy you don't have a problem with this."

"Of course. He's lucky to have someone like you interested in him. Usually it's the bimbos that he attracts."

"I'm definitely not a bimbo."

"Oh god no. Stubborn and willing to walk into danger. But never a bimbo."

The room filling with laughter. "Do you have a plan, to stop this monster?"

"Not exactly. And the monster isn't the only thing we need to worry about. The president of the school. This group he's a part of. They're target is to kill all titans. He's using me to collect them. That's why the others are all dead. Because the titan dies with their host."

"That's awful. And you're going to walk right into this mess?"

"I haven't got a choice. Only I can stop the shadow."

"When you figure out how."

"Exactly."

"The train will be here in…." She lifting up her watch. "Twenty minutes. And it'll take another twenty to get us there."

"Forty? That's plenty of time. Hopefully."

The door sliding open and Flo came in holding a red dress over her forearm. "Ta da. You're going to look amazing in this."

Taking it from her and holding it up. The top would be a tight fit, lines of material swooping to the left hip. Then the dress flared out a touch. Draping to a slit that would run down my left leg. Noticing straps holding the two sides together for the most part.

"You're right, think this will look amazing. Why didn't you wear this one?"

"I was feeling like wearing black today."

"Well it was a good decision." Giving her a quick look before turning around. Feeling my cheeks flushing red.

Flo looking just as nervous as I felt. "It also comes with this." She pulled out a long piece of red fabric. "It'll cover up your tattoos perfectly."

"Even better." I took the dress, the wrap and my toiletries to the showers. Getting rid of all that muck and revitalising myself. Feeling refreshed as I slipped on the dress.

Checking myself out in the mirror. Loving how my thigh looked with the straps sitting across it. Happy that I didn't have much up top since that part of the dress was very snug. Grabbing handfuls of my curly hair and putting it up in a red clip.

Messing with it until it looked great, then I noticed the tattoos on my neck. Three little paw prints. Smiling as I thought about the little Kama. Looking at myself in the mirror. Unclipping some of my hair and letting it hang over my neck. Covering up those paw prints. Giving myself a final check before putting my necklace back on. Carrying a bit of my mum with me.

Heading back to the room. Entering I took in their expressions. Jaws gaping open which quickly turned to smiles. "Damn, I'm a little envious. I never look as good as you do in that dress."

My cheeks going bright red as she kept looking at me. Biting my bottom lip as I turned. "I couldn't reach the zip."

Feeling a hand gently grazing up my spine which made me shiver. Freezing as her touch stopped between my shoulder blades. Then a gentle finger ran over my skin. Tracing the lines of my wings. "These look really cool."

"Thanks. I got a new one." My fingers going to my neck. Feeling hers joining them. Nudging together and sending jolts of electricity through my hormones.

"They're cute."

My fingers entwined with hers and I twisted around. Finding her closer than I thought. Eyes on eyes. Finding myself licking my lips as they suddenly felt dry. "Flo."

"Crys." Those lips of hers curling into a killer smile. My knees feeling a little weak. Leaning forwards, my breath catching quicker until there was a cough.

Both of us looking over to where D was waiting. "Are we leaving? Or do you two need a minute to yourselves?"

My cheeks flaring up in embarrassment. Flo stuck her middle finger up at her but with a giggle. "Let's get going then. We don't want to be late for the dangerous party."

"It's no joke, you two. You'll both do what I say once we're there. Right?"

"Depends if you tell us to leave or help."

"Alright, alright. I get it."

"There's no getting rid of us." Rolling my eyes with a smile. Pulling a pair of red trainers from my wardrobe. "You're wearing trainers with that dress?"

"I don't do high heals and I don't want to break my ankles when fighting."

"Makes sense I guess." Slipping them on before Flo grabbed my hand. Looking down then up into her eyes. Feeling that spark between us flashing again.

"Might even get a dance before the danger happens."

"Yeah?" Watching her tongue run across her bottom lip. D coughing before I could lean in. "Perhaps we can try this when we're alone."

"I'd like that, a lot." Flo letting out her little giggle.

On the way down the elevator stopped here and there. Picking up other people all dressed up for the party. Dresses of all styles and colours. Boys wearing nice shirts and trousers. Some even wearing suits which included my brother. Finding him waiting in the lobby for D.

He looked quite smart and handsome. Lance got a huge hug from my room mate. Then he placed a kissed to her cheek. Wondering how he found it so easy whereas I could barely think straight when Flo looked at me.

"Looking good, brother."

"Me? This is the first time I've seen you in a dress. I'm guessing that its not yours."

"Its mine." Flo bouncing a little on her toes. Feeling her hand cupping against mine tighter.

Lance's eyes dropping to it, seeing the little smile tugging at the corner of his lips. "All three of you look amazing. Really amazing."

Smirking as he gave D a lust-filled look. Hands moving and a flower was pulled from his sleeve like a magic trick. Only it wasn't made from cloth. A rose in full blossom. White contrasting with her black dress. "This is for you."

"Wow. Aren't I the lucky one." She took it and slid it between two of her horns on the side of her head. Looking even more beautiful. Seeing the looks they gave each other. Wondering how long they had been flirting with each other. "Lance, I've got something to tell you on the train."

"Anything I should be worried about?"

"Yes but I'm sure like these two, you won't listen to me saying you need to stay here."

"I feel I would be in more trouble if I suddenly stood up my date."

"Yes, you would." D playfully grabbing his suit jacket and pushing him towards the exit. We followed, laughing as we went. Getting on the train and finding a group of four seats together. Once everyone was on board the train moved from its resting spot.

I filled my brother in what was going to happen tonight at the party. Sharing my knowledge on what was going on behind closed doors. The group the president was a part of and what they wanted. Telling all three of them about the little girl I chatted to. What they were up to in that secret facility.

By the time we arrived at the city they knew everything but we still couldn't come up with a plan. Anything that was mentioned had already been tried when I failed or sounded like a terrible idea. Including Lance's, that I should sit down and have a chat with the thing.

The train arrived just outside the city. Coming out onto a platform made out of wood. The thing put here just for the arrival of Kilroy's guests. Positioned just outside the gates of his monumental property.

Massive black gates opened up. All the students making there way up with teachers dotted about, making sure we all behaved and stayed on the trail. The gardens were bigger than my old village. Big bushes cut into animals.

The whole place looking like a garden zoo. Then there was the mansion at the end of the walkway. The largest building I had ever seen. Looking like a stately home from the country. Not a residence so close to the capital city.

Red bricks, bright white window frames. Trees covered in fir needles towering around the building. Balconies all over the top floor. The perfect place for someone with too much money to reside.   Spotting guards all over the place. Suits walking around with machine guns dangling off their shoulders.

Moving through the entrance. Coming into the lobby which was the size of the school's. A grand staircase ahead of us. Red carpet everywhere. The walls covered in flowery wallpaper. Pieces of furniture that would cost more than my home. So much money dripping everywhere it made me hate Godfrey Kilroy.

It was easier to feel that hate knowing what they were doing behind closed doors. Trying to destroy all those titans out there. Seeing first hand that they weren't just monsters. People only thought that because of the propaganda the group was creating.

If the truth got out then people would change their minds. They could live with the titans in peace. Even help each other out. I needed to find someone who was important, someone that would be listened to. But first we needed to survive what was going to happen tonight.

The line of kids moving through into a massive ball room. Soft music coming from the string band in the corner. My shoes tapping over the dark hardwood flooring. A bar stretching across the wall. As well as two bartenders there were waiters walking around with trays. Trying to understand how someone can live like this when there are others out there not able to scrape together a meal.

The room getting filled with all of us. Standing with my friends. Lance and D were too busy looking into each others eyes. Flo was looking around at the room. Staring up at the gold chandelier that dominated the ceiling.

My eyes were more focused on the people. Noticing adults hanging at the bar. Seeing the pins on their collars and dresses. They weren't at the meeting but they were part of the group. A voice coming out over the speakers.

Every single head turning to the small stage. The

band had stopped playing and William's father was up there with a microphone. "Welcome to you all. It is our pleasure to open our home to you all. To celebrate what the school is accomplishing. Creating these elite teams to help the government in all manner of avenues."

The man started clapping and so did the rest of the adults. Kids smiling and cheering. "All of you can't be at the top of your classes. However, you will all come away from the school with talents you would have never possessed. You can use these talents to further good fortune in your future. Join a police force. The army. Or just use it to grow into a gifted adult."

A tray was brought to him. A single glass of champagne which was lifted into the air. "Obviously, we're not supplying under-aged kids with alcohol tonight. However the bar is fully stocked with all kinds of drinks. I hope you enjoy the party and I will leave you in peace until the scores get announced. So enjoy yourselves, have fun. Dance and have an amazing night. You will all remember this for the rest of your lives. Cheers."

A call of cheers ran through the crowd as Mister Kilroy took a sip of the expensive drink. The band started up again and the room was filled with music. Like a gun starting a race everyone began moving.

Dancing as the music picked up pace. Some heading for the bar to grab drinks. Lance told us he would grab enough for us all. Pulling D and Flo close. "I can't believe they've brought everyone here."

"Crys, calm down. You said yourself that they have defences right? Look at this place. I think we might actually be safe."

"Maybe." Looking around the massive ball room.

One room in the plethora of rooms this man possessed. "Maybe you're right but I still need to look for something. To stop this group."

"Can't you stay. I wanted a dance."

Looking into her puppy dog eyes. Seeing her bottom lip sticking out. "Don't pull that face. That's so unfair."

"Then stay and it'll go away and be replaced with a smile." Laughing as she pulled a massive grin. "See. I know you prefer this face."

"I do." Biting my bottom lip, looking into those eyes. "This is something I need to do. And if I can accomplish it quickly. I'll be right back to have that dance. I promise."

"Alright then, I'm going to hold you to your promise."

"Sounds like a deal to me."

"How are you going to find what you need?"

"There must be an office around here somewhere."

"Sure, as well as multiple other rooms."

My eyes picking out William's face through the crowd. Seeing him surrounded by a crowd of girls. All looking at him with starry eyed expressions. No doubt more at his wealth than him as a person. "I'll find someone who lives here. I'll be back."

"I'll be waiting."

"Good." Giving D a quick look. "You two look after each other. And if trouble hits before I return, follow my brother. He's got the leadership qualities after all."

"Good luck."

Turning and heading through the crowd. Aiming towards William but getting stopped halfway there. A hand turning me around and coming face to face with that chubby bully. His ginger hair gelled to the side. "Troy?"

"Crystal. I'm surprised you showed up after the beating you took from me."

"I'm surprised they allowed you to come along to the party. I was told you would be kicked out."

"My date brought me along." Troy turned and nodded over to one of his friends. "I wasn't about to miss you not being picked for the elite teams."

"What makes you think I care about the elite teams?"

"I saw how you were. How much you tried in class. All those special favours from the president and you still couldn't make it happen."

I laughed. "You still believe those rumours? That the president has a little special spot for me?"

"How else would you explain it?"

"Did you ever hear the rumour that I wasn't human?"

He scoffed. "Of course, everyone did. No one is stupid enough to believe it. The everfae are all killed and sorry but you don't look like one of them."

"So reliant on everyone else's ideas. You should start thinking for yourself. Come up with your own beliefs."

"What are you on about?"

Flicking my curls from my neck, showing him the paw prints. "Where do you think these tattoos come from? There isn't a parlour at the school."

His eyes took in the magical ink I now possessed. "There were plenty of times you were disappearing. Could have gotten them then."

"Nope." Leaning in, fingers wrapping around his shirt. "They come from titans. I am half-everfae. And I don't need these elite teams. I have a much bigger cause. And the fact you'll be heading back to your ordinary life after the party is just icing on the cake."

"I don't believe your lies."

"Finally, your own belief. Keep it up and you'll have two of them. Have fun at the party. Try not to get yourself into trouble. I might not be able to safe you."

Nudging into him as I moved on. Getting to William and having to push through the crowd to grab his attention. Many annoyed looks flashed my way. "Can I have a word with you, William? If I can tear you away from your adoring fans."

"I guess." William gave out apologies and made his way to me. I grabbed his hand and dragged him out of the ball room. The music much quieter out in the lobby. "Why are you dragging me about?"

"I need some help."

"Why would I help you?"

"That's a good question and if I told you the truth you won't believe me."

"So I can go back to the party right? I have plenty of friends wanting to dance with me."

"You know they're only interested in your money. Your family's money, that is. If you didn't live in such a waste of money like this place. None of them would look at you twice."

"It's cute that you're worried about me."

"I'm definitely not worried."

"I see." I was studied for a second. "Why do you think I'm naive? I've grown up with money. With people running around me for attention. Hoping that being my friend will mean they have a better life. Girls showing me affection just because they want to live in a mansion. Believing becoming my girlfriend will involve fancy gifts. Expensive jewellery. Also the parties and the other fancy people they get to meet."

"You know this and you still eat up their attention?"

"Even when it's fake, it's still very enjoyable."

"That's despicable."

"Yeah but it's part of my life. I'm always going to have people like that buzzing around. Why not enjoy it?"

"So as long as both of you are being used, it's okay?"

William let out a laugh, "Exactly. Now what help do you need?"

"Never mind. You're just as shallow as I first thought."

"Hey now. That hurts my feelings, you know."

"You have feelings?"

"Just like everyone else. Didn't I apologise to you?"

"You did."

"So maybe that little hint of humanity warrants a little trust. Try me."

Blowing out a sigh, looking back into the room of dancing students. "Alright. You can't ask me why but I need to find your father's office."

"For?"

"That's asking me why."

"It is, because I want to know."

Feeling like giving him a swift kick to the shin. "I need to find something about a group he's involved with. They're not good people."

"That's not much of a reason for me. I need more."

Seeing how he looked at my arm. His stare moving over Kit's tattoo. Up to the little paw prints on my neck. He knew about my titans already but the way he was looking. Seemed he knew more. "Do you know something?"

"Something? About what?"

"About everfae and titans."

"Maybe."

"How?"

"Let me show you." Up the stairs he led me. Moving along the corridor. Massive paintings hanging on the walls. Some just for the way it looked. Others had family members of William's. Looking noble in their expensive clothes.

"Where are we going?"

"To my father's office."

"Oh." We came across a door. William punched in a code then used his thumb print to gain access. Walking in I was gobsmacked by the furniture. A desk sat against the wall. The wood was veined with gold. Weird little statues ran up the legs.

A mirror covered the other side of the room. Paintings and antiques sat on stands. Things that he brought just for the value. The owner's son walked to one of the paintings. He was sitting there in front of his father and who I assumed was his mother. They looked happy or maybe they were just painted that way. "I didn't see your mum at the party."

"That's because she's dead." My breath catching as he told me, like it was a simple fact. No hint of sadness about it. "Five years ago."

"How?"

"We were on holiday. Camping. Back when my father did things like that. Out in the woods we had the usual bodyguards. A whole team of them to make sure the area was safe. One night a creature attacked our tent."

"What kind of creature?"

"I don't know. All I remember were the teeth. How the tent looked after it was killed. My mum laying there covered in blood." He couldn't hold back any longer and balled his eyes out. Sobbing uncontrollably. Not sure what to do, placing a hand to his shoulder. "My father shut off after it happened. Spent all his time in this room or at work. Blaming titans for the attack."

"Was it definitely a titan?"

"No clue." William sniffed, wiping his eyes. "I've looked into it myself. Looked through the reports my father has. No one knew for sure. His hatred for them is what drives him now. There's no wavering from his mission to kill them all."

"You don't blame them?"

"Even if it was a titan, what the hell was it supposed to do? They're wild animals at the end of the day."

"Not all of them."

Glistening eyes lifting to mine. "Can I meet one of them? Properly I mean."

Nodding with a soft smile. "Sure. This little guy is probably best." Breathing and thinking about the little critter. The fin tattoo on my body itching as he appeared by my feet.

Bending over and picking him up. Giving his chin

a little scratch as it looked up at me. "Wow, that's so cool that it comes out of nowhere."

"It is pretty cool. They're all different. I have one, Kit I call him, who comes out in this bright light."

"That's amazing." William reached out cautiously. Rubbing his own fingers under the chin. Seeing him relax as my titan did nothing but enjoy it. "This is why my father is wrong. They're not all killing machines."

"They aren't. So will you help me look for something. This group he's involved with. Him and the president of the school. It's bad news for titans."

"Last time I was snooping on his computer I found some files. Something about experiments."

"That's perfect. If I can prove that they have been experimenting on little kids."

"Wait, little kids? You don't think he's been doing that, do you?"

Biting my lip, still seeing that sadness. "I've seen it first hand. That's exactly what they're doing in their facilities."

"Here." William moved over to the computer on the desk. A quick fingerprint scan and it pinged to life. Watching as his fingers tapped the buttons. Windows coming up, programs being ran. The password box getting filled automatically.

"Where did you learn to do this kind of thing?"

"Lots of money and lots of time on my hands. You'd be surprised the kind of people you can hire to teach you things." Watching the screen but not really understanding what was happening. Assuming he was breaking into his father's files.

Judging by how long it took there were many

layers of security to get through. The time going on until his fingers stopped moving. William hit enter and a thing popped out of the tower by his feet. "What's that?"

"All the secure files I could find. This is all the evidence you need."

"I can stop that group from hurting any more titans. This is fantastic." Leaping into a hug which caught him by surprise. Feeling his body tense but then relax. Arms coming around me and returning the gesture. "Thank you so much."

"No worries."

Pulling back and seeing his look. Wondering if it was the sadness from his mother's story or something else. "Are you okay doing this? Your father is going to get into a lot of trouble for all this."

"He needs to wake up and realise that there's a life without my mum. He needs to realise that I'm still here. His obsession is robbing him of his soul. I've tried many times already to show him this. This is the only way."

"You sure?"

"Yeah, I'm sure. I know that he's not the only member of this group. They all need to answer for their actions."

"You're a smart kid."

"I know." Laughing but my joy was cut off with the sounds of footsteps. Two sets coming towards the door. We didn't move until we heard the buttons on the keypad being pressed. William shut off the computer then we hurried out onto the balcony.

Shutting the doors quietly just as the office was opened. Peeking where the curtains met the wall. Mister Kilroy came walking in followed by another man.

Hearing the voices through the thin glass. "Is it done?"

"Yes, sir. We moved the transmitter to Mister West's car. When he flees the building to escape the attack the titan will follow him."

"Good. That will teach him to switch off my defences. Thinking he can double cross me. His death will cement my position with the group. Then we can really move forward with our plans."

"Yes, sir."

"Make sure the guests stay in the ball room. None of them can come to harm."

"Why not just turn the defences back on." The guard getting a stare from the man of the house. "Sorry, sir. I'll keep my thoughts to myself."

"Good, you don't get paid to think. Now keep an eye on that traitor. I don't want any more surprises."

The man held a finger to his ear piece. "Sir, the titan has been spotted."

Mister Kilroy came out onto the balcony. Staring off over the massive gardens out the front. "Tell all the guards to get inside. No one is to be harmed. The group was promised no one would be hurt."

"Yes, sir." The guard left the room, leaving the three of us on the balcony.

I stepped forwards. "Something wrong?"

The old man turned around, startled. Looking confused when he saw William out here with me. "What are you two doing in my office?"

"Getting evidence. This group you're part of, they're going down. I'll see to it."

"I knew Ethan's little pet project would come to bite us in the arse."

"I'm no one's pet project."

"Oh please. You only know about your true self because he told you."

"That doesn't mean I belong to him. I'm my own person."

William stepped forwards. "Dad, mum wouldn't want you to do this. She wouldn't want you hurting people."

"What lies has she been telling you, son?"

Godfrey stepped towards his kid but William retreated. "I've been through your computer. I know everything."

"You must understand. Those things can't be trusted. They're monsters."

"The only monster here is you and your friends. Titans have a right to live."

A tear falling from his eye, "You know who had a right to live? Your mother. My wife. She didn't deserve to be ripped apart. We didn't deserve to lose her. I know you feel that piece of life missing. Like a hole in a jigsaw puzzle. Our lives aren't complete with her missing."

"I have two pieces missing. When I lost her, I lost you as well. Can't you just come back to me. Be the father you were before."

"It's too late for that. I do this to honour her life."

"You're doing nothing but honouring her death. Making it a part of our lives. She wouldn't want you to do this and neither do I. That's why we're going to stop you."

The man's eyes flicked past us to the computer. "You stole my files?"

My fingers gripping around that flash drive. "We did. And we'll release them to the government. They'll stop you."

"Give it to me, now!" Kilroy stomped forwards but I saw something over his shoulder. A large shape sent up into the air. It wasn't the shadow titan but it was coming this way. Diving for William and sending us both to the floor as the projectile came plummeting towards the house.

CHAPTER 19

Hearing the brickwork being struck. The heavy object smashing straight through and tumbling out the other side of the building. As I looked I saw that the ballroom hadn't been hit. Jumping up and looking through the destruction.

It was one of the train cars. Looking back to where we disembarked and saw another shape coming through the air. "Get down!" Shoving Mister Kilroy to the floor and joining them. The mansion shaking as another part was destroyed. "We need to get everyone out of here."

"No, this is the safest place."

I looked at the two holes in the building. "You're kidding right?"

"Ethan will flee. He's a coward. This thing will follow him."

"We can't just redirect it. It needs to be stopped."

"It'll be killed by the forces inside the city."

"Stopped, not killed. That's just a little kid who you experimented on. It's not her fault. I'm the only one who can stop her."

"You'll just be killed. That was actually Ethan's plan. Two birds with one stone."

"I'll just have to disappoint him. Where's his car?"

"Why?"

"You had your man put the transmitter in it, the

one the titan is following. Where is it?"

"Around the back of the mansion. It's a black convertible."

"Protect your son for once in your life and keep everyone safe whilst I steer it clear of the city."

Moving towards the balcony doors William grabbed my arm. "Make sure you stay safe."

Eyes flicking to his dad, then back. Giving him a hug before slipping the flash drive in his pocket. "You to."

Running from the balcony and back into the mansion. The second hit had taken out half of the massive staircase. Having to jump down onto one of the expensive side tables. Hearing the wood cracking and tumbling to the floor.

A little amused that something so expensive was just been broken by me. Heading into the ballroom where the guards were keeping all the students inside. Tapping one on the shoulder. "Where's Ethan West?"

"What? I don't take orders from you."

"I don't care. Tell me where he is."

"Get inside the ball room where it's safe." The man turned just as a fist slammed him in the face. His arm twisted and he was dropped with a kick to the back of leg. The man gritting his teeth through the pain.

Smiling as Holbrook flashed a smile. The same height as the guard who was kneeling. "What the hell are you doing?"

"I knew something was going on. The president is over by the bay windows. Here, I brought you a present."

Something was retrieved from behind his back. Seeing the short piece of wood with those amazing patterns in it. "I'm really going to need that."

"Get going. You can do this. I believe in you."

"Thanks." Fingers wrapping around my weapon as I ran through the crowd. Hearing Flo's voice but telling myself to ignore it for now. To save them I needed to get those keys. Coming out the middle to see the bay windows were open.

Moving out onto a large balcony that ran along the ballroom. Peering over the edge and seeing the president running through the back garden. Heading towards some lights that I guessed was the garage.

Hopping over the edge I ran, my dress kicking up and getting caught on some branches. Holding my hand behind me I pushed out a gust of wind. Feeling it pushing me quicker. Cutting through the gardens quick enough to get to the garage just in time.

The far shutter door was opening up. Hitting the button to my left froze it. Then I started closing it. The president spinning to see me. Seeing him mouth a swear word or two. "What are you doing?"

"Running away from your mess I see."

The man climbed out of his vehicle. "You're going to die tonight. Doesn't matter if its by my hands."

Shocked as he pulled out a gun. A shot ringing around the vast space. Hearing the bullet hit the wall to my right. Diving behind a big toolbox on wheels. Hearing more shots, the metal managing to stop the bullets from killing me.

Pushing the thing along until I could hide behind a jeep. "You don't have to do this."

"The hell I don't. Were you expecting me to keep acting? Pretend I don't know what's going on? Tonight was going to be the end for you anyway and I'm getting sick and tired of you. The others knew how to stay in line. You just can't stop sticking your nose into our business. I know you were at the facility. I know you figured it all out."

"Aren't you afraid I'll stop you?"

"Stop me? Have you not seen what's going on? The whole world will see this attack. The death of my friend will make sure they listen to us. The government will appoint our group at the point of the sword. To eradicate all those titans out there. To make us safe again."

"Why do want to kill them? What happened to you?"

"It wasn't the titans. It was the everfae. My mother was one but I wasn't given her talents. It was my little brother who got them. He was so special to my father. Keeping my mum's legacy alive. Keeping the species going forwards. It made me sick. I was tossed aside. Told I was being difficult. Why couldn't I be more like my brother. Every single day I was reminded that I wasn't special."

"That's your reason?"

"You don't think I'm justified? I bet you were brought up with love and affection. My father treated me like I worked for him. Keep the farm ticking over whilst he gave my brother all the opportunities he needed. He was sent off to learn. Giving chance after chance for a better future. I was just expected to take over from my father when he passed."

"Your father loved you."

"No, I was just a replacement for him. But when I killed him the farm went under. His legacy was over and all I had to do was stop my mother's."

"You killed your brother as well?"

"I did. And it was the happiest I've ever felt. So I kept going. Researching and finding more like you and him. Killing them and that's when they found me. DEATH brought me in and gave me a home. Honed my purpose."

"You're just a murderer. How many have you killed?"

"Too many to keep count." Feeling the ground shaking as that shadow titan grew closer to the mansion. "Now I'm going to kill one more."

Hearing more gunfire fill the room. The jeep getting hit until it stopped. Hearing the clip dropping to the floor. "I hate violence but for you I'll make an exception." Coming out around the vehicle. Swiping the weapon from his hands with my short staff.

Dropping under a swinging first and hitting the middle button. It shot open hitting him in the jaw. The bone snapping on impact. Sending him flying into a tumble. The concrete stopping his fall with a thud.

I swung the end and slammed it into his face. His eyes dropping closed and his body going limp. Shrinking my weapon and placing it on the passenger's seat as I climbed into the convertible. I had only been on a few lessons with my father. But it would have to be enough. Starting the engine, putting it into drive and shoving my foot down. The wheels spinning then the car lurched into life.

Shooting out of the garage, finding it hard to keep it on the trail. Trampling through bushes until I aimed towards the gates. The sensor picking up the car and opening just enough to fit through. The scrape of metal running down either side.

The wheels picking up better traction as the gravel gave way to tarmac. Following the meandering path towards the city. Looking over my shoulder I saw the darkness coming for me. Leaving the mansion behind and following that transmitter.

Coming to a T-junction and heading right. Wanting to steer clear of the buildings and all those innocent people. I needed to lead this thing away from the population. My heart racing as my fingers gripped the wheel. Seeing the open space past the Kilroy estate.

My eyes lifting up to try and pinpoint this titan when a shape came down in front of me. It was the rest of the train. One of the cars coming loose and dropping quicker. Hitting the road and tilting towards me.

Turning the wheel and just missing it. But the path was blocked as the other cars came crashing down. That shadow leaning over it, a roar kicking up the air around me. Twisting the wheel sharply sent the back end out.

Coming around and pointing me in the other direction. The pedal was mashed and the car shot from danger. Feeling the ground shaking as that thing came for me. Coming so fast, watching it in the rear-view mirror.

The car coming into the outskirts of the city. Hearing the screams of pedestrians as they ran for their lives. Buildings getting hit and demolished. Trying to keep the car going but the traffic started to build up. Slowing down so I didn't crash but that put me in danger.

Feeling the back of the car getting hit by something. As I turned the wild titan lunged forwards. Kicking up the back of the convertible and sending it flying. Spinning through the air as I clung on for my life.

Hearing my weapon drop and hit the windscreen. Getting kicked off into the distance. The car coming to a crashing stop as it hit into a fountain. Water splashing all over me. Feeling pain pulsing through my body but I ignored it.

The ground shaking as the shadow came for that transmitter. Shifting out and standing in the water. Looking up in enough time to see a tentacle of black coming out and slashing across my arm.

Sent into the air, spinning and hitting the fountain top. The marble stopping me dead, dropping back into the water. Crying out in pain. I sat up in the water and leant back. The car being hit and crushed. Water splashing into the air as I watched.

This thing was distracted for a moment. Looking at my arm where it had been hit. There was no blood but my skin was turning black. The titan must have grown more powerful since we last fought.

Calling to the paw prints on my neck, to the titan within. Feeling the little creature plopping into my lap. "What the hell happened to you?" A smash of metal making him look behind. "Holy hell. What's that?"

"My arm. What's happening to it?" Feeling a numbness emanating from the cut. Spreading over my shoulder and down to my fingertips.

"How am I supposed to know?"

"Can you heal me?"

Kam nodded, pawed up to my wound. Rubbing it's nose over it gently. Eyes shutting then that yellow glow when they were opened. Feeling the numbness in my fingers fading. The colour coming back until the slice was repaired. "Anything else?"

"My weapon. It's a short staff. Fell out of the car. Can you find it, it might be in that direction." Pointing where I heard the noise when it was ejected.

"We'll find it." The weasel jumped onto the side of the fountain. A second jump and he split into three before he landed. The trio running off to find my weapon. I climbed to my feet and saw that the car had ripped into two. The thing digging through until a small piece was ripped free.

A spark as it was squashed into nothing. Breathing in deep and thinking about all the emotions I felt. The most powerful being fear. Channelling it down and shooting out a plume of fire. Hitting it like a flamethrower. The force making it stumble back for a moment.

As I kept firing off I called to all the titans. Feeling them all appearing around me in their different ways. Nodding to the fin covered baby. "You, create tunnels underneath. Make the ground unstable. I want to drop this thing deep underground."

There was no reply but it scurried down into the ground before disappearing to call forth it's bigger counterpart. "Kit and Fujin."

"I won't fight that thing again."

Turning to see him cowering behind me. "No, I won't make you. I want you to get everyone to safety. Out of this area."

"Alright."

"As you wish."

Watching the two of them shooting off to follow my orders. "Belemoth. There's a little girl in all that power. Can you look into her mind. Find out what she fears. Maybe I can use that."

"I'll try." The monkey creature shimmered and vanished from site. Leaving me by myself with this thing. The fire starting to fade as I kept pushing. The shadows growing closer until I felt another whipping attack.

I was sent back past the fountain. Crashing through a cafe window. Tables and chairs breaking my fall which caused me even more pain. I looked at the wound on my chest, happy to see the effects of Kam's healing were still in effect.

The darkness starting to spread but it was quickly pushed back to nothing. The cut healing over. The pain still stayed but at least my body would heal. I just had to make sure I didn't die before it could kick in.

Climbing back through the broken glass. Seeing the shadow monster looking around. Whipping out its body, attacking the buildings. Hearing screams as people were directed away from the mayhem. "Hey!" My call bringing the thing towards me. Eyes deep in that black glowing angry. "Belemoth! Any luck yet!"

"No!" I backed away as this thing stomped forwards. Looking down at the ground as I felt the shake. Seeing parts dipping down but it wasn't caving in yet. Like this titan had no weight to it. I had to make sure this thing stayed where it was.

Calling to my lightning magic. Raising my hands to the sky, clouds coming around above. Darkening until I heard that rumble of thunder. Swinging my arms down and calling to the lightning. Hearing it crack through the air. Striking the ground around the shadow.

Concrete erupting into the sky as I kept it coming. The titan looking shocked and worried as it kept recoiling with each bolt. Caging it, trying to hold it there as I cracked the concrete. The tunnels and the spell causing it to cave in.

The crumble of the space being filled with rubble. The titan lunging forwards but the ground underneath vanished. Breathing out as I let the storm pass by. Moving to the edge cautiously. Looking down, impressed with how deep my titan had made it.

I was able to see my enemy moving around but it was so far down. Leaving the hole and running towards the screams. Coming to a group of people who Kit was trying to help. Running my hand over his body. The larger size of him against my shoulder.

"Hey, it's okay. He's trying to help."

"Are you crazy, that thing is dangerous."

"Not to you." Rubbing my hand under Kit's chin. Stroking his hot fur. "You need to get out of here. It's not safe. Grab anyone you find on your way. Get going!"

"Alright, alright." The group scurrying off.

Still stroking Kit. "Make sure they get out safe."

He paused and looked at me. "Sorry for what I said to you."

"It's okay. You had every right to be upset with me."

"But you're my everfae."

"And you're my titan. Which means I look after you."

"And I look after you. I won't forget that part." Feeling his heated fur as he rubbed his head against my shoulder. His tails whipping lightly as he ran off. The glow of his power shining as he sped up.

Turning back towards the hole. "Belemoth?" Getting nothing in return. Looking down, seeing the black coming. Climbing up the rocky walls of the hole. "Belemoth!"

"One sec!" Taking a deep breath. Looking around, checking for any innocents in the way. Feeling a little relaxed when I saw the area was clear.

Then I felt a slash across my chest. Thudding into the ground and skidding away from the hole. My hand going to the pain. Feeling the rip in my dress down my body. Cracking into a car, the wind being knocked out of my lungs.

Rolling onto my side and taking a few deep breaths. Hissing through the pain, waiting for the numbness to stop spreading. That wound healing up but the pain still rolled through my thoughts. Looking up to see the titan climbing out onto the road.

It roared loudly, the air whooshing over my body. Then it came for me. The ground shaking as it came closer. Breathing in, thinking it was the end until I heard scurrying to my right. Looking and seeing Kam and his brothers.

They scampered along, nudging and knocking the staff to each other until it came soaring to me. My hand grabbing it. Rolling out of the way as a shadowy attack smacked the tarmac. Moving around behind the vehicle.

Lodging the staff into a crack, aiming the top towards the underside of the car. Hitting the button and watching as the weapon launched that vehicle. Flying into the shadow and knocking it back. "Belemoth, you finished yet?"

"Yes." Jumping as the monkey like creature appeared next to me. "The little girl inside is afraid of everything. They experimented on her. Made her fear every single thing in the world. She's attacking before she gets attacked. To save herself from the pain she thinks will come if she waits."

"That's just great." Looking over as this thing was ripping apart the car I chucked. Looking back at Belemoth, eyes looking at the bit of his fur where the brand used to be. Where my mother had used the necklace to bind him in safety. "How did my mum do it?"

"Do what?"

I snapped the necklace from around my neck. Showing him the symbol on the front. "She protected you from death. We can do the same for this girl. To keep her safe in a world where it's just her."

"That will work but you have to get close. Heat up the metal and brand the child."

""Which means I need to get through all that power."

"We can distract her. It's your best option."

"I promised Kit I wouldn't put him in danger again."

"You'll have to. We work as a team. All of us, including you. We know this and we respect you for it. You've put yourself in danger for us. It's our turn."

"But I don't want you to."

"That's not your decision. It's ours." He called out the names of my titans. Even calling the little critter I had sent down into the ground. "We're going to distract this thing so Crystal can get inside."

"Inside?" Seeing how worried Kit looked. "Are you crazy?"

"It needs to be done. No arguments. From any of you." My words aimed at Kit more than any of the others. I knew he was more emotional than the others. "We finish this now, we save these people. But we save this innocent girl as well. From any more pain and experimentation. Go, distract it and make sure you all stay alive. Fujin, get me in there."

"As you wish." Feeling the wind wrap around my body. The others shooting off. Some faster than others. The little critter burrowing under ground. Kam and his brothers shouting at the titan like three annoying siblings.

Kit ran out wide and started launching fireballs with those nine tails. Belemoth was shimmering in and out of sight. Appearing in one place then shifting to another. The black titan looking around in confusion. Roaring but not moving.

Fujin lifted me up, feeling the weight of those wings as they flapped. Bringing me into the air. Rising high above the titan, nearing the tops of the skyscrapers before I was tilted forwards.

Taking a deep breath before we dropped. Shooting down like a bolt of lightning. Feeling the air kicking at my dress. Coming to that thing and then hitting it. The black feeling like oil as it slipped over my skin.

Slowing us down but not stopping until I heard crying. Wings kicked out to halt me in the air, the titan's body shifting around the movement. My eyes searched, the black shadows shifting, opening in places and letting me see through.

Catching the glimpse of a little girl at the very centre. Curled up into a tight ball. "Hey!"

"Noooooo!" Her scream making the storm of black around us shrink. Feeling claustrophobic as it clung to my skin and hair. "Get away from me!"

"I'm not going to hurt you! I'm here to help!"

"No!"

"We need to get closer." Feeling the flaps of wings but it was just drifting through the blackness. Nothing pushing us closer. "You need to calm down so I can help you!"

The little girl lifted her eyes, staring at me through the tears. "Help?"

"Yes, help. I'm just like you. Look." Thrusting out my arm, showing her Kit's tattoo. Then turning my head and showing the paw prints on my neck. "I'm just like you."

"You are?" Tear filled eyes dropped to the black tattoo on her hand. "But, you don't look like me."

"Because of what the bad people did to you. But this doesn't have to be all you are. I know you're scared. It's a scary world. But what if I said you could live somewhere safe. A place you don't have to worry about others. You can live in peace."

"I don't know." I reached out but she pulled further away. "No, don't touch me."

"You're going to need to trust me." Moving my arms like I was swimming, pulling myself through that darkness. Getting closer. Reaching out again but this time she screamed. Feeling a pain as something spiked straight through my leg.

There was no leak of blood but that numbness I had felt before spread quickly. With the shadow spike still in my leg, there was no healing. Reaching down but my fingers sifted through it. My whole leg going numb.

Gritting my teeth as I looked back at the girl. "You're going to kill me, do you want that?"

"No! I just want to be left alone."

"As long as you're in this world. You won't be left alone. But I can help. I can take you to a place where no one will touch you again. Please, I promise you. Please." Hearing a yelp from outside the titan.

Recognising it as Kit's. "No, don't hurt them. They're just trying to help me. Stop hurting them, I beg you. You can hurt me but do not harm them. They are even more like you. In a world that will attack and kill them for simply existing."

"They will?"

"Yes, they're in danger just like you. Coming here and helping me try and stop you, to help you. They risk being seen by someone who has power. Someone who will come after them and me. We are all trying to help you."

Big eyes staring at me. Feeling the slip of pain sliding from my leg. The numbness had spread up my body. Happy that that's where it stopped. Kam's healing taking affect. Already feeling better as the shadows around me loosened. Leaving enough space to slip through.

Fingers touching the girl, feeling her cold skin. Finger combing her hair. Feeling the chaos outside of this cocoon calming down. Calling out to my titans. "Come back to me, it's okay."

The surges of power shifting into my body. Looking at the girl as I kept combing her hair. "Look, this next bit is going to hurt. I promise you this will all be okay and I won't do anything until I have your permission."

Waiting, watching her lift those big eyes. A soft nod then they went back down. Her fingers clutching to my dress and arms. Curling an arm around her, the other holding onto that necklace. The pattern that I had seen burnt into Belemoth's skin against my palm.

Breathing steadily as I brought that fire power to my hand. Engulfing it in heat that didn't hurt. Seeing the metal starting to glow as the fire grew powerful. Pushing all my emotions into that one hand.

The spell creating enough heat, turning the necklace around and pressing it to the little girl's nape. Hearing the burn of skin as it branded her. A scream just escaping her lips when suddenly there was nothing but a rush of air.

The black being sucked into my necklace until there was nothing. The emptiness around me such a contrast. Then I dropped. Falling until Fujin caught me with those wings. Gliding me down to the floor. As my feet touched I felt a twinge of pain in my leg. Looking to see the wound hadn't completely closed.

When I had called Kam back inside my heart, it must have stopped the healing. With the attack being a shadow, there was no bleeding. It would heal over time and probably give me a scar. Something to remember the victory in battle I guess.

Standing upright and taking a deep breath. Looking around at the damage that had been created. So much destruction and I knew how that DEATH group would spin this. They had high officials in their midst.

Blowing out a sigh. At least this titan was safe. Putting the necklace back around my neck. Running my finger over the symbol that still held a little heat. There would be consequences for what happened but at least I did what I set out to do. To protect.

Turning to make my way back to the mansion

when I loud bang rung through the air. My eyes going wide as pain hit my shoulder like a train. Wincing as my legs gave way. Dropping to the tarmac.

My lip quivered as the pain pushed through my chest. The feeling in my fingers faded. Looking up with wide eyes as my brain tried to comprehend what had just happened. Seeing the president of the school walking towards me.

His voice sounding like it was coming through layers of brick. "You might have stopped my plan but you'll still die and so will those filthy titans." The gun was raised again. My lips quivering as I tried to think through the pain.

Breathing out a single word, "Fujin." Feeling the wind leaving me with purpose. Watching as the world around me dimmed. The shape standing there with that gun getting caught up by my titan.

Hearing a dull thud as the gun was dropped. A far away scream as he was lifted further into the air. Then he was let go. The shape moving down so fast and stopping when that horrible splat of body parts.

My eyes drifting closed and not re-opening. The sounds of the world around me fading into nothing. Just the darkness in my mind, taking me in, welcoming me to the silence it offered.

CHAPTER 20

The world around me coming back in one shot. Eyes shooting open. Mouth opening wide as I screamed in pain. My arm feeling like it was about to drop off. Feeling bandages sitting around my shoulder. Red starting to spread as pain shot down to my fingers.

I pulled back the bandages enough to see the stitching on the wound. Dry blood getting washed with the new leak. Pressing my hand over it as I surveyed the room I found myself in. It wasn't the infirmary at the school.

Looking out the window I saw the skyscrapers of Collstar. Leaning back in the bed and swallowing down my dry throat. Seeing the water jug and a glass to my right. Cursing the person who put it on my injured side.

Weak fingers grabbed the jug handle but it slipped as I lifted. Sending it off the edge and clanging across the floor. The water spreading out as the door suddenly shot open. Seeing my brother standing there.

His eyes a little red. "Have you been crying?"

"My sister gets shot, what do you expect?"

"A hug?" His feet carried him quickly and I felt his arms holding me. Hearing a soft sniff from his nose. "I'm more capable than you think."

"I'll never doubt that again but you did get shot. You would be dead if it had hit your heart or your head."

"You're right but I'm alright. Nothing you could

have said would have stopped me. It was what I wanted to do. I know now, it's what I need to do. I can protect them."

"People?"

"The titans. They need me."

"There's plenty of time to think that through. Just focus on getting better. I'm going to give dad the good news."

"Is he here?"

"Of course. You've been out for a few days now. He's asleep downstairs in the waiting room. You've also got some others that will want to come up."

"Tell them to bring a drink and something to eat, please. I'm starving."

"No food until the doctors give you the all clear. But I'll grab you a water." His eyes dropping to the liquid on the floor.

"Thanks." Watching him leave. Waiting for what seemed like forever for the door to open again. My dad walking in with a huge smile on his face. "Dad."

"Hey, pumpkin. It's good to see you awake again. You seem more lucid this time."

"I'm happy to see you to." Getting a second hug.

"It's all over the news what you did. Protecting the city."

"I didn't do it for them."

"You're just like your mother. She would be very proud of the woman you're becoming and so am I. I see a lot of her in you."

"Thanks, so much. I spoke to her."

"What do you mean?"

"Did she tell you about a titan called Belemoth?"

"Of course, she told me everything."

"He let me see her, speak to her. It was like it was actually her. It felt amazing. To experience what she was like."

"She was truly great. So kind and thoughtful. Fierce and brave. Just how you've become. As soon as the doctors give you the all clear I want you back at home with me."

"Alright." Fingers gripping his shirt as he came in for another hug. "I'm sure I'll be told to have lots of rest."

"If they don't tell you, I will."

Smiling wide as Flo came into the room. Replacing my father's arms around me with her own. Tightly squeezed which made me wince in pain. "You look all battered up."

"I feel battered up. I'm really sorry about your dress." Looking around the room and finding it draped over a chair. Seeing the slash marks from my fight. "I kinda ruined it."

"I don't care about the dress."

"Wow, it must be love if she's saying that." D came over and nudged me in the arm. "Glad to see you're okay."

"Me to."

"There's something you should see. I've had it saved for days." She picked up the remote and flicked the television on. Sitting high up in the corner, paused at a news report. She hit play and let it run.

The reporter speaking quickly as shaky images of the fight were shown in the background. Seeing myself and my titans in the city. The destroyed buildings looking even worse from these angles.

Listening to the report. "This unknown girl was filmed fighting a huge monster that was terrorising the

335

CRYSTAL DARKE

city. She put her life on the line with what we can only assume are titans. Putting her as an everfae or something similar. True details of what happened or who she is are being investigated. What we can tell you is that she saved the lives of thousands if not millions who live in Collstar. The origin of this monster was tracked back across the continent. Thanks to her the terror has been brought to an end. More to report as we learn it."

"They have it wrong. The titan wasn't terrorising the city. She was just scared."

"Keep watching." D grabbed the remote and brought up the next recording. The same reporter coming back on the screen only this time she had two visitors on set with her. William and his father.

Watching as they discussed what had happened. The reports William downloaded from his father's computer. The information that would destroy the group. End their experiments and the pain they create.

Watching William do most of the talking. Taking charge of the discussion. Steering it in the right direction. Bringing light to the problem. The reporter trying to change the subject but it wasn't working. William could have just done the report himself.

Footsteps bringing my brother into the room. "I still hate that guy but he did good this time."

"Warming up to him?"

Getting a look as he placed a bottle of water on my table, "I still hate the guy."

Smiling as he went over and stood by D. Noticing his hand gently resting on her hip. Making me think about my own romantic life. Turning and noticing Flo staring at me. My look making her flash a crooked smile.

Quickly turning away and watching the television. Reaching over and slipping my fingers around her hand. A flick of her eyes came to me but she quickly moved them back to the screen as well. Thinking about pulling my hand away but then I felt her fingers entwining with mine. Making me smile.

A voice coming from the doorway making us all turn. "I hate how I look on TV."

"William." Smiling as he walked into the room, followed by someone in a suit. Hair swept to the side. A power tie dominating his shirt. We all watched as he stood there. Rubbing a finger across his thick moustache.

William stood next to him like his personal assistant. "Everyone, this is Scott Cole."

"Hello."

We all greeted him to the room with smiles. My dad stepping forward. "What's a government official like you doing in my daughter's room?"

"Dad, it's okay."

"She's been through a lot and if there's any discussion about repaying the city for damages then you can talk to me."

"Dad." Smiling as he looked over his shoulder. "How about we listen to what he has to say first?"

My father stepped back, sitting on the edge of my bed. Looking at this man as he pulled out something from his jacket. My heart sinking at the thought of my father being right. I was involved in the fight that crumbled buildings and destroyed the Kilroy Mansion.

I was passed the papers, the official allowing me to look through them before he spoke. Seeing they were letters. Voicing support to what I had done. Some of them from groups that are actively trying to create a better place for the titans.

Looking up as his lips moved. "As you can see there are a lot of people out there who label you as a hero. Not for only saving the people in this city and the students at the Kilroy Estate. But for the way you treated the situation."

"How do you mean?"

He looked around at all the faces before him. "Could we possibly chat in private?"

Everyone agreeing and starting to move before I interjected. "You can talk in front of them. They're my family." Feeling fingers clutching my hand tighter from both my father and Flo.

"Alrighty then." The man coming forth and grabbing a seat at the foot of my bed. "I don't know if you know this but there are groups out there. Both in favour of titans and against."

"I've had the displeasure of meeting some members of the latter."

"So we've learnt from Mister Kilroy himself." Eyes flicking to William as he leant against the doorway. He spotted my look and smiled back. "My interest are in the positive groups. They've been going on for years about the need to help titans out there in the world. This event in Collstar has given them more leverage."

"Where do I come into all this?"

"Me and a few others want you to be our link to them. To join the team we're putting together. To go out into the world and find titans. To bring them to our designated nature preserve. Once there, they will be looked after. Protected. Not only from harming others but from people who will cause them harm."

"Sounds like you want to round up all the titans in one spot. What stops these people from attacking this place? Wiping them all out in one single attack." I would have told my brother to stop but it was a valid question. Something I wouldn't have thought to ask.

"There will be a lot of security. We wouldn't suggest this if we hadn't given it a lot of thought. The groups I mentioned in favour of titans are joining together. Creating one massive support group. They will be paid and live on this preserve. A lot of money has gone into creating such a place in the last few days. We anticipate to have it up and running by the end of the week. With a few more constructions happening over the next month or so."

"This all sounds good. What about DEATH? What are you doing to dismantle them and others like them?"

"We already have teams working on that. It will take time but with the evidence from Mister Kilroy and William. It's a great start."

"Okay." Thinking about the repercussions of what Ethan West had done. What he was involved with. The school more than likely ceasing to exist. The elite teams he created might stay in place. However there wouldn't be any new ones. Meaning my friends and my brother did all that hard work for nothing. "I have some conditions."

"I'm not surprised at all. Let me just say, you will have a place to live on the nature preserve. With your family."

"That's very nice of you." Feeling the warmth of joy in my heart at the thought of living with them again.

I had only been gone under a week but I wasn't ready to fly the nest just yet. "That brings me to my main condition."

"I'm all ears."

"I want my own team to help me. They will also live on the preserve. Paid and looked after. If they want to. Including you, William."

"That's very sweet of you but the mansion is already being rebuilt and I've got my own part to play in all this. You're looking at the new head of titans relations at the government."

"That's great."

"So you and William will already be working together. As for the rest of them." His eyes moving around the room. "If they agree. Welcome on board."

"Thank you. When will we start?"

"As soon as you're fully recovered. Your new home will be waiting for you and I'll get the construction crew working on others as soon as I have their answers. Now, I have to get moving. More visits to make and daylight is running out. Have a fast recovery."

"Thank you." A smile to each of us and he left. William waved and followed him. Every one turning to me. "I know it's asking a lot but I'd feel better having you all there with me. I've made friends I never knew I would have. Not to mention meeting you." Giving Flo a smile. My grip squeezing her hand.

"What's going on here?"

"Dad. Now is not the time."

"Oh." My father pulled a sheepish look before he stepped back to the wall. "Carry on."

"So? What do you all think about it?"

My brother rubbing a touch to my shoulder. "I'm

in, someone needs to be there to protect you. Just like mum asked."

A tear threatening to fall at the mention of my mother. "Thanks, bro. What about you D?"

"I need to be there to make sure your brother doesn't fall for someone else." Grinning as she placed a kiss to his cheek. Then gripped his t-shirt, "Or I'll have to mangle him."

"Hey, hey. Don't be beating up the merchandise already. I haven't done anything."

"Just warning you."

"I like a woman with a right hook and a sexy butt."

"Oh god, you two can stop anytime. I already feel rough. Don't need to add nausea as well." Laughing as my brother stuck his middle finger up at me. Looking into Flo's eyes. My other hand coming across and cupping her cheek. "How about it?"

"I'm not ready for this to end. I'd love to help you save as many titans as we can."

"Great. Now, I believe I owe you a dance."

"What?"

Grimacing as I shifted my body. Moving just enough to swing my legs over the bed. Flo's hand keeping me steady as I stood. "A dance. I promised and I'm aiming to keep my promises now."

"You sure?"

"I'm already on my feet." Hanging my arms around her neck, standing close as we started swaying. Moving slowly to the music I imagined playing in my head. Not caring about how awkward everyone else looked. Enjoying the moment.

Looking into her eyes with a smile. "So, do I get to

call you my girlfriend?"

Flo let out a soft giggle. "I like the sound of that."

"Me to." Leaning in and kissing her lips. Surprised at the electric touch. A signal that this was right. The feelings I felt were right and this was the path I was meant to take. From titans to Flo, this was where my life was meant to lead.

BOOKS BY THIS AUTHOR

Leecher Chronicles

Moonlit Blood
Sunlit Blood
Burning Blood
Drowning Blood
Dead Blood

Clearwater Legacy

Shadows in the Light

Printed in Great Britain
by Amazon

32060397R00198